THE NEXT WORST THING

A SWEET, SMALL TOWN ROMANTIC COMEDY

SARA JANE WOODLEY

ELEVENTH AVENUE
PUBLISHING

1

IVY

People say that you know when something feels right.

Me? I pay attention when things feel *wrong*. Dead wrong.

Like, when you meal prep a tuna casserole for a crazy week at work, but you're too busy to eat it until four days later. And by then, the pasta's soggy, the tuna smells weird, and you're actually craving pizza. Or when your grandparents take a step back from running your family's cozy mountain inn, and they make you the new manager... but somehow, you still feel like an imposter. Even though you've been prepping for this for years.

Or when your brother's "all about free spirit" fiancée suddenly decides that she wants burnt orange tiger lilies for their wedding. Tiger lilies are gorgeous, but there's no denying that they'll clash horribly with the rest of the pastel blue decor.

Burnt orange and pastel blue. Talk about opposing sides of an issue.

"Are you absolutely *sure* that's what you want?" I ask again, my voice cracking slightly on the end of my sentence.

"How many times do I have to say it?" Eleanor responds

in a clipped sigh—very unlike her usual calm, monotonous tone—as she throws her wavy brown hair over her shoulder.

"Of course. Sorry." I make a note on my handy wedding planning clipboard. *Find a way to incorporate bright orange into the color scheme...?* This is Eleanor's wedding, and no matter the clashing colors, I'll defer to her and make it work.

In the past couple weeks, I've gone from "venue coordinator" to "low-budget wedding planner." Make that "free wedding planner." Not that I mind much. Aside from wanting to give my brother and his bride the perfect big day, I do have other, slightly selfish, reasons to be doing this.

At this point, it's actually a little surprising that Eleanor's come forth with an opinion at all—she's spent most of our wedding meetings alternating between tap-tapping on her phone and looking unbelievably bored.

"It's moments like this that tell me how much we *need* to get out of this town," Eleanor goes on, checking her sparkling mauve nails.

I swallow, ignoring the jab. And the subsequent sadness at the thought of my big brother, Luke, leaving town. Eleanor's made it no secret that she intends to move them to San Francisco right after the wedding.

I've spent a lot of time wondering whether things might be different if Eleanor and I got along. Would she—and, therefore, Luke—want to stay in Mirror Valley if we were best friends? For some reason, Eleanor and I never jived, and it bothers me given that Luke is pretty much my favorite human on earth (not that I'd tell him that).

I *should* be able to be friends with his fiancée... right?

"Babe, I know it's been a long day, but there's no need to take it out on Ivy," Luke scolds Eleanor gently.

He rarely says her name these days. Luke's been dating Eleanor Wilkes since high school, but since starting her influencer career as "basically a spiritual healer" three years ago, she insists that we call her "Lenore."

Luke loves Eleanor/Lenore to the ends of the earth, and he'd do anything for her, even stop calling her by her given name. And letting her fill his gorgeous ranch house with the TikTok must-haves she promotes. High-waisted "lifting" yoga pants, sets of crystals in a literal rainbow of colors, and enough incense sticks to build a second home (though, if an accident happened and it burned down, Mirror Valley would smell like patchouli for years to come).

I, however, do not love Eleanor/Lenore to that extent. And so, I tend to mentally refer to her as "Elly," a name which she's made clear she appreciates even less.

And yes, it's kind of petty, and I promise I'm not usually like this. But given the woman's passive-aggressive comments and barely-veiled disdain over the past years, it's the only acceptable way that I can retaliate: in private, without her knowing.

"We'll find some tiger lilies for you," I say pleasantly as I add a note to speak with the florist. "Clarissa should be able to order some."

"Thank you, Ivy. Tiger lilies bring good luck. So if you can't find them and our marriage goes down the drain, we'll know who to blame."

She smiles thinly at her own joke and I cough up a half-hearted laugh.

"Didn't you want to show us the gazebo next?" Luke cuts in tiredly.

"That's right." I shoot them both a beaming smile, and Luke's hazel eyes slice through my saccharine gaze. *Take it easy,* I can almost hear him grumble. I whip around and walk towards the French doors at the far end of the lobby. "Follow me."

My heels click-clack on the hardwood floor. It's a bit

ridiculous that I'm showing them around the Inn seeing as Luke and I essentially grew up here.

The Brookrose Inn has been with our family for generations—ever since the founding of Mirror Valley, according to our town's folklore. In fact, it was recently named one of Mirror Valley's heritage sites—an honor that I'm getting printed on all of the Inn's brochures and paperwork. History buffs love stuff like that, and our inn loves history buffs.

Or any buffs, really. Bring on all the buffs.

My grandparents inherited the Inn, and have loved running it for the past forty-plus years. But they're ready to retire and I can't say I blame them. Running an inn is very rewarding, but it's hard work. Or so I've heard, seen, and learned.

I finished my degree in Hospitality Management last year, and I took on managing the Inn a couple weeks ago. With my grandparents taking a step back, it was my turn to step up, and I have a lot of ideas for the Brookrose.

The first? To get the Brookrose on the Colorado Rockies wedding circuit.

In my totally humble (read: biased) opinion, Mirror Valley is the *perfect* place to get married. Picture small town flair, gorgeous mountain backdrop, and a rustic Main Street. The town is attracting more and more tourists by the year, and we should capitalize on that.

Which is why I pitched (okay, begged) my brother to have his wedding here instead of at the courthouse. And after some gentle prodding, lots of puppy dog eyes, and from the goodness in his heart (along with the promise of my home-made snickerdoodles on request for the next five years), he acquiesced.

Hence, the partly selfish motivation to make sure this wedding goes off without a hitch.

The French doors open onto the Brookrose's gorgeous garden and my shoulders relax as I walk towards the gazebo. The warm spring air envelops my body, and the smell of blossoming flowers fills my lungs. There's a good chance I'll be sneezing my head off in a moment—gotta love allergy season—but for now, I want to enjoy this. Winters in Mirror Valley can be harsh, and the early summer is all the more sweet when it arrives.

I stop in front of the gazebo and feel a small bloom of pride. The midday sun is hitting *just* right, setting off the dark brown trim against the white columns. The branches of willow trees dangle just behind. This is where I always dreamed I'd have my own wedding. If I ever get married.

Which, honestly, seems even less likely right now than the *Real Housewives* not wearing fake tan. Unless they use Dorito cheese dust. I can almost imagine them sprinkling it on looking like the guy in that meme—sassy flair and all.

The thought almost makes me laugh uncontrollably.

Can you tell that I haven't eaten much today? I need to find snacks, ASAP.

"So, here's what I'm thinking," I say to extract myself from any more Dorito-related thoughts (except planning to grab Doritos when I have a minute). I hold up my clipboard, but I don't need my notes. "You two will stand there for the ceremony, and the chairs will stretch towards the creek on the far side. That way, no one will be blinded by the sun, and the photographer will have lots of space..."

Luke and Elly both nod along, but their eyes are glazed over. And for the thousandth time, I'm surprised to see it. When I took on a bigger role with wedding planning, I was ready for Elly to be your hyper-involved, super-detail-specific type. So, I over-prepared, made sure I had notes on every little thing. I guess I expected her to be...

Well, I won't say bridezilla. That's rude.

5

But surely, you'd think weddings are a trending topic on TikTok. I've even heard the word "Weddingtok" floating around amongst the happily-paired-ups in Mirror Valley.

Luke says that she's been too busy planning her bachelorette to really get involved with the wedding. Which is fair, I suppose. And it works for me—with my brother taking the lead, it means more time spent with him before he leaves.

Luke's that kind of guy anyway. He likes tradition, cares about doing things "the right way." Having a nice wedding matters to him, just like having a proper Fourth of July barbecue, or a roast turkey at Thanksgiving (and Luke Brooks does make the best roast turkey in all of Colorado). My brother believes that a wedding ceremony with all of his and Elly's loved ones will set the tone for their marriage.

It helps that he's got the money for it. His accounting job might bore me to hear about, but it sure does pay the bills and then some.

This is another point that sets Luke and me apart—where he's a successful CPA with a fiancée and a 401K, I'm a newly-graduated hotel manager who's been single about as long as my house spider, Gary. Though I have noticed Gary getting rather friendly lately with the ladybug who visits my orchids...

Yes, this is my life. Eternal plant and bug mom over here.

The irony is not lost on me that the forever-single girl is planning this wedding. A wedding where I don't even have a date.

After we finish at the gazebo, we walk back towards the Inn. Luke and Elly didn't have much to contribute, but I take notes anyway.

"Let's take a break before the caterer gets here," Luke says. He and Elly are holding hands, and he gazes at her tenderly. "Babe, why don't you go inside and have some lunch? I need to talk to Ivy."

Elly crosses her arms, the flowing fabric of her boho dress shifting with the movement. "Don't take too long, Lukey. You know I hate eating alone."

I fiddle with my notes to give them privacy while they kiss, then Elly floats off inside the Inn. Luke's cheeks are slightly flushed and he's got a sweet grin on his face as he watches her. My heart softens for him. Elly might annoy me sometimes, but I could never fault her for how happy she makes my brother.

"You two are very sweet," I say sincerely. "I'm happy for you."

"Thanks," he says. Then, his expression changes. His smile turns sheepish as he runs his fingers through his dark blond hair. "Listen, I have to tell you something..."

My spine straightens. I'd recognize that tone anywhere —it's Luke's "I did something bad" voice, mixed with a hint of "please don't hate me."

"What did you do?" I grumble.

"Well." He shifts from foot to foot. Luke isn't a shifty person, so this immediately puts me on edge. "You know James?"

My heart slams against my ribcage. "James? James who?" I ask, even though I'm pretty sure I know the answer.

"James Weston."

Ugh. He had to go and say it.

I know I asked, but still.

"Yes, I know James." My voice is clipped.

Luke is apparently fascinated by the bush just behind me. "And you know how he'll be in town for the wedding?"

My lips pinch together. "He's coming back to Mirror Valley?"

"Well, he's not going to miss my wedding, is he?" Luke

gives me a look. "But what I haven't had a chance to tell you yet is he's not just coming back to town. He's coming to the Brookrose."

"Come again?"

"He's staying here. In one of the guest rooms I booked for the wedding."

"I thought you booked those for the out-of-towners."

"Well, if we want to get nitpicky," Luke says. "*Technically,* he is from out of town."

"His parents live here."

"He doesn't. He lives in Denver. *And,*" Luke adds, his voice taking on that same logical, matter-of-fact quality as when he talks about numbers. "He's actually the most out-of-town guest we have, seeing as he was born in England."

"And moved here when he was seven."

"It counts."

I guess... If we're going on *technicalities.*

Mr. and Mrs. Weston are warm, lovely people, and when I was younger and particularly obsessed with British culture, I used to spend hours soaking up their accents and mannerisms. They're an integral part of the Mirror Valley community now, all the more because they introduced our town to Yorkshire pudding and Banoffee pie (trust me, there's no going back to a Banoffee-pie-less existence).

I often wondered how someone like James could be their child. Even his younger twin brothers—Jake and Jesse —are your cream-of-the-crop gentlemen.

James is more of your anti-prince-charming—not quite the villain, but he'd probably drop you on purpose if you were dancing together at the royal ball.

"This can't *really* be a surprise, can it?" my brother asks now. "James is one of my best friends. Of course I'd want him staying here for the wedding."

No, it isn't a surprise. In fact, I think a part of me has

been waiting for this. I've gone out of my way over the years to avoid any James-related topics of conversation, tuned out whenever my brother spoke about him. I should've expected this, but I did the ostrich thing and buried my head in the sand.

The good news is that the wedding isn't for another couple weeks, which means that I have time to prepare myself. When I see him again, I'll be the epitome of "cool as a cucumber." No, something even cooler than that—cool as one of those dragon fruit things. Those are cool, right?

I'm pretty out of touch with anything deemed "trendy" or "on fleek" by kids these days. But if I was a fruit, I think I'd want to be a dragon fruit. Bright pink exterior hiding a speckled black-and-white inside. Plus, the name is *fierce*.

Shut up, brain.

"It makes sense," I finally manage, exhaling a full breath. "And I promise to play nice. This is your wedding, and I want you to be happy, first and foremost."

"Thank you," Luke says, placing a hand on my wrist. "That means a lot to me, Iv. I know how hard this is going to be for you."

I shoot him a look at his teasing tone, and stick my tongue out at him. We might be adults now, but that doesn't mean we don't occasionally give each other a hard time like we're thirteen again. Luke smiles that rare, bright smile of his.

"This isn't about me," I say, tapping my clipboard with finality. "This is about you and the future Mrs. Wilkes-Brooks. We're going to make this the best wedding you could ask for."

"If anyone can put together a dream wedding on short notice, it's you."

He throws an arm over my shoulder as we head back inside. I peek up at my older brother, wondering if he, too, is thinking about our parents and what it'd be like to have them here with us. Big celebrations like this are always bittersweet.

But Luke's expression is neutral, stable. Just like he is. Just like he had to be.

We reach the front desk and I decide to check on a few things for the Inn before the caterer arrives. The Doritos will have to wait, there's just too much to be done.

Luke makes to go to the dining room, then stops mid-step. "Oh, Iv? There's one more thing."

"What's that?"

"You know how the wedding's happening next Saturday?"

"Of course."

"Well, James is arriving a little earlier than the other guests..."

I look up at him, narrow my eyes. "Early like?"

Luke checks his watch. "Early like now."

My jaw drops, but before I can say a word, Luke is gone. Disappeared into the dining room. Leaving me alone, exposed and vulnerable for whenever James Weston strolls in.

2

IVY

I take a long swig of my now-cold coffee, my heart banging out an irregular rhythm.

James Weston is coming here. He's staying at the Brookrose.

Okay, Ivy. It's cool.

Deep breath in, deep breath out. Just like in yoga.

I try to listen to myself, but my mind is already fifteen steps ahead. Breathing isn't nearly as important as damage control.

I flip open the Inn's ancient reservation book—I plan to bring us to the digital age ASAP—and scan through the bookings. Though the wedding is happening next Saturday, Luke's booked out blocks of rooms according to how close he and Elly are with the guests. We have a handful of people arriving this weekend and through next week. This week, we have...

Yes. There is one room booked starting today. With Luke's neat and tidy signature on it. Too tidy, too innocent.

The traitor.

At that moment, the door to the Inn opens, shocking me so bad that my arm jerks and my coffee sloshes upwards. I let out a squawk as the cold liquid drops back on me, staining the front of my white lace blouse.

"No!" I squeak, looking up to see whether the newcomer saw my blunder.

I'm even more mortified when I see that it's none other than Cam Harris—the founder of our town's top cleaning company, and the guy that I've been crushing on for months.

So I do what any smart, reasonable, rational woman would do when she sees her crush and has coffee spilled down her shirt...

I dive behind the front desk.

All thoughts of James Weston are temporarily forgotten as I curl into a ball and pray that Valentina—our capable and wonderful receptionist—comes back from her break soon. Preferably with more coffee that her husband, Ethan, brewed up at his cafe.

Not that coffee matters right now. This is crisis mode x100.

I cross all my fingers, cross my arms, squeeze my eyes shut, and pray that Cam didn't see me.

I hear his footsteps wander through the lobby and I scramble for my phone in my back pocket. Dial the only person on earth who might be able to help me.

"Daisy!" I whisper-shout when my best friend finally picks up.

"Yes. Who is this?" I hear her frown through the phone. "If you're looking to sell me one of those fancy vacuums, I've already got one, thanks."

"No, it's me!"

"Ivy? What's wrong with your voice?"

"Long story. Listen, are you at work?"

"Just finished. Why?"

"Any chance you can pop by the Inn? Cam's just walked in and—"

"Oooooh, Cam," Daisy sings. "Ivy and Cam. You two would have the sweetest couple name. Ivam."

I wince despite myself. There must be something better than *Ivam*.

Cavy?

Nope, that's not great either. Sigh.

"Do you happen to have an extra shirt at the gym?" I say quickly. "I just spilled coffee all over myself. I can't face him like this."

"Again? You need to get your limbs under control around him."

"Easier said than done," I grumble. "I'm cursed, remember?"

Daisy laughs, the sound bubbling through the phone. "You are *not* cursed."

"I am. When it comes to guys, I lose all motor coordination."

"And for those of us who failed biology...?"

"I flail around like a newborn giraffe, but not nearly as cute."

Daisy laughs again. "Ooh! Or one of those weird, tall bugs. Praying mantis."

I cringe, peek around the desk. Cam's at the other side of the lobby, staring at a generic landscape painting. "I'm so jealous of the girls in movies and books who make 'klutzy' look like an adorable character trait. There's always some dude who's ready to fall for a girl who trips and stumbles and knocks things over. Let me tell you, there's nothing cute about it when I'm klutzy."

"I have to agree with you there," Daisy says seriously and I'm not even mad. It's just the truth. "I'm sorry, Iv, but

I'm meeting my sister for a late lunch. Any way I can swing by after?"

I press my lips together. I knew it was a long shot. "That's okay, Dais. Yeah, drop by later, if you'd like." My lips turn down at the corners. "You'll never guess who's checking in toda—"

DING.

I sew my lips shut. Someone—probably Cam—rang the bell on the desk. He's standing, waiting for me.

"Everything okay?" Daisy asks.

Yoga breath in... out...

Oh, who am I kidding? How am I supposed to get out of this one?!

I glance one way, then the other. But there's no way around it.

I have to get up. I have to stand, face Cam, pretend that I wasn't cowering behind the desk, panic-dialing my best friend.

"Gotta go," I squeak.

Take another deep, yoga-rific breath in.

Shoot to a stand and come face-to-face with my crush.

"Hey, Cam," I say in what I hope is a confident, blasé sort of voice.

He looks even cuter close up with his slicked-back blond hair, round brown eyes, and cheek dimples. Most people say that Cam has a baby face, but I don't understand how that could possibly be a bad thing. He dresses so well too, wearing slacks and a dressy blazer no matter the weather. It makes my coffee-stained shirt all the more humiliating.

He cocks an eyebrow, his dark eyes skating from my hair —tied into a limp ponytail—down to the offensive stain. He has the grace to meet my eyes again, and I suddenly have a very real fear that my glasses are horribly lopsided or something. It'd be just my luck.

Luckily, his lips form that adorable grin of his. "Enjoyed your coffee?"

I hesitate for a fraction of a second and then laugh a little too loudly. I gesture down at my shirt, knocking the top of the desk by accident with my knuckles. "Enjoyed *wearing* it."

Ugh. Why am I laughing like a hyena at my own joke?

To my gratification, Cam chuckles. A loud—slightly short, but still nice—chuckle. He fiddles with the cuffs of his navy button-up shirt before placing his hands on the desk and leaning forward.

I have to take an instinctive step back as he towers over me. Cam is very tall and very slim. Some people call him lanky, but I'd say that—if you watched the *Twilight* movies as secretly-religiously as I did in high school—his physique is more akin to Edward than Jacob. He's too busy running his business to run on a treadmill, and I respect that.

"You're funny," he says.

Well, at least I have that going for me.

I tilt my chin up, crossing my arms in an attempt to hide the stain while also appearing cute. Unfortunately, the stain is lower than anticipated, so I end up curling over, caving in my chest so I'm looking at him at an unnatural angle.

Hunchback of Notre Dame is sexy, right?

"So, uh..." I clear my throat. "What can I do for you?"

"I'm here to check our new trainee's work."

"Right!" I say, work-Ivy coming back on shift. I release my hunchback pose and finger through the notes I took while talking to Grams this morning. "Dylan's cleaning Room 11, he should be finishing up soon."

"Great. I'll give him a hand if he needs it." Cam nods and I fall a little more for that can-do attitude of his.

I reach behind the desk for the key. "Room 11 is upstairs and to the right. Check-in's not until 4pm, so there's time."

"No problem. At Clear Reflections, we don't do customer satisfaction, we do customer delight." He grins, all dimples, looking proud as can be. "We'll get it done... Even if it takes all night."

The way he says this, the way he's staring right into my eyes, makes a weird feeling rise up through my body. I stutter over my words. "Well, actually, it can't take all night. Someone's checking in later and all that..."

I trail off into nothing as Cam's smile grows. "I'll give you an update soon. We could talk about it just the two of us. Maybe over a drink at McGarry's."

Oh.

OH!

My extremely slow brain finally clues in and my mouth drops open. "A drink? Wi—with me?"

Cam nods. "Unless there's another cute front desk girl I can ask."

Okay, so *technically* I'm the manager now. But I wouldn't expect Cam to just remember my promotion. He's only ever dealt with my grandparents as the managers— they're the ones who signed the contract with his cleaning company.

And yes, I want to meet him for a drink, but I'm rusty at this whole "say yes to the date" business (though *Say Yes to the Dress* is one of my favorite TV shows, when I have time to watch it). I'm assuming the crying and laughing and snotting and resounding "yes" thing is a no-go for dating?

I keep my smile flirty, stand with my hip jutted out. I go to place my hand on the desk oh-so-cutely. "I could be talked into i—"

My hand lands on the reservation book, which then falls to the floor under my weight.

Suddenly, I'm plunging sideways through the air, and I stumble. My hip bumps into the wall behind me, sending pain radiating down my leg. "Oof!"

Luckily, I manage to regain my balance before I'm flopped unceremoniously onto the floor with the rest of my dignity.

I wince as I rub my sore hip. My cheeks are burning when I finally bring myself to look at Cam.

His deep, round eyes are concerned. Though if it's for my injury or for my sanity, I can't tell. "You okay?" he asks.

I wave a hand, even as I subtly lift my leg to relieve some of the pressure on my hip. "I'm fine! Totally fine. I meant to do that."

Cam nods. "I better check on Dylan. See you later."

With that, he walks up the stairs, and I smile after him, still rubbing my hip.

As soon as he's out of sight, I turn away, cursing my un-adorable klutziness for the millionth time.

Cam Harris was trying to ask me out, wasn't he? And I had to go and put my hand where it didn't belong. Did I just ruin my one and only shot?

All of a sudden, there's a clap.

A slow, persistent clap, just behind me.

My heart sinks to my tiptoes and my stomach clenches into a ball. *For the love of all that is good and holy... Please, please don't let that be who I think it is.*

The clapping continues and I finally find the courage to turn around.

And there he is. The one person I hoped I'd never have to see again. My nemesis. The devil in disguise. My brother's best friend.

James *freaking* Weston.

17

3

JAMES

I'm staring. I know I'm staring.

I should stop... but I can't.

You know that feeling when you put something down and leave the room, but when you come back for it, it isn't there anymore? That's *kind of* close to where I'm at right now.

I'm not sure what I was expecting when I crossed paths with Ivy Brooks again. Apparently, my brain froze her in time, because I was picturing the blue jean capris, the colorful T-shirt with clashing patterns, the bright blue eyeshadow, and the braces. I imagined her slightly chubby apple cheeks, her wide, green eyes that were a little too big for her face.

And the bangs. I forgot about the bangs.

I'm surprised I haven't seen my best friend's little sister once in the past eight years. But when Luke told me that he was getting married, I knew I'd have to see her again.

On my one-a-day flight from Denver to the tiny Mirror Valley airport, I didn't think about it, threw myself into work. Mostly because I have a lot to get done, even while on "vacation." I actually went into the office this morning before my flight, and am still wearing my work clothes.

Which means that I am sticking out like a sore thumb.

Don't get me wrong, people in Mirror Valley wear suits... to weddings, funerals, and church on Sunday. My hometown is the kind of place for well-worn jeans with the bottoms frayed out, comfy flannel shirts, and baseball caps with faded logos. As much as I like wearing designer suits in the city, every time I come back—a rare occurrence, honestly—it's like my jeans somehow fit me better here.

So, when I walked into the Brookrose, all I was thinking about was changing into a Henley and my favorite blue jeans.

Until I saw the woman behind the front desk and stopped in my tracks.

I'd recognize her anywhere. Her chocolate brown hair is longer now, and tied in a messy ponytail so strands fall around her face. She's grown into her emerald eyes, still huge and wide behind Coke-bottle glasses. And her cheeks aren't as chubby, but her golden constellation of freckles are brighter than ever.

Is it just me or is she taller? Can women grow after they turn sixteen?

If anyone could do it, it's Ivy.

Thankfully, she doesn't see me staring—I would hear about it otherwise. She's too busy talking to the guy on the other side of the desk, waving her hands around as she speaks. I used to make fun of her for that, ask if she was conjuring spells or something.

I've since learned that moving your hands while talking is a sign of intelligence.

Yeah. That checks out.

Ivy giggles and runs her fingers through her ponytail, and I realize what's going on—she *likes* this guy.

A smile spreads across my lips as I watch the show; it would be rude to interrupt. I size him up—funny enough, he too is wearing a suit. Must be an out-of-towner.

As for Ivy, her flirting technique clearly hasn't changed since high school—lots of fidgeting, and playing with her hair, and laughing that sweet, light giggle that makes all eyes within a five-mile radius turn to her.

It's working—the guy's eating it up. I'm not surprised when he asks her out.

I'm also not surprised by her response—to keel over sideways into the wall.

Classic Ivy.

I can't help myself. I have to clap.

Who wouldn't clap for that?

Now, as she stares at me, shock written across her face, all I can think is that this is the last thing I could've expected. The cute, quirky teenage girl I went to school with has turned into this animated, beautiful woman. With a coffee stain in the shape of Australia on her blouse.

And really, this is the perfect way for Ivy and me to see each other again all these years later. After everything that's happened, everything we put each other through.

"Hey, Brooks," I say, and the name rolls off my tongue. Muscle memory. "Long time, no see."

4

IVY

I stare at the mirage of a person in front of me for a long moment. Too long. Then, I open my mouth, unsure what exactly is going to come out.

"Jaaaaaaames!" I slather in this high falsetto I don't recognize. Guess we're going the kill-em-with-kindness route. "How are you, old bean?"

I've watched too many British films.

James leans back against the door and looks at me. Really looks at me. Trails those cool, blue-green eyes down my body in a way that makes me want to fidget and cover myself up. His eyes have to be one of his most disarming qualities—calm, still and unassuming as a tropical ocean, but with so many mysteries lurking beneath the surface. They might as well be MI6 agents, the both of them.

Shut up, brain.

"Good to see you," he says, and that deep voice resonates through my body.

There it is. The lilt of his faded English accent.

"Isn't it?" I say sweetly as I pick up the reservation book from the floor, plop it on the desk and throw it open, strictly business. I promised Luke that I would be nice, and I wouldn't break that promise. "You're wanting to check in?"

"Who was that?" James asks instead of answering my really very simple question.

"Who?" I blink, pushing my glasses up my nose.

"That guy who went upstairs." James's full lips twitch as he approaches. His stride is long and casual. "The man who I *think* you were trying to flirt with."

He sidles up to the desk, so close that I can almost smell what I'm sure is some overpowering musky cologne. I look up at him—how on earth is the guy so tall? Doesn't he have a castle atop a beanstalk to protect?

Okay, he's about the same height as Cam. But he's more muscular, so he just screams "fee-fi-fo-fum."

"I don't know what you're talking about," I say.

"Sure you do." James's eyes are still traveling over me, lazily exploring my face before meeting my gaze. The icy turquoise of his irises shoots right through me like daggers. "You were wriggling around like a drunk orangutan."

That's actually probably the most accurate description I've heard of my attempts at flirting.

I steel myself. I can be nice and still draw my line in the sand. "That's not any of your business."

James's lips quirk, his eyes still locked on mine. Something clenches deep in my stomach. "Guess you're right. It's not my business anymore."

There's a heavy, loaded silence as we glare at each other, and then I look away. I lay my finger on the reservation book and scan down until I see Luke's tidy signature again. "You're staying in one of our King rooms. Should be nice and spacious for all your jockstraps and soccer gear."

His eyes dance. "Don't you mean 'football' gear?"

My nostrils flare. Of course he would say that. There was a period in high school—at the peak of my Anglophilic phase—where I'd refuse to call it "soccer" and only referred to it as "football." Given that James was the top athlete on our high school soccer team, he liked to give me a hard time about it.

On top of everything else we argued about.

"I mean what I mean," I say flippantly. Like that makes any sense at all. I make a note on the reservation book. "You only reserved for one guest, so if you're bringing a lady friend, you'll have to pay extra."

"Nope, just me."

"Really." I stand straight, hands on my hips. "Going to the wedding solo? Couldn't find a date?"

James's lips twitch again, rather distractingly, although I'm too focused on gloating to pay much attention. "Something like that."

I can't help myself. I smile smugly. "Oh, James, don't you worry. You'll find a woman who's willing to put up with you someday."

He chuckles. "Does this mean you've got a date? Maybe BabyFace McGee over there?"

Yikes. I did not think this through. Because he's right, I don't have a date either, but I won't be telling him that. "What did I say about minding your business?"

Before James can respond, I turn on my heel and file through the keys, looking for Room 6. I take a moment to gather myself, catch my breath.

Slow down, this is James. You haven't seen each other in years, no need to fall back on old patterns. Be nice.

But why, oh why, didn't Luke tell me? I had no time to get ready. No time to take my hair down, put in my contacts, even change my shirt. No chance of throwing on that cool, confident glimmer and shine I always imagined I'd have when I saw James again.

Nope. Instead, he's seeing the girl in the movie before

23

the glamorous makeover. It's not that I care what he thinks, but I'm vulnerable in one too many places right now.

I sneak a glance over my shoulder.

Cowbells. He looks good.

His black hair's all grown-out and spiky in a way that looks like he's just woken up and run his fingers through it. He's gained muscle since the last time I saw him—especially in the upper body and arm regions. And though he's wearing nice slacks and a white dress shirt with the top button undone to show off a triangle of his firm chest, he looks right at home in our cozy country inn.

Though with that level of cockiness, he probably makes himself at home wherever he goes. Probably thinks he rightfully belongs on Her Majesty's throne.

The scoreboard is clear: James - 1, Ivy - 0.

"You know it's rude to stare, right?" he asks.

My cheeks flush a furious shade of red as I turn back to the keys. I fiddle some more, pretending I didn't hear him, then grab the right one. I throw the key at him. "There you go. Room 6 is just down the hall on the left."

"You're not going to show me to my room?"

"Surely, you can find it yourself. Or are you prone to getting lost in small spaces?"

"I was under the impression that the Brookrose was one of the top-rated hotels in the area for its hospitality." James tsks, shaking his head. "What a disappointment."

I press my lips together. Man, he drives me up the wall!

We haven't seen each other in years but he knows *exactly* which of my buttons to push. It's like he somehow senses how important it is to me that I run the Inn to perfection.

Letting out a small, frustrated breath, I sidle around the desk and gesture down the hallway with a deep bow. "Follow me, sir."

"I like when you call me that."

I shoot him another glare before turning on my heel and strutting away. James is light on his feet—probably all those stupid calf muscles—but he's behind me, keeping my pace.

"Number 6, huh?" I can hear him smirking. "Is that referring to something?"

I roll my eyes, though he can't see it. "What would it be referring to?"

"Well, I believe you were six when we first met. I wouldn't put it past you to give me this room as a way of declaring your everlasting love for me."

I almost gag. "Guh. Puke."

James chuckles. When he speaks again, his tone is conversational. "Are you excited for the wedding?"

"Luke and El—Lenore's wedding?" I say. "What do you think?"

"I think you're over the moon about it."

There's a serious note in James's voice that I can't quite work out. I look over my shoulder at him, but his face is the Switzerland of expressions, so I shrug. "I want Luke to be happy."

"I get that. I was pretty honored when he asked me to be his best man—Oof!"

James lets out a grunt as he runs into me, feinting sideways so as not to knock me over. Because my legs have stopped working. I'm frozen in the middle of the hallway, my heart leaping. "He did *what*?"

"Asked me to be his best man. You didn't know that?"

Freaking Luke!

"Yeah. Of course. I knew that," I find myself saying, even as I imagine the different ways I might lightly poison my brother with my next batch of snickerdoodles. A small dose of laxatives should do the trick.

"It's not a big deal." James shrugs. "I'll be helping with wedding errands so I won't be around much."

I sigh miserably. "I am also helping with wedding planning."

James's eyes widen a fraction. "Oh."

"So we'll be seeing a lot of each other."

"Looks like it."

"Great. Wonderful." My head bobs up and down. I gesture stiffly towards Room 6. "There you are. Go nuts."

"I will." James shoots me a dazzling smile. "I'll see you soon for the meeting with the caterer."

"Can't wait." I match his smile, holding up an overenthusiastic thumbs up. Then, I march back down the hallway, hoping that my stride hides the fact that I'm currently dying inside.

You know how I said that I felt it when things were wrong?

Well, James Weston definitely goes on the *wrong* list. And now, I have to spend the next couple of weeks pretending that I can get along with the guy. Pretending that he hadn't made it his personal life mission in high school to make me miserable.

Wonderful, indeed.

5

JAMES

I vy storms off down the hallway, her short black heels click-clacking and her hips swaying in time with her ponytail. I'm almost tempted to say something else.

Almost.

But I hold back. Because we're adults now, and this is Luke's wedding, and I need to be on my best behavior around her. I *will* be on my best behavior around her. No teasing, no feuding, no giving her a hard time.

I shake myself off as I let myself into my room. Press my back against the door and exhale loudly once, twice.

When I was playing soccer in college, my coach got me into these loud breathing exercises, and I still do them when I'm stressed or under pressure.

The key is to choose your moments. For example, *don't* do them when you're in your office after a big meeting, and you're set to have lunch with the cute account exec down the hall that you've just started dating.

There's a chance Cheryl thought I was in labor. We didn't go out again.

I go to the bed and unzip my bag. I have a few minutes before the meeting with the caterer, just long enough to get changed. I automatically check my phone and see that there aren't any messages... Yet.

I'm *technically* on vacation—Jen from HR told me that I had too much overtime carried over from last year and then handed me literal folders of brochures to all-inclusives in Hawaii with no Wi-Fi coverage. I think Jen was trying to tell me to get a life.

A few days later, Luke called and asked me to be his best man. I booked two weeks off so I could be in Mirror Valley for all the wedding events, but I plan to work while I'm here. Don't tell Jen.

As I get changed, my thoughts briefly flit away from work and back to Ivy. Just mild observations, and questions like—how do I recognize that guy with the baby face she was flirting with? How does she manage to look so put together even with a huge coffee stain on her shirt? And why does she choose to wear glasses that cover ninety-five percent of her face?

The glasses look good on her, of course. Ivy could make a carrot costume look good. Which she did when she worked for Mirror Grocery for those two high school summers.

Ivy's got a sweet, doe-eyed look to her, but experience as her nemesis has taught me that her personality is something fierce. Sure, I might've given her a hard time in high school, but she wasn't afraid to give it right back. It's an intriguing combination—one that I'm sure many people are drawn towards.

Not me, though. Ivy hates me, and I hate her. Our relationship is easy in that sense—I don't have to think about it. Anytime I've thought about her over the years, I've filed those thoughts away in a secure mental lockbox. "Enemy" is safer than pretty much any other label when it comes to your best friend's little sister.

I decide that I won't spend any more time thinking of her. This is Luke's wedding, and I'm going to be the best best man.

I'm shuffling my fingers through my hair, trying to make it less airplane-y, when my phone rings with the signature tone I set for my boss.

"Martin," I answer the call using my polished, serious work voice.

"Howdy, James." Our company's Senior Director of Marketing always uses this greeting, no matter how far he is from Texas. "How's it feel being home?"

I turn away from my reflection, start to pace. "Good. I'm all settled at the hotel."

"And the flight?"

"Productive. Managed to finish the Samson proposal."

"Excellent," Martin says. "I know you're on vacation— wink wink—but this news couldn't wait."

"What's up?" I respond smoothly. I've been working with Penumbra Hospitality since I graduated college. My reachability—especially on vacation—is likely one of the reasons I'm being considered for this promotion. If I get it, I'll be the youngest person in Penumbra's history to be a director.

Martin takes a breath and there's a scuffle as he switches the phone from one ear to the other. I bite my thumbnail and take a seat on the edge of the bed, leg bouncing.

"I finally heard from Xavier about your presentation. The 'start small, go big' campaign."

Xavier. My boss's boss.

No big deal.

I try to play it cool. "And?"

"He loved it."

My leg stops bouncing. "Really."

"The entire C-suite was impressed and, last I heard,

29

there's been some serious talk about moving forward with it. And on who should lead the project."

"Who are they thinking?" My voice is calm, much calmer than I'm feeling. Which is something like a hyperactive Corgi running towards a stick three times his size.

"Obviously, it'll fall on the future Director of Marketing Strategy and Optimization. I don't want to give anything away, nothing's set in stone. But I will say that it's looking very promising for you."

A smile tugs at my lips. "I'm happy to hear that."

"You should be. Have a beer on me tonight, will you?"

"Thanks, Martin."

I hang up the phone. Then, I launch back onto my feet and pace around double time.

There's a weird pressure in my chest, a whirl of emotions I can't get straight. I should be happy about the likely promotion. I should be bouncing off the walls with excitement, and pumping my fist at the accomplishment. I should be running around with my big stick, knocking into trees and unwittingly tripping people.

Instead, there's a niggling feeling that's growing stronger and stronger, no matter how much I try to ignore it. Something about the win feels... off.

I've worked with Penumbra for the past four years and learned a lot. I've excelled in all of my positions, gone for exactly what I wanted and achieved it. Martin has pretty much said that if I continue working this way, I'll be quick to rise through the ranks. Which sounds great to me; taking things slow and patient is not my forté.

But lately, questions about my future have been popping into my head at the most inconvenient times. Questions like—"do I want this?" and "what next?" and "aren't I a little young to be having a midlife crisis?" I figured I'd be closer to fifty when it came up, and then I'd dive into the Amazon for a couple months and come out a changed man with an impressive beard.

Nope. These days, whenever I think about my future, it's like I'm looking through a kaleidoscope. With fewer fun and bright colors.

So I do what I always do. Squash those questions away to the back corners of my mind.

DING!

I pick up my phone and check the text.

Luke: Dude, you coming?

Right. The meeting with the caterer.

James: Be right there.

I'm excited to see Luke... less so about seeing his fiancée. Eleanor and I never hit it off. There was something about her that felt fake to me—like she was hiding something, holding back parts of herself. But I'd never tell Luke that, it isn't my place. As long as she's authentic with him, that's what matters.

In the past, I've wondered whether I was jealous of their relationship. Luke and Eleanor have been building and growing and working on creating a life together.

Meanwhile, I did the bachelor thing. Had casual relationships, and casual breakups. But love? Never, and I don't think it's on the cards for me. There's always been something missing.

As I enter the Inn's dining room, I spot Luke, Eleanor, Ivy and a lady who must be the caterer standing by one of the tables. Ivy's let her hair down and it cascades down her back in waves. She's taken her glasses off, and she's wearing a forest green athletic tank top that hugs her body.

"Sorry I'm late," I say. "Hope you weren't waiting."

Ivy's emerald eyes swivel towards me and she fixes me with a glare. I don't drop her gaze as I walk up next to her.

Close enough to smell her soft, sweet scent, but not so close that we're touching.

Luke smacks my palm. "We were just about to start."

The caterer—a tall, fit woman with huge blonde hair and a lot of makeup—steps forward. "I take it you're the best man?"

I duck my head. "James."

"Ooh!" She giggles. "I love that accent. Are you English?"

"I was born in England, but I live in Denver now."

"Well," she says, her eyes sparkling. "It's nice to meet you, James. I'm Charlotte."

Beside me, I can almost feel Ivy rolling her eyes. Charlotte begins by saying that she wants to confirm the final guestlist for the wedding. As she takes out a prim pink-and-white folder, I make extra effort to keep my eyes on her.

"You're a second away from drooling," Ivy hisses as Charlotte flips through her folder.

"What's it to you?"

"Nothing. It's just hard to pay attention when you're panting right next to me."

I have to hold back a snort. "This is just like that SAT prep course. You never could keep from talking to me. Maybe that's why you failed the SATs."

This has the desired reaction. Ivy splutters a few times, her cheeks growing red. "You don't *fail* the SATs, genius, it's score-based. This explains why you needed a soccer scholarship to get into college."

I hold a hand to my heart. "Oof. Getting me where it hurts."

Ivy opens her mouth to retort when Luke fixes us both with a glare.

I bow my head in remorse. I made a vow that I would behave around Ivy—the last thing I want is to cause Luke any additional stress around his wedding. I can't let myself get sucked in like this, can't fall into old and familiar patterns.

Ivy and I are just like this, though. It's a constant challenge, a give-and-take, a push-and-pull that I kind of hate, but also kind of enjoy at the same time.

Is that my toxic trait? Maybe. But I'm trying to be better.

I resolve, once again, to behave myself. I shoot Ivy a sideways glance, and to my surprise, she's smiling too. A second later, though, the smile's gone, and she's focused again on the caterer.

I follow her lead, even as I wonder what she's thinking.

6

IVY

How on earth did she get her hair like that?

H I stare in wonder as Charlotte checks the guestlist with Luke.

I should be paying attention, but I'm mesmerized. Her ash-blonde hair leaps out of her head like a fountain, and then falls delicately to her shoulders.

I absent-mindedly finger a lock of my own dull brown hair. Sure, it's a little greasy today and I could've done with running a brush through it, but I like being a brunette. I've never dyed my hair, barely done anything more than cut it myself over the years. But Charlotte's amazing bouffant is making me second guess that decision.

Although while she pulls off the hairstyle effortlessly, I have a feeling I'd look more like an oompa loompa.

"Okay, everyone." Charlotte with the big hair claps delicately to get our attention. I get the feeling she does everything like that—delicately. "I hope you're hungry. I brought a few cake tasters from our baker to celebrate being in the home stretch. I thought it would be a fun game to try them all and guess which cake you've selected for the big day."

Luke's eyes light up—my brother has a serious sweet

34

tooth. Though he doesn't indulge often given his "strict exercise regimen."

"If we *have* to," he says, smiling at Elly, who grins at him in return.

I line up behind Luke and Elly at one end of the table, where a series of eight pink boxes are laid out with a small cake in each. My stomach is grumbling with a fervor even I'm impressed with, and my mouth is watering.

We each take one of the dainty white plates I'd polished earlier, though I try not to notice Elly grimace at hers with something resembling distaste. She scratches at a spot I can't see on the surface, then places the plate on the table and takes a new one.

As we serve ourselves, I realize that James hasn't lined up with us. I glance over my shoulder, and see why: he's occupied with Charlotte. He says something that makes her laugh, and she places a hand—once again, delicately—on his bare forearm.

It takes everything in me not to roll my eyes. I'm sure he's loving this. Charlotte looks like a prima ballerina, complete with cute button nose, perfect posture, and long, toned legs. On top of that, she's not falling over herself while flirting with him.

I wonder if he'll ask Charlotte to be his date for the wedding. If they were to get married in turn, they'd have cute babies. The only newborns with abs of steel.

"You're so funny!" she twinkles, her hand moving slowly down his forearm.

Oh, good. James must've told her about his lifelong battle with raging athlete's foot.

Never mind, that's rude. I'm sure he has perfectly nice feet. Or devil hooves, who's to know?

James brings out this side of me. Just as he did in high school.

Our feud was legendary. Four long years of taunting and teasing, of embarrassing the other in front of crushes, and sabotaging each others' dates.

Nothing I did ever felt like enough, though. No matter how many times I tried to get James back for the night he started it all, I couldn't. I went to great lengths to make him look bad, but he'd just smile that annoying little grin of his, and give it right back.

He was untouchable. Unflappable.

It was infuriating.

And I had lots of opportunities too. Girls were constantly throwing themselves at James. Maybe it was the piercing turquoise eyes, or the soccer muscles, or the English accent. Unfortunately, he was blessed with symmetrical features so, scientifically speaking, he was always objectively attractive.

But I digress.

According to Luke—when something he said about James over the years *did* slip through my filter—the attention never stopped. James was a serial dater in high school, through college, and it looks like he still hasn't changed one bit.

Meanwhile, my dating history is as empty and lifeless as poor almost-planet Pluto. But I've decided that I should at least *try* and be in a relationship. I've used my well-worn "I'm too busy studying/working/reading" excuse for years, ignoring any inclinations towards dating.

But I can't exactly ignore the fact that Luke is getting married, and it's only a matter of time before Daisy pairs up with someone too. Soon, I'll truly be alone.

Just me and Gary. If he doesn't go off with Miss Ladybug.

"What do you think, babe? Do you know which one we picked?" Luke's voice pulls me from my thoughts.

"Uh. The strawberry shortcake one?" Elly responds.

"No, we got the lemon with strawberries."

"Oh, yeah. That works."

"Did you want strawberry shortcake?"

Elly stifles a yawn. "No. I mean, whatever. It's just a cake."

Luke pauses for a second. "Our wedding cake."

"I know, I know." Elly waves a hand, agitated. "I'm sorry, Lukey, I'm just tired. We did a lot today. Can I go meet Francesca now? She's got *so* many ideas for the bachelorette and she won't stop texting me about it."

Ah, yes. The bachelorette. Just me, Elly, her maid of honor Francesca, and a couple of her other college friends. Guaranteed fun.

Sorry, I shouldn't be sarcastic. I'm sure it'll be a great time.

"Sure, love," Luke says to Elly. "Whatever you want."

She gets up on her tiptoes to kiss my brother on the cheek. "I'll be back later, don't wait up."

Elly grabs her bag and races out of the room, seeming happier than she has all day.

I wait a moment before I sidle up to my brother. "You okay?"

"Absolutely. Why?"

"I don't know. That seemed kind of... abrupt."

He chuckles. "That's just Lenore being Lenore."

Luke turns away to grab more cake, and my stomach twists slightly. I love my brother with every fiber of my being, and if he says he's happy, I believe him.

Luke and Elly have an interesting relationship. She was there for him through a lot of the hardships—when he failed that calculus course, when his pet iguana died, on our parents' birthdays, the anniversary of their deaths, and our family holidays. Elly has always been there for my brother, and I respect her for that.

But there's something about her I could never trust, no matter how hard I tried. And trust me, I tried, especially since they announced their engagement two years ago. I tried to get over that feeling and get to know Elly. But all I ever got was false laughter, and smiles that didn't reach her eyes.

"Hey, we're down a person," a deep voice says behind me.

The sentence leaves my mouth before I can think it. "Observant little thing, aren't you?"

"Careful who you're calling little," James says wryly, standing next to me for effect. He looks at Luke. "Where's Eleanor?"

"She has some important stuff to get done," Luke says.

James's eyebrows rise. "More important than her own wedding?"

Luke shrugs.

"How's it going over here?" Charlotte's voice tinkles as she inserts herself between James and me. She's talking to him, though he's the one person who hasn't tasted the cakes.

I roll my eyes, then catch James watching me with a smirk.

"Delicious," Luke says, apparently unaware of anything but his plate. He scoops the last bite of cake into his mouth. "I'll be right back, have to use the facilities."

And with that tasteful exit, Luke strides out of the room.

"Speaking of facilities," Charlotte says in a sexy voice that does *not* match the conversation topic. "I have a question about the kitchen. Maybe we can go check it out, the two of us."

"Actually." James nods towards me. "Ivy's the venue coordinator. You can ask her about it."

"Ivy?"

"That would be me." I step around her awkwardly and she looks at me with wide eyes that say she forgot I was here.

"Oh. Great. I'm wondering whether your walk-in is eight-by-eight or eight-by-ten? My team needs eight-by-ten for this amount of guests so if you have the smaller one, we'll bring a couple of portable fridges."

"Let me check." I grab my clipboard and rifle through, trying to find the notes about our kitchen.

Lights. No. *Tents.* No. *Garden & Gazebo.* No, no, no.

Charlotte raises a brow. "Well?"

"Sorry, I don't have it right here. I'll have to go check."

"Yeah, best do that." Charlotte laughs again, batting her eyelashes at James. "So funny, I don't think I've worked with a venue coordinator who didn't have this kind of info on hand for the caterer."

My cheeks flare red again and a wave of humiliation soars through my body. I know this is a small thing, but being caught unprepared is one of my worst fears. That, and skateboarding (don't ask). All the more when someone is laughing at my expense because of it.

Charlotte's placed her hand back on James, and her intent is now clear—laughing at me is her attempt to bond with him. I look away, flustered and upset. If the past is anything to go by, he'll be joining in any minute now.

Instead, that deep voice cuts firmly through Charlotte's laugh. "It's not a big deal. Far as I know, only the chef or F&B manager would know something like that. Besides, Luke's our numbers guy."

Is he... defending me?

Surprised, I sneak a glance in James's direction.

"The kitchen is literally right there," he continues. "You could check the fridge yourself. In fact..." He takes Charlotte by the elbow and points her in the direction of the kitchen. "Why don't you? We'll be out here, chatting about other super specific wedding details."

Charlotte splutters for a moment, but as James turns away, she seems to realize that she's talked herself into a hole. She pads off towards the kitchen, looking every bit the dog with its tail between its legs.

I look up at James. "Did you just... do something to help me?"

"Don't be so surprised. I can be a good person," he says with a wink.

I shake my head. "Color me shocked."

"And now, this means you owe me."

"I *knew* you had to have an ulterior motive."

James laughs. It occurs to me that it's not a terrible sound—rich and smooth, like melted dark chocolate.

What? No. I blame the cakes for that wayward thought.

I cross my arms in a way that probably looks more confident than I feel. Especially in a tank top that shows off more of my body than I'm comfortable with. As much as I don't like to be so casually dressed for work, it was this or the shirt that's really a coffee stain, and somehow this felt more put-together.

"So you thinking of asking her to the wedding?" I ask wryly, nodding towards the kitchen.

A smirk plays on James's lips. "Why so curious? Getting some ideas in that brilliant head of yours?"

Is that a compliment?

I decide not to read into it, and smile back at him sweetly. "James, don't be ridiculous. We're far older and wiser than we were in high school, I would never revert back to that immature behavior. But if I did, you wouldn't see it coming."

Soon, Luke and Charlotte come back to the dining room. It might just be me, but it looks like she's reapplied her lipstick.

For the rest of the meeting, she backs off of me and concentrates all her efforts on James. And while he effortlessly charms her with that accent and flirty smile, I get a weird urge. A small desire to maybe go back to the ways of high-school-Ivy. Just for a second. Just because, clearly, James can do no wrong when it comes to Charlotte with the big hair, and because I kind of want a laugh.

I remind myself that I'm not in high school anymore, and what happened is in the past. I am a twenty-five-year-old woman with a wedding on her hands and an inn to run.

But as much as I try to overcome and be the bigger person, when the meeting's over, I find myself placing a foot in James's path anyway. He trips, stumbles, then catches his footing again.

And I walk out with my head held high, like I did nothing wrong.

7

JAMES

Charlotte's been talking about her bikini collection for the past twenty-seven minutes.

"The pink frilly one was *perfect* for my gap year in Europe," Charlotte's saying. "The beaches there are unreal. Have you been? It literally changed my life."

"Hm," I mumble. I'm trying to pay attention, really I am...

While also low-key looking for an exit strategy.

"And did I tell you about the time that my bathing suit top accidentally untied at the beach? You should've been there, it was so embarrassing." She flutters her long eyelashes and stares me down with a gleam in her eye.

I realize she's waiting for me to say something. "That's a shame," I offer.

Honestly, I don't know what to say about any of this. Don't get me wrong, I have absolutely nothing against a woman in a bikini, or a full-piece, or whatever she feels most comfortable wearing.

But all I can think about right now is how snooty she was to Ivy. Ivy's only *just* taken over managing the Brookrose, how would she be expected to know the dimensions of a fridge? Unless she was a fridge salesperson, which would be a pretty niche dream to have, but I'm not here to judge.

I waited for Ivy to laugh, to make a joke about not knowing something so nitty-gritty specific. But instead, her face fell, and for a shadow of a second, she looked so intensely vulnerable that it made my heart twist. All the more because Charlotte was laughing at her, which felt like a rather uncomfortable deja vu...

I had to step in, say something.

Apparently, this is another thing that hasn't changed. Ivy used to get so flustered when she was caught off guard. I remember, when I was a senior and she was a junior, she was doing some Model UN debate thing in front of the school and someone on the opposing team called her out for not knowing the population of Ghana.

She went home that evening and memorized the entire Ghana Wikipedia page. I'm sure that, if you asked her a question about Ghana today, she'd have all the facts you could ever want to know. And several you probably couldn't care less to know.

"So, James. What do you think?" Charlotte purrs, running a manicured fingernail down my bare bicep. It kind of tickles and I pull my arm across my chest to scratch it, pretending I'm stretching.

"Think about what?"

"Weren't you listening?" She giggles and elbows me lightly in the abs.

I really wasn't.

"Sorry, I zoned out for a moment." I shrug apologetically.

"'For a moment'," she repeats, imitating my accent but with a bizarre, Spanish-adjacent twinge. "I was asking if you'd like to go to the beach with me tomorrow."

"Mirror Valley doesn't have a beach."

"I happen to know of one. A *private* one."

My forehead puckers. "Thanks, but I'm going to be busy with wedding stuff over the next few days." Or weeks. Or months. Or years. "Speaking of, I've been meaning to talk to Luke about the..." What do best men do again? I rack my brain, then remember something from my uncle's wedding. "Boutonnieres!"

Charlotte blinks. "The what?"

"The boutonnieres," I say firmly, like I know exactly what I'm talking about. Which, I'm guessing, is some sort of food item? "Luke wanted to talk about the boutonnieres before he leaves today. So I better get to that. Can't be choosing the wrong... topping or something."

"Topping?" She frowns.

Maybe I've got it wrong. But, I'm halfway through, can't back out now. I paste on a bright smile. "I'll see you later. Thanks again for the cakes."

With that, I jog out of the room.

As I cross the lobby and head towards the French doors, I give my head a shake. What is going on with me? Normally, I'd be flattered by Charlotte's attention and would have said yes to the beach invite. But even before she was rude to Ivy, I was thinking that I'd turn her down if she asked me out.

I've been turning down a lot of dates lately. I'm kind of over these superficial, surface-level relationships that don't go anywhere.

I bust through the doors and walk into the Brookrose garden.

Man, I forgot how magical this place is.

Growing up, the Brookrose was the place to spend lazy Saturdays and weekday evenings. Luke, Ivy and I would play tag and soccer, and in the winter, we'd have epic snowball fights. Funny enough, Ivy and I made an awesome team. Though once we got to high school and our bickering kicked off, she was never on my team again.

Their grandparents, Richard and Maggie, always had chocolate chip cookies and glasses of milk on hand. And their parents? They were the kind of people who read their kids to sleep at night, the kind who'd jump into puddles with them after a rainstorm.

They were great. Not that I remember them all that well.

A familiar pang of sympathy rockets through my body. No one expected the accident in the mountains... especially not on that day, when the sun was shining and everything looked perfect.

Luke and Ivy dealt with their grief in such different ways. Luke became rigid, averse to any sort of change, where Ivy gained this intensely independent, perfectionist streak. The same streak that probably led her to chastise herself for not knowing whether the fridge was eight-by-six or ten-by-eighteen (FYI, I don't know fridge dimensions, either).

It's part of the reason I've always had a protective instinct for Ivy. Sure, she might hate me, and we might be enemies, but at the end of the day, I would never want to see her seriously hurt. I would never want her to be unhappy.

As I stroll through the garden, I let the breeze chase away those thoughts. For a minute, I can pretend that this is all that matters—nature, sunlight, the smell of freshly-cut grass. Forget about work, forget about high school, forget about my future...

I'm approaching the gazebo when I see Ivy. She's clutching her clipboard to her chest and frowning up at the top of the structure like it personally offended her.

I should keep walking, but I turn in her direction. "In my line of work, we call that a roof," I say conversationally.

She barely glances at me. "I didn't know that clowns do construction."

"Ha ha." I roll my eyes. "You seem a little lost."

"As do you. Shouldn't you be somewhere flirting your mouth off?"

I can't help myself, I shoot her a wicked smile. "I can start, if that's what you want."

Her cheeks redden slightly and she takes a step onto the top stair so we're eye to eye. "Your flirting leaves much to be desired."

"Based on that performance earlier, so does yours."

"Jerk," she mutters under her breath. Then, she changes tack, and a bright, angelic smile crosses her lips. A smile so beautiful that my heart picks up speed. Because I know that it's leading to something. "I saw your stumble before. I do hope that isn't the reason Charlotte rejected you."

I knew it. I *knew* she tripped me.

I bite my lip to keep from smiling. "Who says Charlotte rejected me? I'm in high demand, Brooks, but the boutonnieres can't wait."

"What boutonnieres?"

"Don't worry about it, it's the best man's job. And I promise, I'll pick the best flavor."

At this, Ivy's eyebrows shoot all the way up. She raises a hand to cover her mouth, placing her index on her full bottom lip. It's kind of distracting. "Oh, the best flavor... What would that be?"

I assess her, unsure what she's playing at. Does she really want to know what my favorite flavor is? I decide to answer honestly. "I'm thinking salted caramel. I love salted caramel."

"So do I," she responds off-hand. "But tell me, James. What exactly *is* a boutonniere?"

I pause, searching her face. She looks back at me innocently, her eyes wide, emerald pools that I could imagine diving into on a hot day. "A boutonniere is like a brownie lollipop thing," I hazard a guess.

At this, Ivy snorts. A full-on snort that would impress the guys in my rec soccer league. "Here I was thinking that a boutonniere was a sort of flower decoration that you pin onto a jacket. Silly me."

I raise my eyebrows. Ivy's poking fun at me, but I'm genuinely curious. "Like a corsage?"

Her mocking smile turns into something more pensive. "A boutonniere is like..."

She frowns at the garden and I realize that she's going to show me.

Ivy was always good about sharing her knowledge—though she likely does it less smugly with other people.

She steps past me, bends to a rose bush nearby, and gently picks a white bloom along with a few strands of grass. She collects the bundle in her hand and returns to her position on the top stair. "You'd wear it like this."

Ivy presses her palm to my chest, directly above my heart, and something in me jumps. A warmth spreads out from where her fingers lie, through my chest and down my limbs. It's not unpleasant, just... unexpected.

She drops her hand and I realize I'm holding my breath. There's a loaded silence that feels awkward, though it might just be me.

"Ivy!"

Her gaze falls on a point behind me and her face registers surprise followed by something I've never seen in her before. Her eyes soften and she smiles this sweet, glowing smile.

I turn to see the guy from earlier walking towards us.

"Hey, Cam," Ivy says in a melodic voice that makes my chest do another weird jump. Maybe I should cut down on the caffeine.

Ivy brushes past me, meeting the guy a few steps away so I can't hear their conversation.

I should walk away, leave the two of them to what I'm sure is going to be a weird flirtation. But I find myself leaning against the wall of the gazebo, watching them.

How do I recognize this guy, and why can't I place him? It's nagging at me. There's something so familiar about his huge brown eyes, the gelled hair, the dimply grin.

He looks like the grown-up version of the Gerber baby. Maybe that's it.

As I watch, Ivy crosses her legs, one in front of the other. Then, unbelievably, she twists her arms around themselves. It looks like she's trying to be a human pretzel or something.

When she tries to move, she almost falls side-first into the fern next to her.

I've never seen someone so short be all elbows and knees quite like Ivy.

I'm about to turn away, give them privacy, when the guy takes a big step forward. He's literally towering over Ivy, not even bending towards her or anything. Understandably, with his height, this sends her off-kilter even more and she shrinks up.

It's like he's asserting his dominance. And he's been monopolizing the conversation—for every word Ivy says, he seems to say ten.

I can just picture him mansplaining something to her...
Stop it, James.

I reel myself in, calm the surge of protectiveness that feels at once familiar and ancient.

It isn't my place to get in the way, isn't any of my business. Goodness knows my protective streak towards Ivy hasn't served either of us well in the past. My interference started our stupid feud, and I've regretted it countless times. I was young and dumb then. It's not an excuse or an explanation, but there it is.

All I ever really wanted was for Ivy to be safe and happy. And right now, this guy is looking at her like conversation is the last thing on his mind. She's finally saying something, but every time she looks away, his eyes drop down her body hungrily.

Yeah, I've seen that look. I don't like it.

But Ivy and I are both adults now. And even though that high school kid in me is itching to do something, do what I would've done so many years ago, I hold back.

Until I remember what happened in the dining room.

"I saw your little stumble earlier."

Ivy got me by tripping me, so it's only fair that I get her back, right? Even the playing field before we go back to being grown-ups?

Before I can stop myself—and reassess what I'm sure is *very* flawed reasoning—I'm already taking a step forward. Within seconds, I'm by Ivy's side, interrupting the guy's speech about what Elon Musk's been up to recently.

"Ivy, right?" I ask innocently.

She turns towards me, annoyance flashing in her eyes. "What?"

"It *is* you!" I say enthusiastically. "I wasn't sure. I couldn't tell from the back."

Her nostrils flare dangerously. "James. What're you doing?"

I ignore her question. "You look different in your photos. Still gorgeous, just maybe a little... shorter than expected."

Ivy squeaks indignantly and I look at the guy, extend a hand. "I'm James. How do you know Ivy?"

The man's expression is almost as priceless as Ivy's. His eyes are narrowed to slits and he's looking between the two of us, head swiveling back and forth. "What's going on here?"

Ivy presses a hand to my bicep, shoving me away with surprising force. "Ignore him, Cam."

"Oh, don't be shy," I say teasingly, grabbing her hand and pulling her back towards me. I wrap my arms around her waist loosely so her back is pressed against my chest. Her light, fruity scent almost trips me up, but I keep going. "Imagine telling this story at our wedding."

Cam jerks back. "Wedding?"

"Yeah." I nod helpfully. "You know, that thing you do when you love someone."

Ivy's fuming. "He knows what a wedding is."

Cam's still staring at us, frowning like he's trying to do complex division involving apples and oranges. Finally, he exhales impatiently. "I'm going to go. Dylan's wrapped up in Room 11 and everything looks good. I'll send you the details tomorrow, that cool?"

Ivy's been struggling in my arms, but now, she stops. Deflates. "That's cool," she says miserably.

"Great. I'll see you around."

With that, Cam salutes to Ivy, nods at me, then marches away.

"Seriously?" I ask as I let her go. "*That* guy?"

She whirls around, her face like thunder, and swats at me with her clipboard. "He's nice and smart, you absolute jerk! And you had to ruin it. What is *wrong* with you?"

I hold up my hands to protect myself, shielding my face. "Ouch. Watch the clipboard, Brooks!"

"You deserve it!"

My actions are catching up with me, and I realize what I've done. I did *not* think that through—my old patterns just took over. "I'm sorry, you're right. I shouldn't have done that."

"Shouldn't have done what? I want to hear you say it."

"I shouldn't have gotten in the way. It won't happen again. I'm really sorry."

"Really really?"

"With cherries on top."

She finally stops attacking me and places her hands on her waist. "That was so rude, James."

"I know." I open my palms, feeling terrible. "I slipped up. Repressed, or whatever the word is—"

"Regressed."

"Exactly. I'm sorry."

She shakes her head. "I thought we were over what happened in high school."

"We are. It's done. I don't want to restart our feud, and I will never embarrass you in front of Cam again. Promise."

"Good." Ivy nods resolutely. "Because you know that I'll get you back twice as hard."

My lips twitch. "I do know. And I'll leave you alone now, promise, I won't get in the way. You and Cam can go off and be together."

At this, Ivy hesitates, her face going slack. But a second later, she sets her jaw. "Exactly. Because... maybe a relationship is exactly what I want with Cam."

"Good for you," I say sincerely.

"Yes. It *is* good for me."

Now, she's smiling smugly, and I let her bask in the win for a moment.

"So we're decided," I say. "We won't get in each other's way anymore. We'll be civilized, mature people."

"Agreed."

"We won't pretend we're on a blind date with the other person, or scare away potential dates, or..." I pause for a second. "Sabotage each other, say by, tripping the other person."

Her eyes widen and she looks away quickly, picking at the edge of her clipboard. "Right."

"Awesome. See you later. Mate."

With that, I give Ivy a friendly little punch on the shoulder and walk back towards the Inn. Just as I'm about to go inside, I glance back towards her.

Ivy's still standing where I left her, between a fern and a rose bush. She's gathered her hair over one shoulder and is biting her pinky fingernail, lost in thought.

A ray of sunlight is shining on her, illuminating the lighter streaks in her hair and setting her naturally tan skin alight. She looks... pretty. I can see why Cam's been flirting with her. There's something that feels off to me about the guy, but it's not my problem.

I turn away and head inside, glad that Ivy and I are putting our old battles to rest.

Ivy: Hey, *pal*. Just wanted to remind you that Luke and Eleanor are expecting us to meet with the photographer tomorrow.

James: Who is this?

Ivy: Are you serious?

James: Charlotte, right?

Ivy: You're a jerk.

James: Oh, Ivy! Good to hear from you.

Ivy: Trust me, contacting you was the last thing I wanted to do. But seeing as we're being mature and civilized now, I figured we could communicate as friends.

James: Right you are. So what's happening tomorrow?

Ivy: We're meeting at noon to finalize the plan for the wedding photos.

James: I'll be there. Will that Cam guy be coming as well?

Ivy: Not tomorrow. It'll just be the four of us, plus Daisy.

James: Sounds good. I'm glad we're friends now.

Ivy: Right. Friends don't make friends look bad in front of the people they like.

James: I am sorry again. I don't know what came over me.

Ivy: Stupidity?

James: Apparently. I just didn't love how he was looking at you like he couldn't care less what you were talking about.

James: But I don't know the guy, and I'm sorry for jumping to conclusions. I will stay on non-jumping-ground going forward.

Ivy: Good. Because I'm a grown woman, I can take care of myself.

James: You're right, Brooks. I know you can.

8

IVY

The Brookrose doesn't look like your classic mountain inn.

For one thing, it's pink.

Well, not actually. The building is made of bricks, but next to the other buildings on the street—all earthy, neutral colors—the sandy-coral walls of the Brookrose stand out like a bright pink beacon. The white trim and blue accents—remnants of an unfortunate eighties makeover—don't exactly help the situation.

But I love the look of the Inn, from the blue "Welcome" sign all the way to the yellow staircase leading to the front door.

When I was little, I used to pretend that the Brookrose was an English country manor. With the brick walls and the garden out back, all you'd need is to get rid of the blues and whites, and maybe paint the front staircase. Grow some vines.

It's in a great location too—nestled at the end of Main Street, right next to the creek that ambles through town. Shops spread down either side of the road, connected to their neighbors by wood awnings with hanging flowers.

There's a chill this morning, so the cafes and restaurants haven't put their chairs out yet, but when they do, the lively atmosphere is contagious.

"Morning, Ivy!"

I half-turn to see Valentina walking towards me, her dark curly hair falling around her shoulders and her brown eyes bright. She's wearing a floral dress, and I remember the days when she only wore stiff suits to work.

"Aren't you off today?" she asks as we share a hug. Val's a couple years younger than me, but we've become close working at the Brookrose.

"I'm meeting Daisy here for a wedding errand. We're headed to Morning Bell, so I'll say hi to the hubby for you."

Val's cheeks turn rosy pink, as they always do when Ethan comes up in conversation. "Please do! And this is good, the last thing you should be doing is worrying about the Brookrose. The wedding is taking a lot of your time, huh?"

"It's worth it. And I'm hoping this wedding is just the start... But we'll talk about that at our next team meeting."

Val raises an eyebrow. "Intriguing." Then, her eyes drop to the box in my hands and widen slightly. "Are those peanut butter chocolate brownies?!"

I chuckle. "They're snickerdoodles for Luke. He's been so stressed lately, I figured he could do with some sweets."

Minus laxatives, I might add. He has enough going on right now.

"Probably for the best." She sighs. "Ethan's been baking a lot for the cafe and I've stolen more baked goods than I'd care to admit. That man is too good to me."

"He loves you. Sounds like he's treating you right."

Val beams, her eyes taking on a faraway quality. Then, she shakes her head. "I should get inside."

"Have a great day. And I'm around if you need anything!"

Val waves as she enters the Inn and I sigh happily.

My apartment is a few streets away, but the Brookrose is my home. I learned to ride a bike here, with my dad giving me a running start. Every November, my mom and I would decorate the lobby for Christmas, and then bake cookies in the kitchen. And on winter evenings, I'd curl up in the worn, plushy sofa chairs in front of the fireplace, reading books or studying.

The Inn is my past, my present, and I want it to be my future too. This wedding—and everything that comes after it—is my chance to prove to my grandparents, to our town, to *myself*, that I can do this. That I can run the Inn, just like my parents would have wanted.

No imposter syndrome here. No, sir.

This what I've studied so hard for, what I've thought of and dreamed about for years. The Brookrose is our family's business, and Luke and I knew that we'd be inheriting it once our grandparents retired. With Luke pursuing his own career and getting ready to leave Mirror Valley with Elly, managing the Inn would fall to me.

I wouldn't have it any other way.

After graduation, I got a job offer from one of the country's top hotel chains in New York, but my mind, and my heart, were made up. Mirror Valley is my family, my community, my home. In some ways, I'd say I'm blessed because I learned how precious that is at a young age. Yes, the circumstances around that life lesson were pretty horrible and gut-wrenching, but I'm trying to focus on the bright side.

Which is this: when you find your home, the place where your heart truly belongs, it's impossible to turn your back on it.

"Surprise!"

A pair of arms wrap around my waist so forcefully that I almost drop the box of snickerdoodles.

I laugh as Daisy twirls me around. I follow through with the movement, spinning out gracefully.

See? I'm not a complete mess all the time. Only around men I might want to date.

Great.

"Ready to go?" she sings.

"Ready as I'll ever be."

Daisy and I stroll down Main Street towards our favorite coffee shop. Morning Bell Cafe is a franchise based out of Montana, and Ethan opened the Mirror Valley location a few months ago. It's done really well—partly because Ethan's a wonderful teddy bear of a person and everyone in town loves him.

"Are you excited for the photo shoot?" Daisy asks after we place our orders with the barista. Ethan's out running an errand, so I asked her to pass on our hello.

"It's *not* a photo shoot. We're just meeting the photographer and finalizing details for the big day. Boring logistical stuff."

Daisy rolls her eyes. "So glad you invited me."

"You know I appreciate having you around for this kind of stuff. Not to mention, you're a good buffer with Elly. And James." I shiver involuntarily, then hold up the box of cookies. "Plus, I made snickerdoodles! They're for Luke, but I'm sure he'll be happy to share—"

Daisy snatches the box, opens the lid, and grabs one before I can react. "Too late now."

She munches into the cookie happily and I roll my eyes, taking the box back. "It's a good thing you and Luke get along so well. He's picky about who he shares his treats with."

"Ah, that old softie can't say no to me."

I hold back from saying that Luke's inability to say no likely stems from her infallibly sweet nature rather than from him being a "softie." Luke has a tendency to be blunt with the people who annoy him, but Daisy always manages to escape any chastising. She's never concerned herself about annoying Luke, and really, he never seems annoyed with her.

It helps that being angry with Daisy would basically be equivalent to picking a fight with that puss-in-boots character from *Shrek*. Those big eyes have you forgetting why you were even mad in the first place.

"I do have an ulterior motive in asking you to come today," I admit as I take my clipboard out of of my bag. Yes, I take it with me everywhere. And yes, I have a special pink and green carry case for it. "I have a plan."

"I knew it," Daisy jokes. Then, she leans in. "I'm a sucker for a good Ivy Brooks gameplan. Let's hear it."

I flip through my papers until I reach the page titled: *Rockies Wedding Plan A.* "I've been tracking all the weddings in the area, and if we want to get Brookrose on the wedding circuit, we need to get it featured in the Colorado Rockies Wedding Review."

"Which is...?"

"A magazine."

Daisy snaps her fingers. "The fancy one with the perfume tabs that Ria stocks at the salon?"

"That's the one. We need to get Luke and Eleanor's wedding in there."

At that moment, the barista calls out our names. We take our drinks and head outside, but right as I'm about to launch into my brilliant three-step plan, I notice Daisy frowning at my hand. "What?"

"You always get the same thing. You don't want to try something new?"

I swirl my straw around my drink. "Don't be knocking the iced chai."

"Wouldn't dare! I'm just saying that, if you step out of your comfort zone, you might find something you like even *more* than iced chai. Like this smoothie." She holds up her cup proudly. "I'm not usually a smoothie person, but I figured, why not try it? YOLO and all that."

I groan. "Don't be using that young person lingo on me."

She raises an eyebrow. "I don't think 'YOLO' is even young person lingo anymore. That trend came and went."

"And I'm happy I missed it."

"Well, my point is... sometimes, it's worth the risk to find something you love more."

Easy for her to say.

I love my best friend to pieces. But sometimes, I could believe that our plant-based names—the reason we got paired together in second grade and have been inseparable ever since—is the only thing we have in common.

She and I are opposites on almost every level. She's lean and leggy, with straight blonde hair and blue eyes that scream "2000s era romcom lead," where I'm more your garden-variety, unexceptional-yet-jaded best friend. She works at the gym in town while balancing two or three side gigs and volunteer positions, and I'm struggling to manage the Inn alone. She's an eternal optimist, the ray of sunshine peeking out on the cloudiest days, while I'm constantly looking out for the tornadoes, tsunamis and hurricanes.

Plus, she didn't grow up with an annoying manchild calling her short, and it shows.

I shrug. "I don't see the point if you've already found perfection."

"Perfection is subjective, Iv."

"I may not know much, but I *know* that's not true. Perfection is universal, measurable. And achievable in the right circumstances."

Daisy nods slowly, considering my point. Perfectionism is a life tool for me—where the thought of making something perfect usually scares or overwhelms people, it's my security blanket. Striving for perfection is my safe space. As long as I'm working to be the best at something, I'm moving forward.

Finally, Daisy shrugs. "Agree to disagree."

I hold up my drink for a cheers. This is another reason Daisy and I get along so well—we can have our opposing views, but we love each other regardless.

Daisy takes a long pull of her drink. She winces as she swallows, then coughs quietly. "Ugh."

"What's wrong?"

"Nothing." Daisy frowns at her cup. "This just wasn't what I was expecting. I thought I ordered the kiwi smoothie, but this tastes like a whole lot of spinach. And... garlic?"

I hold out my drink, keeping my "I told you so" locked safely in my mouth. "Want some chai?"

Daisy pokes at the smoothie with disdain. "That's okay, I'll survive. I think the barista was new, maybe this was her first kiwi smoothie."

She continues to poke and prod at her drink, looking unbelievably sad. I peer at her sympathetically, then walk back to Morning Bell, grab an extra cup, and pour half of my chai in it. I give her the half-full cup before we start walking again.

"Where were we?" Daisy asks, slurping away. "Right. You were about to let me in on the gameplan."

"Yes, so I'm seeing a three-pronged approach." I hold up three fingers and count down as I go. "Step one: we need to plan and host a beautiful wedding, in line with what Luke and Eleanor want."

Daisy nods. "Check."

"Step two: we need to write a concise yet appealing description of the Inn to send to the magazine."

"I'm assuming that *will* be a check?"

"I've already started working on it. The final prong is the photographer."

"What do you mean?"

"If I'm going to propose that they feature the Brookrose in the Wedding Review, we need good photos to send. Which means that the photographer is *key*. We need someone who can take initiative, who has an eye for these things."

Daisy's brow clears. "And that's why you need me..."

"Yes. I'd love to have a second opinion. Obviously, Luke and Elly will be thinking of their wedding and I don't want to put this on them. So, I'm hoping you can step in if something seems off with the photographer or if I miss anything."

"At your service, ma'am."

I giggle and elbow her lightly. I'm excited to meet the photographer—I have high hopes that if we get the photos *just right* on Luke and Elly's wedding day, we'll be a shoo-in for the magazine.

My grandparents don't know my plan yet—I'm keeping it safely under wraps and on a need-to-know basis for now. Which will hopefully make it all the more dramatic when I show them the magazine feature, and hopefully, get us on the wedding circuit.

You know the "grand gesture"? The big dramatic moment at the end of romance books and movies? Yeah, that's essentially what I'm envisioning for this. Risking everything, putting in all this effort, just to show how dedicated I am and how much I love our inn.

Is that weird? Tells you a lot about the state of my dating life, I guess.

"Speaking of the wedding..." Daisy says. "How did everything go with the *gu-uy*?"

My smile fades. "Ugh. As expected, he hasn't changed one bit. He's still infuriating, immature, cocky, and arrogant. He was literally flirting with the caterer right in front of everyone. *And* he had the audacity to pretend to be, like, a blind date of mine when I was talking to Cam. He's the most vile human."

I stop the flow of words and clear my throat, remembering my resolution to be kind.

"But now that I have that off my chest, you won't hear another word against him. James and I have agreed to be friendly for Luke's wedding. So, he's... great?"

Daisy's stopped walking, and I turn back to face her. Her lips are twitching in such a way that I have to glance around to make sure that James isn't peeping around a corner.

"What?" I ask self-consciously.

"I was talking about Cam."

"Oh." I pause, take a long sip of chai. "Well, that went pretty much as expected too. I lost my balance and toppled over in reception, then couldn't think of a single thing to say when I ran into him again..."

At that moment, James pops uninvited back into my head. Specifically, his text—when he said that he didn't like how Cam was looking at me as we chatted in the garden.

It threw me off. The message sounded borderline protective, which is strange given our past. And when coupled with that weird burst of electricity I felt when I put my hand to his chest (which is way too firm, honestly), it's even stranger.

My skin heats as I remember having his arms around me

63

when he *should* have been minding his own business. The warmth spreads like a fire down to my toes and fingers. Because I hate him. And he makes me angry.

What does James know anyway? Sure, Cam doesn't always scream "fascinating conversation," and maybe he occasionally doesn't seem to be listening. But he's intelligent and well-spoken and dedicated to his job. Which I can sympathize with.

That's why I want to make things work with him. A relationship with Cam would be smooth, easy. He doesn't seem like the romantic type—the type to evoke or express big emotions or get all lovey-dovey. But who needs that? We'd get along great.

Just as soon as I stop all the fidgeting and knocking things over.

"I don't get it," I say, frustrated. "I'm usually fine standing on my two feet, but when I'm around Cam—or any attractive guy—I'm a mess."

Daisy's eyes sparkle. "You seem just fine when you're around James."

"That's because he's not attractive," I say stubbornly.

"That's a lie and you know it."

I press my lips together. Even I can't argue that point—if James was attractive in high school, he's only become more so with age. Like really old wine, probably. With his thick hair, piercing eyes, and the little chin dimple that makes him look at once regal and up to no good, James is pretty much the full package for most women.

But I can also acknowledge that I've been thinking about him *way* too much over the last couple days. I have to put these thoughts away. James is meaningless, inconsequential. Like any one star in the sky—unrecognizable except in terms of proximity to other stars.

"Hey, isn't that Luke?" Daisy asks.

My brother is indeed jogging towards us from the opposite direction. He waves. "You guys made it!"

I glance around. "Where's that wonderfully kind, intelligent, and respectable best man of yours?" Luke gives me a look and I smile sheepishly. "Too much?"

"*Way* too much. But I appreciate the effort." We all fall into step towards the photo studio. "James is meeting us there. He's on a call with work again."

"His circus coming to town?" Okay, *that* was the last dig, I swear.

Luke sighs.

"And what about Lenore?" Daisy asks.

"She's also running late; some makeup crisis. She'll be there as soon as possible." His eyes drop to the box in my hands. "Are those snickerdoodles?"

I hand him the box. "As promised."

"Thanks, sis. You're the best." He pops the lid and shoves a couple cookies in his mouth. Daisy steals another one for herself.

I finally register what my brother's wearing, and that there's a light sheen of sweat on his forehead. "You didn't change out of your gym clothes for this?"

"I lost track of time. I was mid-workout when I got a notification about the appointment."

He lifts a corner of his jersey and wipes his face, showing off a slice of his midsection. At that moment, Daisy swallows the wrong way and starts coughing.

I roll my eyes. "Gross, Luke. No one needs to see your abs."

"Pretty good, right?" Luke waggles his eyebrows. "Been working on my core a lot lately."

"I don't understand why you're so obsessed with the gym these days."

"It's a proven way to work off stress. Dais, you work there. What's your professional opinion?"

"Uh..." Daisy gasps, still sounding strangled. "Core work is important?"

Luke gives me a triumphant nod, then goes serious again. "Anyway. Let's see what the photographer's got for us. I asked Lenore to book her, and she didn't have many details—just said that it's a new business and the photographer goes by 'Madame Francoise.' I don't know much about wedding photos, so hopefully she and Lenore have some ideas."

"It'll be great," I say. "I've got a list we can go over until Lenore arrives anyway."

"Of course you do." Luke chuckles, tugging his fingers through his hair—a habit he's had since we were kids. "Let's get this over with."

"That's the spirit." Daisy links one arm with his and the other with mine. "This'll be an adventure."

An adventure's right. I can't wait to see what this "Madame Francoise" has in store for us.

The bell above the door tinkles as Daisy, Luke and I file into the photo studio. It smells like fresh paint and carpet, mixed with a flower perfume I vaguely recognize. Daisy and Luke are bickering over some movie, but I tuned them out minutes ago. The two of them often get into these little ping-pong conversations and I've learned to stay out of it.

"That's so not the point," Luke says as he holds the door open for her.

"Isn't it? Sometimes, you gotta look below the surface, Luke," Daisy retorts.

"Like I said the other day—"

"Guys," I interrupt. "As thrilling as this conversation is, maybe you want to put it on the backburner for now?"

Luke raises a brow, his hazel eyes sparking as he shoots Daisy a quick smile. "Fine."

While we wait for Madame Francoise to make her appearance, I take a look around the storefront.

The space is newly-renovated, with butter yellow walls, a teak reception desk, and bookshelves stacked with a haphazard arrangement of photo frames and random items —a fur hat, a set of candles, a silk scarf. Above the desk, there's a huge, flat-screen TV cycling through a slideshow of photos.

I stroll around the shop, examining Madame Francoise's style. Photos stare back at me—of happy, posed families, black-and-white graduations, and odd, historical-looking sepia shots taken on Main Street.

Eventually, I reach the back wall, where rows of glass shelves are lit with small spotlights. Each shelf carries a collection of dark, artsy photos. Clearly, these are the featured shots—the ones Madame Francoise is most proud to display.

As I look closer, my jaw hits the floor.

"Luke..." I say slowly. "What do you know about Madame Francoise?"

Luke is still at the front, staring at a close-up of a dog's face as it leaps for a treat. "Uh, not much. Just that Lenore got her number from someone in town."

"I don't see any wedding photos, though," Daisy says.

I swallow thickly. "I don't think Madame Francoise specializes in wedding photography."

Luke peers at me. "What do you mean?"

I gesture towards the wall behind me, and Daisy comes closer. Her eyes go wide. "Oh," she mutters. "Oh, my."

Luke comes up next. His face goes slack. "What in the—"

"Bonjour!"

The voice is sharp and high-pitched, and I nearly jump out of my skin. Luke, Daisy and I whirl around guiltily, like we've all been caught doing something bad.

When I see the woman approaching us, I do a double take. "Fran?"

Fran Bellamy is the last person I expected to see here. She's comfortably in her seventies, and is one of those older people who couldn't care less what anyone thinks of them. She used to work as an administrator at Mirror Valley's police and fire department—our town is so small, you just need the one—but since retiring, she spends her days hosting book clubs, playing bridge, and knitting everything from clothes to stuffed cacti.

Apparently, she's now added "photographer" to her list of accolades.

She smiles at us grandly, her arms extended. She's wearing a full denim outfit—her jacket covered in artsy patches and badges that each have their own wild, colorful story. Her dyed fire-engine-red hair is tied back with a massive clip, and her rhinestone-rimmed glasses are perched down her nose.

"Mais oui!" she exclaims—likely the only French she knows. "Sorry to keep you waiting."

"No problem," I squeak, my back to the wall of the photos.

Fran comes to me first and kisses me on both cheeks, like they do in Europe. "Ivy, good to see you." She proceeds to Luke, and finally Daisy. "Where is Eleanor?" She rolls the r on Eleanor's name and I can't help but wonder how Elly will feel about that whenever she arrives.

"Lenore," Luke corrects automatically. "She'll be here soon."

Fran takes a look down his body, registering his workout clothes. "Dear boy, there was no need to run a marathon before coming here."

Daisy snorts and I cover my smile. Fran isn't exactly known for being tactful—"*Life's too short for niceties, darlin'!*" She gets away with it because she's kind of like the town's eccentric grandmother. Which makes me all the more uneasy about having her as the photographer, but I'd like to give her a chance anyway.

"Sorry. Lost track of time," Luke says tightly.

"So what can I help you with today?"

"We're here about the wedding photos," I say, though it comes out sounding like a question.

"Ah, so this is for a wedding!" Fran claps her hands. "Eleanor was vague in her email, I wasn't sure."

I look at Daisy and Luke in alarm. Luke's expression is now mildly surprised. "You *do* know that we need you next Saturday, right?"

"Yes, yes. Eleanor mentioned that." Fran waves a hand so the bangles on her wrist clang together.

"And do you have experience taking uh... wedding photos?" Daisy asks, peeking over her shoulder at the back wall again.

Fran catches the movement and sweeps towards us. She manages to gather all three of us under her arms, and cranks us towards the wall. "Of course, I've taken photos for weddings before. But as you can see, I do have another speciality..."

"Yes." I shift on my feet. I wish I could look literally anywhere else, but the photos are directly in front of my eyes. Meanwhile, both Luke and Daisy are staring at a point

69

just above the photos. Ah, to be tall. "It looks like you do a lot of—"

"Boudoir photos, yes!" she exclaims, then waggles her eyebrows at Luke. "Maybe for the first anniversary, hm?"

Luke looks horrified.

"Let's head to the back and get started." Fran finally releases us and I turn away. I'm all about women being proud of their beautiful, God-given shapes, but the thought of my photo up there fills me with a discomfort I can't even begin to describe. I don't have *nearly* enough confidence for that.

Luke, Daisy and I follow Fran to the back of the studio, where a large room is set up with photography equipment, various props, and a box of clothing. It actually looks pretty professional.

"What got you into photography?" I ask as Fran gets set up, a look of determined concentration on her face.

"I've been interested in photography since you were in diapers, darlin'. I finally decided to go for it. Life is too short to waste a single moment, and I'm seventy years young. There couldn't be a better time to dive in."

Daisy looks at me pointedly. "Good for you for trying something new."

I roll my eyes at her while Fran laughs a big, booming laugh.

"That's what life's about!" she guffaws. "Taking risks, being brave, grabbing opportunities when they come up and never looking back. We all have regrets, of course, but I always say, by the time the good Lord takes me, I hope I've learned the lessons I need to learn, and lived the life I've been given to live. And laughed a lot along the way."

We all continue to chat while Fran finishes getting set up.

Finally, she claps. "Wonderful. Now, I will ask you to pose."

"Pose?!" I frown. "I thought we were just running through the plan for the big day."

"Why yes. But a part of that is making sure that I have everything I need. I'll ask one of you to get on the set and pose in the different lighting."

"Not it," Daisy says, pressing a finger to her nose.

I'm jerking my own hand up to my face when I notice Luke already has his finger on his nose and is looking at me smugly.

Crap. I do *not* look good in photos.

Granted, I put in more effort today—donned my protective armor, so to speak, as James is supposed to be here. I've pulled my freshly-washed hair into a sleek ponytail, have a base layer of makeup, and am wearing a smart white t-shirt and cargo-style green pants.

But there are photogenic people and non-photogenic people, and I fall comfortably into the second camp.

Still, there's a clear loser (me), so I approach Fran with hesitation.

"Stand over there. By the couch," she orders, pointing across the set. I awkwardly walk over. "Great. Now turn to the side."

I follow her directions and she adjusts the camera. The shutter clicks, she barks out more orders, makes more adjustments, and the shutter clicks again.

My skin is crawling, but I grin and bear it. Once we're through with these photos, we can move onto more serious business.

"Ah," Fran mutters as she steps away from the camera. "I need to try with a different lens. One moment."

With that, she unlocks a side door and disappears.

"Wow, Ivy..." The laughter in Luke's voice is clear as day.

"Shut it."

"You're a natural." Daisy snorts.

I peer through the darkness, trying to see their faces past the blinding spotlights. "You have no idea how uncomfortable this is."

"So make yourself comfortable," Daisy suggests, and I finally see her. She's taking Fran's place behind the camera. "Go on, do something nutty."

"What?"

"Let loose a little. It'll be fun."

I cross my arms. "I don't think so."

"Come on, sis," Luke taunts, appearing next to Daisy. "Why not? Things have been so serious lately with the wedding."

"So why don't you come up here and 'let loose' then?"

"Because I'm the groom," Luke answers helpfully. "Look, I'll go after you. Check out all the props and costumes—you can have some serious fun with this."

"Do it, do it," Daisy starts to chant.

I look warily at the box of clothing on the other side of the couch. At the top of the pile sits a pirate hat, various wigs, and what looks like a silk nighty. "I mean... I just..."

"Do it, do it!" Daisy chants louder, and this time, Luke joins in.

I roll my eyes, exasperated. "Okay, okay! Fine." I chuckle. "But I'm only doing this for you. And you have to promise to delete *all* the photos before Fran comes back."

"Yay!" They both cheer.

I sink down behind the couch. I'm not sure what I'm doing—impromptu photo shoots are *very* much outside of my comfort zone. But Daisy said I never try anything new, so hopefully this'll put that argument to rest for the next little while, at least.

I throw on a cape, a Marie Antoinette-looking wig of tall, white hair, and a cane. Then, I rise from behind the couch, stepping mechanically into the spotlight.

"Woooo!" Daisy hollers as Luke does a wolf-whistle. "Work it!"

I roll my eyes. "This is so cringey!"

"Who cares? No one's here to see it."

I roll my eyes again. Then, summoning an attitude I don't recognize in myself, I strike a ridiculous pose. This garners more laughter and cheers, so I start to do a little dance, twirling around and making faces.

This has to be one of the weirdest moments of my life, but it's making Luke laugh in a way that I haven't heard him laugh in a long time, so it's worth the embarrassment.

I find my groove, gaining confidence from heaven knows where, and I continue to strut around. I channel my inner Victoria's Secret model, pretending that I could really be this sure of myself. If I'm honest, it's kind of liberating. It's nice to try something so out of character.

Soon, I'm smiling at the camera for real, and laughing so hard my insides hurt.

9

JAMES

"This is great news for you, James. You should be proud."

I nod. "Thanks, Martin."

"Now, enjoy being home. The last thing I want to do is disrupt your vacation time, so I won't contact you again until you're back in the office."

He barks out a laugh and I smirk, knowing full well that I'll be hearing from him before that. "No problem. Chat soon."

I hang up and stick my phone in my back pocket. I've been pacing outside the photo studio for the past five minutes while Martin gave me an update on my "start small" campaign. It's already in motion, and Xavier is putting together a team to work on it.

Exciting stuff. And yet, for the entire conversation, all I could think about was Cadbury chocolate...

Last night, I had a dream about England. I don't think of it often; I barely remember the years I spent there as a kid. But in my dream, I packed up and moved there.

I didn't hate the idea.

But this is crazy. I can't just move to England.

Though my dad would be all about it. His one true love in life—after my mother—is English Cadbury chocolate. "*It tastes different!*" he insists, and heaven forbid anyone attempts to fool him with Cadbury chocolate from North America.

Having a son in England to send him endless amounts would probably be enough to sell him on the whole idea.

I give my head a shake. I'm *not* the type of person who uproots their life based on a dream. I'm the person who sees what they want and goes for it. Just like I did with soccer. Just like I'm doing at Penumbra.

I banish any more—clearly irrational—thoughts of moving away from Denver, then stand straight. Smile. Take one of my long, loud breaths in...

And realize I've startled a child.

I high-tail it into the photo studio to escape any embarrassment. Maybe I should reconsider the yoga breaths.

"Hello?" I call.

Nothing. I walk into the store slowly, wondering if I'm in the right place.

"Luke? Ivy?"

Still nothing.

The room is kind of a mess and smells vaguely like paint thinner beneath heavy perfume. Photo frames are spread around, which means that this has to be the photo studio. Or a proud grandparent rented out a storefront to display photos of their loved ones.

I smile at the thought. Until I approach the back wall.

Crikey. The photos over here are definitely *not* in the endearing grandparent category.

I move along quickly and continue my wander around. It's not until I'm in front of the reception desk that I freeze. Above the desk, there's a massive, flat-screen TV.

And front and center is a photo of Ivy Brooks.

But not just any Ivy Brooks—this is Ivy Brooks in a wig, posing with a cane.

The photo fades out and another takes its place. A close-up of Ivy with her eyes crossed. Then, one with her tongue out.

I watch, mesmerized, as the photos cycle through. When did she take these? And why? I realize I'm smiling. Not because this is embarrassing for her, or because she looks ridiculous, but because she looks... happy.

I can almost hear her laughter in the poses she's making, visualize her cracking up as she moves, the sparkle in her eyes.

The stress and tension in my shoulders melts away as the slideshow continues. Ivy's a perfectionist, she likes things to look polished. I can't remember the last time I saw her like this—with her guard down, being a little goofy.

Not that she'd ever willingly do this in front of me.

With that thought, I turn away, knowing she'd be mortified if she knew that I'd seen these photos.

Finally, I see a door that says "Studio." Bingo.

I step into the back room, which is dark aside from a large space in the center, lit up by huge spotlights. And in the middle of it stands Ivy with the wig and cane, dancing and blowing kisses at the camera.

My heart skips as I watch her, drawn in. A cape sits lopsided over her shoulders, and the wig keeps tipping off her head. My eyes skim over her, from her ponytail, down her slender, capri-clad legs, to her heeled sandals.

"James?"

Luke's voice startles me, and I see him shielding his eyes and peering through the darkness from where he and Daisy are standing behind the camera.

Immediately, Ivy squeaks and dives behind the couch.

Cover blown.

"Yeah." I clear my throat, stepping forward. "Just walked in."

Luke walks over and gives me a fist bump. "We're waiting for the photographer to come back."

"And where's Ivy?" I ask innocently.

"I'm here!" Ivy suddenly shoots up from behind the couch, minus the costume. "I was inspecting the props. Making sure everything's good and sturdy. Like this couch, you know..." she trails off, losing steam. "It needs to be... solid."

"Sure, sure." I nod along like I'm buying her role as Couch Quality Control Specialist.

Luke turns to me with a barely disguised eye roll. "You didn't see Lenore out there, did you?"

"She's not here?"

Luke runs his fingers through his hair, tugging at the ends. "She's on her way. I'll call her again."

I press my lips together as Luke dials Eleanor's number and walks away.

Then, I catch Ivy looking at Daisy with wild eyes, and Daisy nods surreptitiously. Before I can ask what's going on, she exclaims, "hey, James! Good to see you. How's work?"

My brow furrows. I like Daisy, but we've never been all that close. Definitely not close enough for her current level of enthusiasm. "Uh... same old."

"Great, great," she says, fiddling manically with the camera. Okay, she's definitely putting up a front.

Right then, she gives Ivy a sneaky thumbs up.

What's that all about?

"Ah, we have a latecomer," a voice booms behind me. "Welcome! I'm Madame Francoise."

I turn to face the woman sweeping into the darkened

room. I register her red hair and her denim outfit, and my eyes go wide. "Franny?"

She stops walking, swivels to look at me. "Jamie?"

I smile wide, wrapping her in a hug. "Good to see you."

"You too, my boy!"

Ivy hops out of the spotlight and walks towards us. "You know each other?"

"Of course, darlin'!" Fran chortles. "This one, he made quite the impression at the department growing up."

"Bit of a juvenile delinquent, was he?" Ivy smiles angelically.

"Nothing like that. James was one of our top student volunteers. Used to play on the soccer league for the annual fundraiser and everything. Went above and beyond, helped with so many of our programs."

Ivy blinks. Tilts her head at me in surprise. "You did?"

I shake my head at the older woman. "Fran, come on. I've got an image to keep up, remember?"

"Sorry, my boy. My lips are sealed and your reputation is safe." She spots Luke walking back towards us. "Enough chit-chat. Shall we get back to discussing the big day?"

Luke nods. "Lenore's on her way."

"Wonderful. Let's get started and catch her up whenever she joins us."

Fran returns to her spot behind the camera but Ivy stays put for a moment. For some reason, I feel extra aware of her —of her coconutty scent, of where her arm almost brushes against mine. She refuses to meet my eyes, even as her chin is tilted up defiantly. I can't see her freckles in the darkness.

"What?" I finally ask.

"Did you..." She clears her throat. "Did you see anything? When you walked in?"

I keep my face neutral. "See any of what?"

Ivy nods once, but I catch the relief in her expression. An unexpected pang twists my stomach.

"Nothing, nothing at all," she says.

She turns on her heel and joins Fran, Luke and Daisy by the camera. I walk a step behind her, unsettled. I have a feeling that her smiling face and laughter will be engraved in my mind in a way that I won't be forgetting anytime soon.

10

IVY

"Now that we have a few solo shots, let's move onto the next step," Fran is saying when I rejoin the group.

"Next step?" Luke asks. He's tugging on the ends of his hair again, and checking his Apple watch every two seconds. I hope Elly gets here soon—Luke's fiancée should be with him, instead of a ragtag team of his best man, sister/unofficial wedding planner, and sister's best friend.

And let's not forget Fran. To be fair, you could never forget Fran.

"Photos of the bride and groom, obviously!" she says, staring at him over her rhinestone-rimmed glasses. "But, seeing as the bride isn't here yet, we'll have to improvise."

I hold my breath.

Please choose Daisy, please choose Daisy...

"Ivy, darlin'. You're the obvious choice, seeing as you're so... comfortable in front of the camera." A knowing smile crosses Fran's lips and I have to look away, my face pinched.

Daisy gave me a thumbs up—she'd deleted those ridiculous, goofy photos we took. Unless Fran is somehow clairvoyant, which I wouldn't put past her.

"I've already had my turn." I force a laugh. "Surely, someone else wants to go."

"Come on, Brooks. You can do it," James prods. He's standing behind my left shoulder, and when I turn to shoot him a look, he's smiling innocently.

A little *too* innocently.

He said he didn't see anything when he walked in. The absolute worst thing would be James Weston witnessing my not-so-Victoria's-Secret moment in the spotlight.

I decide to believe him, because the alternative is far, far too embarrassing.

"Go on. Don't keep us all waiting," Fran orders. I meet her gaze and, for a fraction of a second, I could swear I see something there. A mischievous little gleam, like she's got something up her sleeve.

But the next moment, she's fiddling with her camera again.

I press my lips into a grim line and march back into the spotlight, fiddling with my ponytail. James is looking at me, and I narrow my eyes back at him.

"Now, we need someone to pose with you..." Fran muses as she looks at our little group.

"Daisy can pose with me."

Fran guffaws. "Unless Daisy can pass for Luke—"

"No problem," she interrupts, her voice so low, it cracks. "I can be Luke. I love taxes. So many taxes. Get the IRS on the phone STAT and ASAP."

Even through the darkness, I see Luke's raised eyebrow. "I don't sound like that."

James slaps him on the shoulder. "Dude, she's got you pegged."

"Anyway," Fran continues. "As... valiant as your efforts are, dear, you won't make the cut. And for obvious reasons, we can't have Luke up there posing with Ivy. So that leaves..."

Oh, no.

Please, no.

I'd sooner do couple's photos with the donut mascot guy outside the car dealership who always smells vaguely of old cheese.

I shake my head vigorously. "Fran, I don't think that's—"

"I'd love to!" James cuts through my protests, sounding more gleeful than he should.

He practically skips onto the set and walks towards me. As he approaches, I'm blown away, once again, by how tall he is. And strong. He walks towards me purposefully, like he might just pick me up and sling me over his shoulder, caveman-style.

My eyes scan his body without permission, taking in his long, confident stride and his wicked smile. He could make a convincing caveman—just add a perma-dumbstruck expression and patchwork furs. Instead, he's wearing blue jeans and a light gray Henley that sets off the tan on his muscled forearms.

His eyes lock with mine and in the depths of his oceanic gaze, I see a shimmer of something I really don't like.

He stands next to me and I find I'm holding my breath.

"Let's start by having you stand together." Fran nods. "Maybe holding hands?"

"I can do you one better," James says. Then, before I can say or do anything, he steps behind me and wraps his arms around my waist so my back is flush with his firm front.

Well, that's the second time this week that I'm pressed against James Weston. And it's the second time that my heart races to feel the heat of his body, my bare skin separated from his by just a couple thin layers of clothing...

Being this close to him, he doesn't actually smell like overpowering cologne. He smells like fresh laundry, and a hint of sandalwood.

My head starts to spin and I realize I haven't inhaled in awhile.

Yoga breaths, I tell myself. *Keep breathing, Ivy.*

Unfortunately, my body decides that the breath I need to take is one of those long, loud ones in your nostrils that you only ever do when practicing yoga at home. Alone. With no witnesses.

This is what I get for spending more time staring at my phone screen in "Do Not Disturb" mode than the instructor in my yoga videos.

James chuckles at the noise, making his abs flex against me in a way I don't appreciate.

"Wooooo!" Daisy does a long wolf-whistle.

Meanwhile, Luke shakes his head, his arms crossed. I can imagine what he's thinking—James and I, with our never-ending bickering and our childish games, are poor replacements for him and Eleanor.

All of a sudden, James takes a sharp inhale and his arms tighten slightly against me. I've just placed my hands on his forearms... Could this little pose of ours be affecting him too?

I don't know what to do with that, so I take the smallest step away from him and file the thought away in my mental folder titled "do NOT open."

"Fantastic!" Fran exclaims as the shutter clicks. "Brava. Dance my puppets."

Isn't this just every girl's dream? Posing in a lovey-dovey way with her nemesis at the whims of a septuagenarian.

We all peak sometime.

The shutter continues to click, and I stand firm, my body stiff and unyielding. I will *not* lean back into James. I will *not* become comfortable or at ease in his arms. And I will *not* acknowledge that his fresh, clean, warm scent is making my insides do weird things.

"You're naturals, the both of you!" Fran goes on, animated.

Doubt that. On my part, at least. James always looks like he just stepped out of a Netflix show for hot people.

"Now, relax into the posture," Fran says.

Nope. Not doing that. I've drawn my line.

But James obeys, stepping the slightest bit closer so he's not quite pressed against me, but grazing my back. Somehow, the feeling is even more potent, and while I know I should step away, there's an alarmingly insistent part of me that wants to close the gap.

What is happening?!

Unfortunately, Fran isn't done. "Now, look at each other as if you were the bride and groom."

"Are you kidding me?" I squeak.

"What was that?" James asks. Is it just me or is his voice a little husky?

"Nothing." I shake my head, thinking fast. "I just... My neck hurts. From yoga."

"That's okay, Brooks." His voice is almost gentle. "Tilt your head a bit and I'll meet you halfway."

My nostrils flare, the overachiever in me taking over. "No. I can do this."

I twist my neck around so I'm staring straight at James and he smiles down at me, amused. "Yeah. That looks normal—you gawking at me."

"I do not gawk," I say flippantly. "I am a lady."

"Of course you are." James nods seriously. "But you

don't have to do everything all the time. Let me help you. This'll be more comfortable, promise."

He tilts his head forward, so his jawline and his lips are close to my face. Very, very nice lips. And the chin dimple. What is it about a chin dimple that's so freaking attractive—

Nope! Ivy, what is going on with you?

I must've eaten bad shrimp or something.

Not that I like shrimp. See? James is getting me all flustered.

Our scoreboard must now read: Ivy - o, James - 23.

"Okay. Look up at me," James says. "You can even glare at me, if that's easier for you."

"She did say to be natural," I respond automatically.

Good. Being catty with James is far safer than where my mind was going a moment ago.

"Just remember," he whispers. "The sooner this is over, the sooner we can get on with our lives."

Now *that's* something I can get on board with. I follow James's advice and tilt my head as instructed. And he's right, of course—this feels a lot nicer for my neck.

I start off shooting him daggers, but his eyes have this curious gleam to them and the fight in me starts to ebb.

I look up at him, my mind blank for once.

SLAM.

"I'm here!"

I leap out of James's arms like a startled frog, and he steps in the opposite direction.

I'm glad everyone's paying attention to Elly's arrival, because I need a second. As soon as I get my bearings, I march away from James without giving him a glance—I don't know what would happen if I did.

My entire body's vibrating, my skin is hypersensitive. And my breath?

Very irregular and un-yoga-like.

"Babe, so glad you're here!" Luke says as he wraps Elly in a hug. She hugs him back, closing her eyes blissfully, and a deeply unsettling feeling rises through me. For the first time, I think I might understand how it feels to be wrapped in someone's arms like that.

Though, for me, it happened very much with the wrong person.

"Sorry." Elly steps out of the hug, but holds tight to Luke's hand. "The makeup artist canceled and Franscesca was having a quasi-panic attack."

"So you don't have anyone to do your makeup for the wedding?"

"Oh... No, I'll be doing my own makeup that day. Franscesca scheduled a makeup artist for the bachelorette, and she's the one that canceled. But crisis averted: Ana is getting her cousin to do our makeup." Elly smiles. "She works on movie sets in LA. It's going to be *amazing*."

Luke tucks a strand of hair behind her ear. "I'm glad it worked out."

"Same." She faces the rest of us and the corners of her eyes tighten. "So what're we doing here? I saw the photos outside, seems like James and Ivy are getting cozy."

What photos outside?

I reflexively cast James a glance over my shoulder to see if he's as confused as I am. Instead, he's shifting back and forth on his feet, brushing at an imaginary speck of dust on his shirt like he doesn't care to be a part of this conversation. He almost looks...

Guilty.

I frown at Eleanor, a bad feeling in my stomach. "What photos? What do you mean?"

"You know... the photos taken in here are being shown on that TV screen in the shop." She shrugs. "While I was waiting, I saw a whole series of you two hugging."

Wait.

No.

If the photos of James and me were being projected on that huge TV for the world to see, then wouldn't my goofy photos from earlier...

My stomach lurches and a burning-hot wave of embarrassment rolls across every inch of my skin.

I whirl around to face James, who is now apparently fascinated with something on the ceiling. "But you..." I splutter. "You said..."

He finally looks at me, and the truth is right there in his eyes.

Why, oh why, can't the floor open up and swallow me right now? I'd even take a spontaneous alien capture. Anything but having to stand here and process this.

The costume, the strutting, the stupid faces... James saw it all.

Oh my goodness. I never let my guard down around *anyone* except my closest friends and family. James is pretty much the furthest he could possibly be from that.

This is what I get for acting so stupid in front of the camera. How many chinks did he find in my armor? How many jokes is he going to make? I can't even bear the thought.

Unfortunately, the ground does not open up, and I am not taken away by aliens. Instead, Fran claps her hands, like she couldn't care less about my current fatal state of mortification. "Chop, chop, everyone. These photos aren't going to plan themselves."

Everyone gathers around Fran, and I stand all the way across the circle from James. I don't dare shoot him a single look, give him a moment of my time. Instead, I focus on the one thing I can control—making this wedding the best it can be.

11

JAMES

"Hey man, wait up!"

The voice pulls me from my thoughts. Thoughts which were *not* revolving around Ivy.

I turn to see Luke jogging out of the photo studio. He holds up a hand and I smack it.

"I thought you were staying back with Eleanor and Franny to go over the plan one more time."

"Lenore," Luke corrects. "She wanted to speak with Fran about the bridesmaid photos. Ana, Francesca, and Leona have very specific requests, I guess. Took it as my cue to bow out, and besides, I figured we could do something." He picks at his watch. "Sorry I haven't had a chance to catch up with you lately. All this wedding planning has been hectic."

"Don't worry about it. I'm your best man, here to wait on you hand and foot and all that."

"And I'll happily return the favor someday."

I smile tightly. I definitely don't have the same optimism when it comes to my love life. I would never get married just to do it, to check off a box on my life bucket list. If and when I get married, it'll be for love. And I don't see love breaking down my door anytime soon.

We walk down Main Street, headed for McGarry's Pub. Neither of us drink much, but the music is fun, lively, and not too loud, and they've got pool tables and dartboards where Luke and I spend hours whenever I'm in town.

"How're you feeling about everything?" I ask when we've racked up. I place my cue carefully and break. I take another shot and the white ball hits a solid, which sinks into a corner pocket. "Sounds like Ivy's got it under control, huh?"

I take another shot, but this one doesn't sink.

Luke steps up to the table. "Classic Ivy—she covers all the bases and then some."

"So she hasn't changed."

"Nope."

"She still single, then?" The question is out of my mouth before I can think about the possible consequences. AKA, making Luke think something that he shouldn't. AKA, that I might be fishing for information.

Which I'm not.

I assume Ivy's single given her flirtatious attempts with Babyface, but who's to know? And this is just idle chit-chat anyway.

"Single as ever." Luke shrugs, and I'm slightly relieved at his easygoing response. "I'm starting to think her one true love in life is the Brookrose. Which suits me just fine."

He shoots and the cue ball bounces off the far end of the table, then hits a stripe into a pocket.

"Why do you say that?"

"She's my baby sister. I already know that no guy is ever going to be good enough for her. So if she chooses to be single, that means much less work for me hunting down her boyfriends and giving them the third degree."

Here's the thing about Luke—he might seem like your standard-issue CPA, and while he is smart and logical, he's also jacked and fiercely protective of his family. Richard Brooks is tough as nails, but he's getting older, and seeing as Luke and Ivy's dad passed away years ago, it makes sense that the role of "stern dad" has fallen on Luke.

Needless to say, I would not want to be on the receiving end of his "third degree," whatever that entails.

"Right," I say, my throat weirdly dry. "Well, the Brookrose seems to be keeping her busy, especially now that your grandparents are retiring." I bend over the table and take another shot, but the cue ball misses the target by a mile. "Aren't you meant to be inheriting half of the Inn with her?"

Luke pauses for a moment, then picks up the cue chalk. He keeps his eyes on the table, as though he's planning his next move, but his eyes are troubled. "Kind of a touchy thing. I'm thinking of giving up my share."

My eyebrows shoot up. "Really?"

"Yeah... It just doesn't make sense for me to be a part-owner of the Brookrose if Lenore and I are moving away after the wedding. Besides, Ivy's got her degree in hospitality, she should take on full management of the Inn. As much as I love it, it seems only fair to relinquish my part."

"Tough decision. Have you talked to your grandparents about it?"

"They seemed sad, but they understand," Luke says soberly. "They only want what's best for Ivy and me, and they know I'm moving soon to start my life with Lenore. Now, *that's* going to be the fun conversation."

"You haven't told her?"

"I'm waiting for the right time. Lenore has a soft spot for the Inn; she was thrilled when I told her that I'd be inheriting half of the business whenever our grandparents retire.

But now that it's happening, I can't imagine being a part-owner. I'm sure she'll understand."

"Good luck." I pat Luke on the back, then sidle around the table and line up another shot.

"Hey, can you do something for me?" he asks as I focus on the cue ball.

"Anything, man."

"Can you keep an eye on Ivy while you're here?"

I take a bad shot and almost tear through the lining on the table.

I clear my throat and stand straight. "What do you mean?"

"Well, you guys used to argue all the time, but I know you have her best interests at heart. I want to make sure that she isn't killing herself with this wedding. I've heard her talk about this wedding magazine thing she has planned and I'm worried she'll burn herself out. Normally, I'd be watching out for her, but obviously, there's a lot going on these days. I know you also feel a little protective of her sometimes, so I thought you might look out for her."

Hmm. Best not to mention the weird spike in my heart rate when I had her in my arms earlier.

Caffeine, remember? I just need to cut down on caffeine.

I focus on Luke. "Of course, man. I'll make sure she's alright."

"Thanks, you're a lifesaver. The girl doesn't know when to stop, but when Madame Francoise was taking photos, she actually seemed to relax at a certain point. It was refreshing to see that. Whatever you were doing or whatever you said to her, it was good."

I stare down at the pool table because looking at Luke right now is not an option.

It was cocky of me to wrap my arms around Ivy, to step

into the protective bubble she has around herself. But it was also cocky because I didn't realize how much it would affect me to have her body pressed against mine. To smell her shampoo that I could only describe as "sexy coconut." Which feels ridiculous, even aside from conjuring images of a coconut sunning itself on a beach with a piña colada.

And her high ponytail. What is it about a high ponytail that is so insanely attractive?

When she placed her hands on my forearms, I had to steady my breath because her touch did that thing again. Like waves of electricity across my skin.

All I wanted was to draw her closer and closer. But I couldn't. Not only because we had an audience which included her protective older brother and my best friend, but also because she wouldn't want that. And I'm not in the business of crossing those kinds of lines.

I realize I've been staring at the pool table without giving Luke a response, so I look up. "Right. Yeah. I got you. And her. I'll watch out for her."

"Thanks, James." His expression softens slightly. "I've always trusted you, you're like a brother to me."

I shake my head, suddenly overcome. Neither of us are big emoters, but Luke I practically grew up together, were on the same soccer team through high school. We went our separate ways for college and in our careers, but we've stayed close. I would trust him with my life.

"Anytime," I manage. Then, I clear my throat. "Can I give you some advice, though?"

"Shoot."

"Ivy's an adult, she can take care of herself," I say this slowly because it's a reminder to myself as well as to Luke. "When you move away, don't stress about her too much. She's much more capable than either of us give her credit for."

Luke nods, considering my words. "I've been worried about leaving her, but maybe you're right. It's time that I hang back and trust that she's got this."

"Exactly. Anyway, let's wrap this up. You've got a workout to get back to, and I have to figure out a rental car for tomorrow."

Luke raises a brow. "Why are you renting a car?"

"Visiting my parents. Mum and Dad don't drive much anymore, and I figured I'd go for a scenic tour around Mirror Valley. See the sights before we get busy with wedding stuff."

"You should take Betsy."

"You *still* have Betsy?"

"Of course I do. She's vintage."

"Vintage is not the same as 'ancient and falling apart.'"

Luke laughs. "I fixed her up. She's good as new."

I doubt that. Betsy is Luke's beloved red pickup. She's literally as old as I am.

"Besides," Luke continues. "She might sell someday for a good buck. You know how those old car collectors can be."

I chuckle. "I'd love to take Betsy. It's been awhile since I had a 'will I make it or will the car fall apart beneath me' sort of adventure."

"Great. Now, are you going to rack up or am I?"

12

JAMES

When I get to Luke's house early the next morning, Betsy's parked in the driveway. Her red paint shimmers in the sunlight, and the silver bumper is polished and gleaming. I have to hand it to Luke, he did a great job—the rust is gone, she's got a fresh coat of paint, and the brand new tires are still a uniform black.

Luke messaged early to say that he was doing some errands and wouldn't be able to hand off the keys. He didn't say where he was leaving them, so I walk around to the driver's side to start searching.

It doesn't take me long. The keys are in the ignition.

The joys of small town life—you can trust your neighbors. If I left a car with keys in the ignition in Denver, it'd be gone within a half hour.

I slide onto the newly-upholstered white leather bench seat and clutch the steering wheel. To my surprise, it has that signature new car scent. You could almost forget that, a decade ago, it smelled like old potato chips, sweaty soccer uniforms, and other unnameable teenage boy smells.

The pickup starts easily, and the motor purrs. Nothing like the clanking and banging around that it used to do.

"Well done, Luke," I mutter as I put the truck in gear.

As I drive towards the other end of town, I press the button for the radio. Blaring static fills the cab and it's everything I can do not to slam my palms over my ears.

"Yeesh!" I grunt as I turn it off. Luke must not have gotten around to fixing that yet.

On a whim, I click the "Play" button. I doubt there's a cassette in there, but it's worth a try.

I'm gratified to hear the opening chords of a song.

Good ol' Luke. If anyone's going to keep their old cassettes, it's him.

As the music plays, my smile grows wider.

No way. Is my best friend *still* obsessed with ABBA?

I laugh to myself as I crank the volume. Luke's always had a weird, unexplainable love for ABBA. Growing up, the happy, poppy electronic music was so completely out of character for him that it made me laugh.

Apparently, his secret love has never died.

I'm whistling along with the tune, and the breeze washes over me from the open window. My shoulders relax, and I smile at the road. It used to be a long, winding gravel road that circled town so you didn't have to drive on Main Street when it was chock-full of people. Now, it's paved, and there are even a few houses built along it.

Mirror Valley has grown a lot over the years. In Denver, people have started talking about how Mirror Valley is the "Cradle of the Mountains" or whatever the slogan is. I'm proud to have grown up here.

My parents are still in the house where I grew up—a small yellow bungalow with a slate-gray roof. Two flags hang outside—one American, and the other a Union Jack as a nod to where we came from.

My mom insisted that I stay with them on this visit, but Luke wanted me close to the Inn for the wedding, and I couldn't say no. In retrospect, there *might* have also been a quiet, subconscious part of me that wanted to see if Ivy would be working there.

I still feel bad for how everything went down at the photo studio yesterday. I should've said that I saw her goofy photos, but I couldn't bring myself to do it—make her feel shame about a moment when she looked so happy and sure of herself.

But after Eleanor burst that bubble, she looked at me with such intense betrayal in her eyes that I immediately regretted it. I should've told her, if for no other reason than to be honest and upfront with her.

Being around Ivy these days is turning out to be more complicated than I anticipated. No less because there are certain things that I really, really shouldn't be feeling when I'm close to her.

At that moment, I'm distracted by something ahead.

A blue car is stopped on the side of the road, and smoke is billowing out of the hood. Someone's standing just in front of the car, peering into the hood.

I pull up behind it and cut the engine. Take a step out of the car. "Hey there! You okay?"

A familiar face pops out from behind the hood, and my eyes widen.

"Ivy?"

"Yeah?" she asks, stepping out into the deserted road.

I'm momentarily distracted by how cute she looks. She's wearing pink shorts, a white top with a cartoon cactus on it, and a gray sweater tied around her waist. She goes to tuck her hair behind her ears, but it's gathered in a high ponytail again, emphasizing the curves of her rosy cheeks, her extra wide eyes. My chest does another weird jump.

I should get back in my truck, send someone else to help given that I can't seem to do anything right by her these days. But I can't talk myself into leaving. I want to help her; it's the right thing to do.

Plus, even if my thoughts are sometimes slightly more than friendly towards her, Luke would want me to help. Right?

I'm teetering with indecision when I notice Ivy blinking and winking at me rather aggressively. She screws her eyes up, squinting.

"Need a hand?" I ask cautiously.

"No, thanks. I've got this."

I'm about to turn when she winks again. "Are you sure?"

"Absolutely. I can do this."

Another wink!

That's it. Whatever her deal is, I'm not leaving her here alone. "I think I've got some tools in the back," I say firmly.

Now, she narrows her eyes to slits and tilts her face forward. "James?"

I stare at her for a long moment. Glance down at myself as though to double check, then look at her again. Her eyes are still all squinty. "Uhm... yeah. You hit your head or something?"

"Ugh, I should've known you'd show up," she huffs. "I'm fine, thank you. My car just... made a weird noise, then started smoking. I stopped right away."

She winks with her other eye.

If I didn't know better, I'd say this was another of her weird flirting attempts. But I do know better—this is Ivy, and she wouldn't flirt with me if I was the last man on earth.

I go to the truck bed, grab Luke's tools, and walk towards her. "I'm helping you, Brooks. Whether you like it or not."

13

IVY

James Weston *would* show up in my hour of need.

And just like the anti-prince-charming he is, he's being all stubborn about it. I can't even glare at him properly because my contacts are dried out from staring at the engine for so long, trying to figure out what could've gone wrong.

So here I am, winking and blinking like a maniac. James probably thinks I'm into him or something. Which I'm not, obviously.

If I was, I would've fallen into the ditch in one of my failed attempts to be cute by now.

Shut up, brain.

"You don't have to help me," I say in a voice that's meant to be strong and sure, but actually comes out a little desperate. I clear my throat. "I'm fine. I don't need a man to help me with my car troubles. I'm a modern twenty-first century woman."

"I realize that," James says and there's something in his voice that makes me blush. "And I have no doubt that you can handle this on your own. I'm just here as a helping hand in case you need it. An assistant, if you will."

"Well, I don't need you to *assist* me with anything," I retort.

Even through my dried contacts, I see James's wicked smile. "I'll be on my way then."

"Good day to you, sir."

He turns on his heel and I look back at the engine, slightly overwhelmed. But I can do this, I have to do this. I don't need his help. I'll figure this out on my own... somehow. My grandparents gave me their old car a month ago and I haven't had the chance to read the manual yet, but I resolve to study every little thing about car maintenance when I get back to the Inn.

"If I had to guess," James throws over his shoulder. "I'd say you're low on coolant."

Coolant.

Of course. Why didn't I think of that?

Unfortunately, there's no extra coolant in the car, which means that I need to pick some up at a gas station. And even more unfortunately, this is a quiet road—since I broke down ten minutes ago, there hasn't been a single car that's come by.

I hear James's car door open and I grit my teeth. Pop my head back out from behind the hood. "Do you... do you have any coolant?"

He's standing just inside the door of his truck, which looks suspiciously like Luke's pickup, Betsy. "I don't, but there's a gas station up the road by my parents'. You want a ride?"

I pause for a long moment. A ride with James? Alone? It's been a long time since James and I spent any time together—Luke or Daisy have always been with us. What would we talk about? Can I stand to be trapped in a car with him?

As I look at my poor excuse for a ride—the hood up and

the engine still emitting little puffs—I know that I have to do it. It'll be fine. I told my grandparents that I'd visit them today, and I can't say when the next person might come along this road. Could be hours.

Catching a ride with James is a means to an end. A sacrifice for the greater good of seeing my family.

"Tick tock," James says, as though sensing that I'm coming around to the idea.

"Okay, fine. But no being weird or annoying. Obviously, you and I don't get along, so let's be adults about it and sit in silence in our respective seats."

I refuse to acknowledge that I don't want him anywhere close to me because his proximity does weird things to my mind and body. Like makes me want to be even closer to him. Or, it did yesterday when we were at the photo studio.

Why, oh why, did Fran order us to stand so close together? It felt like that scene from the freaking *Titanic*, except that I'm no Kate Winslet and James is *certainly* not Leo.

"I'll do my best." He nods solemnly.

"That doesn't sound convincing." I walk around to the passenger door and immediately see why. I forgot that Betsy has a bench seat. A *small* bench seat. "Oh."

"Hop in!" he says.

With some reluctance, I sit next to him on the bench seat. Because of the small space, his leg is pressed against mine. He's wearing jeans again today, and a green shirt that makes his eyes look extra turquoise. His hair's captured under a backwards baseball cap. This close to him, I can see the fine lines starting to form around his eyes, the little freckle on his cheek, a faded tan line from his sunglasses.

We start driving and the cab fills with his cozy sandal-wood scent. I find myself wanting to relax back into the seat, enjoy the ride, but I force myself to sit straight. Not to give in.

"Music?" James suddenly asks.

"Sure."

He turns up the volume and I snort. "ABBA? Really?"

"I thought you said we should sit in silence."

I press my lips together. "Right."

Not even thirty seconds have passed before James says, "what do you have against ABBA?"

"Nothing. And definitely nothing I'd tell Luke. It was a huge ruckus when Elly said she wouldn't listen to them anymore. Luke says it's because he overplayed their music and it soured her on them."

James shoots me an amused look. "Elly?"

"Sorry. I meant Lenore."

"No you didn't."

"No, I didn't." A chuckle escapes me. "But that's another thing you probably shouldn't tell Luke."

"My lips are sealed," James says wryly. "And speaking of our favorite couple, can I assume that Cam is your date to the wedding?"

I tense up for a moment. Ugh. Why couldn't James have a bad memory? I would've loved for him to forget that little conversation. "Uh... yeah. Probably."

"Probably?" He cocks an eyebrow at me. "You don't know?"

"Not yet," I say defensively. "But he'll be my date, I think. Once I ask him."

"Can I give you some advice?"

I pause. "James Weston, are you offering to give me *dating* advice? You know this goes against our entire history, don't you?"

"I do." He laughs. Then, he looks at me, and there's something in his eyes I can't quite decipher. He looks back at the road quickly. "We're friends now, so I figured I'd offer you my two cents if you want it."

"Oh, go on." I wave my hand for him to proceed. *This oughta be good.*

"You're short—"

"I *know.*" I give an exasperated sigh. "Move on with that."

"Let me finish." He chuckles. "You're short, but from what I saw when you were around him, it was like you were trying to make yourself even smaller."

"You lost me."

"I'm saying... don't be afraid to take up space, Brooks. Especially not around the guys you like. You deserve to have someone like you for you, instead of trying to hide yourself away. Or pretzel into a bizarre shape."

I want to say something smart, reject his observation, but the words die in my throat. I've never thought of it that way—is *that* why I'm so klutzy and awkward when talking to cute guys? I'm trying to subconsciously make myself smaller, less noticeable?

Weirdly, the words ring true on some level. Maybe there's a part of me that doesn't want to show these guys who I really am...

I pull myself out of that thought process and resolve to do some journaling whenever I have time. But I can't let James know that he's got me thinking, so I reach for the first thing that comes to mind. "And what about Charlotte with the big hair?" I blurt.

"Charlotte with the big hair?"

Great. Another one of my weird nicknames makes an appearance. "Yeah," I say, then feel the need to elaborate. "Like, Becky... With the good hair?"

James stares at the road blankly.

"From *Lemonade*?"

He gives me a look like he's concerned for my sanity.

"By Beyoncé?"

Nope. Nothing. He's completely unphased.

"Hello! This was a major moment. You don't know what I'm talking about?"

James rolls his eyes. "Sorry. Guess I was too busy working and living and listening to the classics."

I'm already scrolling through my playlists. "This, my friend, *is* a classic. Hold onto your seat."

I put on *Lemonade* and turn the volume all the way up on my phone. The song blasts through the cab of the car and it's everything I can do not to belt along. But I won't, because I sing off-key and I don't want to give James even a smidge more ammunition to make fun of me.

As the song comes to an end, I turn down the volume.

"So?" I ask, more eager than I should be.

James chuckles. "I get it. It's a good song. And I heard the line about Becky."

I smile, satisfied, and sit back. "So? What about Charlotte?"

"What about her?"

"You bringing her to the wedding or what?"

James shakes his head. "I don't think so."

"Why not?" I taunt him. "Tall, pretty and fit isn't your type?"

"Not quite." James chuckles, but it doesn't sound very sincere.

I roll my eyes. "Yeah, right."

He scratches his chin. "Nah. I always saw myself with another kind of girl. Brunette. Wears glasses. Too smart for her own good. Short."

My heart jumps to my throat. That sounds familiar. Very familiar.

But, he couldn't be describing...

"Honestly?" he continues with a smile before I can say anything. "I don't think I want a date."

My lungs expand with oxygen again. He was joking, obviously joking. I lean into the conversation. "That's not what I'd expect to hear from a bachelor living his happy single life."

"Who says I'm a 'happy' bachelor?"

All at once, the air in the cab changes slightly, gets more weighted. James seems pensive now, even though his lips are quirked.

Meanwhile, I'm thrown for a loop. I expected him to go on, and on, and on about the models and athletes and high-powered business women he's dated. Between playing college soccer, having a thriving career, and living in a bustling city like Denver, I'm sure he has his pick of beautiful, intelligent women.

But if he's serious—which it *looks* like he is—I don't know how to take that information. I examine him closely, trying to see if he's putting up a front as a set up for a joke.

"I figured you were satisfied with the money, fame, and glory. And the dating that entails," I venture. I have to admit that a part of me is morbidly curious about this side of James.

"Used to be." He's got a faraway smile. "But that's not what life's about, is it?"

I'm surprised by his honesty. "I guess not."

"It's part of the reason I quit soccer. I didn't want to be one of those athletes who retires in their thirties and essentially has to start over with a new career."

"Yeah... I get that."

A silence settles between us again and I'm not sure what to say next. James and I never get real with each other, it isn't a part of our relationship dynamics. There's only one time that it ever seemed like we might get to a deeper level. But that same day, he kicked off our legendary feud.

I shake myself off. I can't be having thoughts like this—even being curious about him is dangerous. James Weston is and always has been the sneaky raisin in a chocolate chip cookie, the wrinkle in your sock when you're wearing tight boots, the mosquito in your tent on a summer night.

He's the one person that I know I can't rely on or trust, and in a weird way, I count on that. It's the one, infallible, unalterable part of my life. I can't afford to go around thinking he might be a decent person underneath it all.

Even if he picks me up from the side of the road when my car breaks down...

"Well, that got heavy." He chuckles and turns up ABBA again—SOS. Fitting. "We should be at the gas station soon."

"Good, good," is all I can manage as I stare out the window.

14

JAMES

I'm humming along to the ABBA song on the radio when Ivy suddenly shoots sideways across the seat so she's leaning across me. Her coconut scent is wafting right in front of me, but I stay focused on the road and not the excitement on her face.

"That's your parents' place, right?"

I glance out the window at their yellow bungalow. The gas station is just down the road. "Yeah."

"Let's stop and say hi," she insists.

"Why?"

"Because I see your mom around town a lot and she always mentions that I should pop in if I'm in the area." She checks her watch. "Besides, my grandparents already know I'm going to be late, and they'd want me to stop and say hi to Darlene."

Darlene? Since when are Mum and Ivy on a first-name basis?

Ivy's staring at me so intently, her eyes beckoning pools of green and her face so close I can smell her vanilla chapstick. I can't say no. "Whatever makes you happy."

I pull into the empty lane next to us, and do a sharp U-turn.

Ivy clearly wasn't expecting this, and she topples into my lap. My reflexes kick in, and I catch her before her head hits the driver's side window. She grasps my arm and thigh as she straightens up.

"What was that about?" she demands angrily.

"You said you wanted to visit my parents."

"I wasn't expecting you to do a super illegal U-turn and almost kill us both."

I chuckle and gesture to the completely empty country road we're driving on. "No one else is around, we're safe as could be."

"Still. Rules are rules for a reason."

I cock an eyebrow at her. "Here I was thinking rules were made to be broken."

She purses her lips. "You're trouble, James Weston."

"I think you like it."

Ivy ignores the flirtatious comment and smoothes down her shirt, but I swear her cheeks are pink.

I smile to myself as I remember the *Lemonade* song. Ivy's lips were clamped shut the entire time, but I heard her humming. It was hard not to—the girl has many talents, but an ear for music is not one of them. She's as tone deaf as they come.

We pull into the driveway and Ivy launches herself out of the car. She strides down the pathway, head held high, then pauses on the top porch stair. She half-turns and lifts an eyebrow. "You coming or watching the flowers grow?"

With a smirk, I jog to catch up with her. "We don't have to stay long."

"It'll be nice to see Darlene and Tom again."

This time, I have to call her out. "Darlene and Tom, huh?"

She shoots me an innocent grin. "Don't you know? Your parents and I are tight. Best friends. So you better watch yourself because I don't keep secrets from my friends."

I tap my nose. "I'll be on my best behavior."

"Don't be making empty promises, James."

"Wouldn't dare. Not to a *lady*."

Ivy shakes her head and sticks her tongue out at me.

Sticks her tongue out! Like we're five!

I'm laughing when the front door suddenly opens. Ivy puts her tongue back in her mouth guiltily.

"Thought I heard voices!" Mum exclaims, tucking her short blonde hair behind her ears.

She gathers Ivy and me into her arms, hugging us. Her perfume is sweet and familiar, and all at once, I'm happy to be home.

"Good to see you, Mum," I mutter against her hair.

She steps back, one hand holding Ivy's and the other holding mine. Her red patterned sweater has a sprinkling of flour across the front, and one of her bunny slippers is still missing an ear—result of an unfortunate meeting with the neighbor's poodle pup last year.

"Look at the two of you—you both look guilty as ever," she chortles. "I'd be quick to believe you're still kids, having just pranked each other or something."

Ivy squeezes Mum's hand with both of hers. "Darlene, I hope it's okay that I've dropped by. I thought I'd say hi since I was in the area."

"I'm so glad you did, dear girl. And you're right on time —the scones have only a few minutes left and I was about to check on the clotted cream." Mum puts an arm around Ivy's shoulders and drives her inside, leaving me alone on the porch. She shouts over her shoulder. "Close the door behind you, James? Your father's just popped out to the shop; he should be back soon."

As their voices disappear into the kitchen, I almost laugh out loud. Of course, her first-born child comes back to Mirror Valley and she'd rather spend time with Ivy.

Mum always liked Ivy, and clearly, they've gotten closer over time. Don't get me wrong, Mum loves my brothers and me, but she wanted a daughter, and instead, was blessed with three tall, loud, stinky boys. None of whom are married or have serious girlfriends.

Ivy's probably a breath of fresh air for her.

I shut the door and take in our cozy entryway. The walls are lined with family photos—holidays, Christmases, family dinners and trips. A vase of flowers sits on the crowded cupboard next to the stairs. I smile, enjoying the warm, slightly stuffy and very familiar smells of my childhood.

I arrive in the kitchen to find Ivy sitting at the counter, her legs crossed beneath her. She's telling Mum about her car breaking down, and Mum's making those sympathetic motherly noises, hands on her hips.

It's like I'm on the edge of one of those scenes in a snow globe—just add snow. And weird caricature faces with too-big eyes. They kind of freak me out.

Yeah. THAT'S what you should be focusing on right now, James.

Ivy looks more at home than I can even remember feeling. But Ivy has a *life* here. Her parents passed when she was young, but our town rallied around Luke and her, taking them under their wings. It's a beautiful thing to see people come together like that, and a feeling of something like homesickness mixed with nostalgia balls in my stomach.

Mum notices me in the doorway and waves me in. "Let me take a look at you!"

She grabs my hands and scans down my body, her eyes like X-rays that are perfectly attuned to catching any ailment. She does this every single time we see each other after a couple weeks or months have gone by.

My brothers and I call it the "DW body scan", and my last one happened at Christmas.

Her blue eyes finish their perusal, and satisfied, she gives me another hug. "How are you, Jamie? You're looking well."

Mum and I catch up for a few minutes, and Ivy bustles in the background, grabbing a glass of water, checking on the clotted cream, tending to the scones. Eventually, the oven beeps and Mum goes over to help. They chat as they take the scones out of the oven, and Ivy laughs—a big, deep belly laugh. The kind of laugh that's genuine and full and sweet.

I'd like to make her laugh like that.

Just like I enjoyed having a real conversation with her in the car. For a minute, there were no pretenses, no walls up. Just chatting, like we could be friends instead of two relative-strangers who constantly plot the other's demise.

We have a long way to go before we get there. More on my part than on hers. What happened all those years ago... I hurt her badly, and I wish I could tell her the full story. It bothers me to think that that day might still affect her.

But with all our fights and bickering, even if I told her the truth, she wouldn't believe me. Would think I'm making something up to hurt her, which could just damage things further. I wouldn't blame her for being doubtful. Our relationship has never been strong in the trust department.

At that moment, my phone rings. Mum and Ivy look at me with wide-eyed surprise and I shrug apologetically. "It's work. I should take this."

"On your holiday?" Mum tsks. "Hurry back, the scones are almost ready."

I jog upstairs to my old bedroom, shut the door, and answer the call.

"Howdy!" Martin drawls. "Sorry for the cold call. You're not busy, are you?"

I bite the inside of my cheek and glance towards the door. I give him my automatic answer. "Nope, free as a bird."

"Fantastic. First off, I wanted to chat with you about someone on your team—Samuel..."

Martin goes on about Samuel and I half-listen, answering his questions with ease. As he speaks, I look around my bedroom. It hasn't changed since I was a teen, though it's tidier now. The same plaid bedspread covers the bed, and the desk is littered with books and soccer medals. On the nightstand, there's the red London bus that I used to roll around when I was supposed to be doing homework.

I'm looking at the posters on my wall—man, I was so into those emo-rock bands—when Martin says something that catches my attention. "Sorry, what was that?"

"Service not great over there in small-town-ville?" Martin laughs heartily. Then, he goes serious all of a sudden. "But seriously, is the service not good there?"

I blink at the change in his tone. Since when does Martin care about phone service? "Uh... no, it's fine. I was just shifting the phone to my other ear and missed what you said."

"Oh." The relief in his voice is unmistakable, and I chalk it up as another of his weird eccentricities. When it comes to Martin, sometimes it's better not to ask. "I was just about to tell you the big news and the main reason that I'm calling."

I sit on the bed, my muscles tense.

"Xavier and I have been speaking with the team all

111

week about this new position," Martin says gravely. "And we've finally come to a decision..."

"You have?" I keep my voice steady.

"Yes. We know who we want as our next Director."

Anticipation pounds in my temples. "Who are you thinking?"

Martin takes a long, deep inhale, and it feels like he's preparing to give me bad news. I hold my breath, waiting for the final verdict.

Then, he very calmly says, "Daryl from Accounting."

I freeze for a moment, uncomprehending. Accounting? Why on earth would *Daryl* from *Accounting* move into a senior marketing role?

"I'm sorry?" I finally choke out.

At once, Martin bursts into laughter, the sound booming into the phone so loud that I have to hold it away from my ear. "I'm kidding! Daryl has a long way to go if he ever wants to take on a marketing position, believe you me. James, we picked *you*."

I'm still reeling. "Seriously?"

"Yes. We want you as the new Director of Marketing Strategy and Optimization." Martin sounds all too pleased with himself. "Xavier and I have been watching you. You're just like us—hungry, ambitious, you'd do anything to make the sale. The 'start small, go big' campaign was too good to pass up, and who better to lead it than the person who first envisioned it."

"Wow, I can't believe this."

"And seeing as you can't stop singing his praises, Samuel will obviously step into your old role."

I shake my head slowly. "This is amazing news. Thank you, Martin."

"Thank Xavier. He's the one who's run off with the idea like a dog with a bone."

"Will do, as soon as I'm back in the office."

"And when will that be? Obviously, we'd like to get started on this project right away. But you've got your buddy's wedding..."

"The wedding is next Saturday, but I'm not supposed—"

"Excellent!" Martin cuts me off, distracted. I hear him typing in the background. "We'll see you the following Monday, then. Xavier is anxious to get moving ASAP."

I pause for a moment. If they want me to start with a new role next Monday, I'll want to leave right after the wedding so I have Sunday to prep. It's not an ideal situation, but duty calls. "I'll be there."

"Fantastic. I better run. I'll see you next week, and I promise that *this* is the last you'll hear from me. Need you fresh and rested!"

Ivy's words pop into my head—"*don't make empty promises.*" I don't think Martin's aware of that particular rule. "Sounds good, Martin. I'll chat to you later."

"Enjoy the rest of your time in Mirror Valley."

I hang up the phone, and my brow furrows. Odd, I don't remember telling him that Mirror Valley was my hometown. Must've mentioned it in passing.

I finger the cool plastic on my phone, my blood pounding in my ears. This is incredible news.

I did it—I'm the youngest director at Penumbra Hospitality.

All of those years of hard work—the late nights, stressful meetings, dealing with a range of problems at all hours of the day and night... it's paid off. I finally got my dream role.

And I am completely in over my head.

No, seriously. As excited as I want to be by the promotion, what I'm feeling is a new level of overwhelmed. Because while I'm sure everything will be good as gravy as soon as I start, that same niggling feeling of uncertainty is growing stronger.

The next step is a Senior Director role, but even optimistically, I won't reach that until I'm, like, thirty-five. Do I want to spend another decade working at this? Do I even *want* to be a Senior Director?

I toss my phone from one hand to the other, my stomach twisting into a knot, as much as I wish it wasn't.

I've wanted this promotion for so long. But now what?

Knock, knock.

The sound at my door shocks me back to life.

"One sec." I pocket my phone and run my fingers through my hair. Exhale a long, loud breath.

"Ew, James. What're you doing in there?"

Ivy's tone makes me smile, and the ball of stress in my stomach temporarily unclenches. I open the door and come face-to-face with her. Well, face-to-chest.

I lean against the doorframe, but unfortunately, it's slightly smaller than my 6'2" so I have to tilt my head awkwardly. "Don't you know it's rude to eavesdrop?"

"I wasn't eavesdropping, you weirdo. Your labor breaths are just *that* loud."

I bite my lip and Ivy's gaze drops to my mouth in irritation. "Those aren't labor breaths, they're yoga breaths."

"*You* do yoga?"

"Sometimes." I step out of the room so I can stretch my hands above my head, bending one way, then the other. "Helps with soccer."

Ivy's eyes drop to my abdomen, where I realize the bottom of my shirt's lifted. I drop my arms again as her eyes meet mine like two fiery emerald balls of anger. She tilts her chin defiantly. "Well, you're doing the stretch wrong."

I raise an eyebrow. "Care to demonstrate? How should I be stretching?"

Ivy assesses the small hallway, and for a second, it looks like she might launch into a full stretching session. But she places her hands on her hips. "I can't show you here. But I *can* tell you that you're doing it wrong."

"Well, I'd love to learn some of these expert-level yoga skills at a later time. Keen for a yoga-off?"

Ivy shakes her head slowly. "Competitive as ever, James Weston. But you're on."

I hold up a fist and she bumps it. Both of our faces drop at the same time.

We used to do this when we were young. Whenever we'd make a bet or challenge each other to something, we'd make it official via fist-bump. It was our thing.

"Anyway." Ivy clears her throat, blowing past the awkward moment. "Can you bring me to the gas station now? I should get over to see my grandparents, and I'm sure your mom wants some alone time with you. She said she'll keep the scones warm for when you come back."

"The things I do for you."

James: You alive?

Ivy: Hi to you too.

James: Just wanted to make sure you weren't still stuck by the side of the road having to flag down truckers for a ride. You never know whose car you might get into.

Ivy: I think my luck ran out when I had to get into a car with you.

James: Hey now, Betsy didn't even break down once.

Ivy: Betsy's not the problem.

Ivy: This is Mirror Valley though, you think I'd get kidnapped?

James: I'd like to see them try—I'd come with popcorn and everything. I can just imagine you going on about the mud flaps on their truck or something for so long that they'd end up leaving.

Ivy: Gee, so kind of you to offer to witness my kidnapping.

James: Anytime. How're your grandparents?

Ivy: Is that a serious question?

James: Only if you're willing to give a serious answer.

Ivy: *thinking emoji*

Ivy: They're doing well and they were happy I stopped by your parents' and said hi. They handed off a few more tasks to me—I think they're excited for retirement.

James: They should be. They've worked hard, and they have lots to be proud of.

Ivy: That's what I told them.

James: Also, Luke just messaged asking if you and I could hit up the night market on Thursday for a wedding errand. You game?

Ivy: Just you and me?

James: He asked Daisy too, but she's busy.

Ivy: Great. I'll be sure to bring some chocolate to make spending time with you bearable :)

James: Do what you gotta do, Brooks.

15

JAMES

Knowing Ivy, she's going to arrive at the Mirror Valley Night Market five minutes before we're scheduled to meet. She's one of those "early is on time, on time is late" kinda people.

Me? I'm partial to rolling in riiight at the last minute.

But I'll admit that I planned my evening so that I'd get to the market *six* minutes before our meeting time. Just because it would throw her off, and seeing her surprise would be worth it. She might smile, maybe even laugh.

For some reason, I haven't been able to stop thinking about it. Her laugh has been playing in my head on repeat ever since we visited my parents a couple days ago. It'd be annoying if it wasn't so weirdly addicting. I'm craving the full, breathy, hiccuping sound of it.

Ivy and I haven't seen each other in years, but we've fallen back into a groove like no time has passed at all. And yet, one thing's changed, because after what happened at the photo studio and in the car, I can no longer deny that I'm attracted to her.

It's that darn high ponytail, I swear.

I have to keep reminding myself, over and over, that she's Luke's sister. But I need to keep my distance. Keep away from her and this draw I feel towards her.

Between work and best man duties, I thought it would be easy. Until Luke asked if the two of us could go on this errand. I'll have to be good. Just this one little allowance to see her smile, and I'll be on my best behavior for the rest of the evening.

Because I don't have Ivy's freakish internal clock, I arrive at the school field way ahead of time. Luke lent me Betsy again, so I park her in the center of the lot, get out, and lean against the bumper to wait for Ivy. The sun'll be setting soon, and the mountain peaks behind the school are turning a gorgeous yellow-orange.

Don't get me wrong, I love living in the city, love the excitement of Denver. But there's something about Mirror Valley, being surrounded by mountains and ranchlands. It's salt of the earth.

A familiar blue car pulls up next to me and Ivy steps out. She grasps around for her purse and I notice that she's wearing her glasses again—those Coke-bottle ones that make her eyes look huge. She seems frazzled. "Sorry I'm late."

I check my watch. "Four minutes before 7pm? Wowwww, Brooks. You've let me down."

"And *you* can put a sock in it," she grumbles as she zips her oversized purse.

I smirk, looking her up and down. She's wearing a huge, tie-dye off-the-shoulder sweater. "Long day?" I ask.

"Wouldn't you like to know."

"I would, actually."

Ivy looks at me for a long moment. Yeah, I guess that was out of character—me being friendly instead of dry and sarcastic. But I don't care. I'm genuinely curious about why she's dressed like she's about to sell me on peace, love, and Rock n' Roll.

Ivy purses her lips, then swiftly gathers her hair and ties it up into a high ponytail.

I swallow.

It's nothing. Really nothing.

"Ugh, it's been a day," she finally says, exhaling. "One of my contacts ripped, so that was uncomfortable. Then, there was an issue with a bathroom faucet in one of the guest rooms. The plumber was fixing it and I tried to help, but my clothes got soaked. Thank goodness Val happened to bring this sweater to work today." She shakes her head, dejected. Then, as an afterthought, "I *need* to bring a backup outfit to work."

"I was wondering why I didn't see you."

"Well, that'd be why." She shoots me a look. "I haven't seen you much at all. Luke keeping you busy?"

"Something like that." I decide not to go into the specifics—I've been wrapping up work in my old positon to help me get ahead for my promotion. Not exactly exciting stuff.

Ivy nods, and I swear a shadow crosses her expression, but she looks away.

"Shall we get started?" she asks as she pulls her beloved clipboard out of her bag. Seriously, she's practically cuddling it. "What does Luke need from the market?"

I keep my eyes carefully trained on hers. "He wants us to do a little treasure hunt."

At once, she lights up, just like I knew she would. "What kind of treasure hunt?"

"For something old, something new, something borrowed—"

"And something blue."

There it is. Her smile.

Of course, Luke didn't make it sound nearly as fun as this. He asked if Ivy and I could get to the market, grab a bunch of stuff we thought Eleanor might like, and bring it back so she could choose what she wanted. But I figured it's the perfect opportunity to make this into a game, a fun competition. Something Ivy would enjoy.

"Shouldn't the bride be doing this?" she asks as she stashes her clipboard back in her bag.

"Yeah, but Elly's got lots going on with the bachelorette. Luke's busy too, so he asked for help."

"Elly?" Ivy quirks a brow.

I shrug. "Oops."

She shakes her head but then bites her pillowy bottom lip, like we're sharing a secret. My heart does that jump again and something fiery expands through my chest and down my limbs.

Nope, don't go there.

I clear my throat. "Ready?"

We start walking across the parking lot towards the fence circling the school field, where the market takes place every Thursday evening in the spring and summer. Her arm almost knocks against mine, a fact which I am trying very hard to ignore.

"Do you know the meaning behind the 'something old, something new' tradition?" she asks.

"I'm sure I've heard it, but I can't remember."

"It's an old English rhyme, meant to ward off the Evil Eye."

"Like Sauron from *Lord of the Rings*?"

Ivy snorts, then covers her mouth. "The Evil Eye was thought to be a curse that could make the bride infertile."

She glances at me. "I can't believe you just whipped out an LOTR reference. You sound like Luke."

I hold back from knocking against her. "You pick up a thing or two being best friends for years."

Ivy rolls her eyes.

"Have you heard that that's not the full saying?" I ask in return. "The full rhyme goes 'something old, something new, something borrowed, something blue, a sixpence in your shoe.'"

Ivy stops walking, eyes wide with wonder. "I've never heard that."

"Mum's mentioned it a few times. She put a sixpence in her shoe when she married Dad, and she still has it. Framed it, even."

"She framed a coin?"

"Yeah, it's on the mantle at home in all its glory. You didn't see it?" Now, I knock my arm against hers without thinking. "You should ask next time. She'd be delighted to tell you all the nitty gritty details. Maybe even take it out so you can hold it."

Ivy wrinkles her nose. "Ah, just what every girl wants—an old foot coin."

We get to the fence and pass through to the market. By now, the mountains are pink, and the fairy lights strung above the stalls are on, casting the field in a warm light. Conversations and laughter fill the air, and the intermingling smells of hot dogs, barbecue, and french fries make my stomach grumble though I just had dinner.

"There's Daisy's sister." Ivy points at someone just inside the market. "Dee!"

Among a crowd of people clamoring around one of the food stalls, a girl with long blond hair looks over her shoulder. She smiles, then runs over, tugging a tall, athletic guy behind her. "Come *on*, Noah," she grumbles at him. "We'll come back for your fried onion later!"

Dee wraps Ivy in a hug, and then looks at me. "Ohmygosh, James! You're back?"

"Just for the wedding. I'm here until Saturday evening." I nod at the dark-haired man next to Dee. I briefly remember him from school—he's a lot taller than he was the last time I saw him. "Noah Jackson, right? Played on the baseball team?"

He ducks his head. "That's right."

"What're you guys doing at the market?" Ivy asks.

"*Someone* was freaking out over Daisy's birthday present." Noah chuckles.

"Yeah, well *someone* doesn't enjoy doing everything at the last minute." Dee sighs, hands on her hips. "I swear. If you weren't my oldest friend, I'd drop you in a heartbeat."

"I have *way* too much blackmail material on you for that." Noah winks at Dee then turns to us. "What are you two doing here? Didn't you used to, like, hate each other to the ends of the earth or something?"

"Still do," I say brightly, and Ivy rolls her eyes. "We're picking up some last minute stuff for the wedding."

"You've come to the right place," Dee says, gesturing around the crowded market stalls. "The market is *on* tonight. Lots of good stuff."

"Speaking of..." Noah says, practically vibrating with excitement. "The main reason I'm here is for a fried onion and they might run out." He nods at Ivy and me. "See you guys at the wedding?"

Noah grabs Dee's hand and pulls her back to the line at the food stall.

"Look at that, Brooks. That could be us," I tease. "Imagine, being friends instead of hating each other."

Ivy turns to me, emerald eyes sparkling. "Where's the

fun in that? If we were friends, I'd have no one to compete with. And speaking of..." She places her hands on her hips, all business. "Let's get on with this treasure hunt, Weston."

"Alright. You want to take something old and new, and I'll look for borrowed and blue?"

Ivy screws up her face. "Hang on, I know people here. I can probably get something borrowed more easily."

She makes a good point—I haven't seen many of these people in years. "Cool, so you take borrowed and blue, and we'll meet back here in ten."

"In ten." Ivy extends her fist, then seems to realize what she's done and drops her hand quickly. Before I can think about it, I extend mine towards her with a wry smile. She rolls her eyes and fist bumps me, and I shouldn't be as happy about that as I am.

I lean in close and drop my voice. "Ready, set..."

Her eyes light up with the spirit of competition. It gets me even more amped up.

"GO!"

Ivy shoots off towards the crowd in the market, and I follow her. As she disappears into the crowd, splitting off one way, I go the other.

This is just a stupid game, but I can't remember the last time I had fun like this. The last time I was in a competition like this—where there weren't any real stakes, but I was taking it so seriously. As seriously as I knew Ivy was taking it.

I used to think that Ivy's determination and competitive side were irritating. But as I jog around the market, feeling like I'm twelve again, it occurs to me that I never believed it. Those qualities were what I liked and admired most about her. I like that she challenges me, that we have these games.

At some point, I come across Ivy stopped at a stall, chatting with the vendor. Even though I'm losing time, I stop and watch her for a moment. Watch the way she runs her fingers over the objects, how she leans in to speak with the vendor. Watch her smile.

That strange heat expands through my chest again. I force myself to turn away.

16

IVY

Time is ticking. My ten minutes are counting down.

And finding something borrowed that Elly might like is turning out to be a *much* harder task than expected.

I was under the impression that the bride gets family heirlooms or gifts from friends for her something borrowed, so I can't help but wonder why Luke sent us to the market for this particular item.

It makes it all the more important that I find something Elly will enjoy having with her on her wedding day. Something borrowed, and meaningful, and symbolic of love, and small enough to fit on her person, and cute.

No pressure.

I look around the stalls, mind racing even as a small smile plays on my lips. Daisy and I often stroll through the market together on Thursday evenings, mugs of hot chocolate and fresh cookies in hand. I use the opportunity to find decorative pieces for the lobby or the guest rooms, and Daisy makes fun of me for working on my time off.

But today, work is the last thing on my mind. I'm here on a treasure hunt—something I never thought I'd be doing at this age. Probably says a lot about my relationship with James that we play such childish games.

I don't want to consider what it means that a part of me is actually *enjoying* this.

I shake off the feeling and refocus. I've already found something blue, but I need to get my head in the game.

Four minutes and nineteen seconds left.

I'm passing by the Beau Luxe home decor market stall when I get an idea.

"Hey, Gemma," I call to the pretty, dark-haired vendor as I walk up. Gemma Myers was in Luke and James's grade growing up, and she was known for her fashionable outfits—which, to be fair, isn't hard in Mirror Valley. Throw on a pair of nice jeans and a clean flannel shirt, and you might as well have stepped off a runway in Milan.

But that's beside the point—Gemma and Elly used to be friends when they were on the cheer squad together in school. Something from Gemma would likely mean a lot to her.

"Ivyyy." Gemma smiles, her lips shining with a freshly-applied coat of lip gloss. She's wearing an adorable navy striped jumpsuit. Where she finds these clothes, I don't know.

"How's it going?" I ask brightly, then I glance around. "Where's Renée?"

Gemma shrugs one shoulder. "She just left to find Raymond. He installed a shelf in Beau Luxe that's not quite straight, so the pillow display keeps sliding off. Gave Mrs. Perez a scare yesterday when the pillows fell on her." She rolls her eyes. "Drama."

Poor Mrs. Perez. I keep my expression neutral as I politely ask, "and how's Willie?"

"Good! I forgot you guys used to be friends. He got out of the hospital a few days ago and is adjusting to the cast.

128

His arm should be healed in a few months, and he can get right back to 'carving.'" She uses air quotes. "My brother's never going to grow out of the skate park."

I offer a laugh. Well, I wouldn't go so far as to say that Willie and I were *friends*, but I definitely knew him much better than I knew Gemma growing up...

The thought of that skate park still makes me cringe with a discomfort I refuse to acknowledge.

"I'm glad he's okay," I say sincerely. Then, I lean in close. "Listen, I have a bit of a weird ask. I was ordering tiger lilies the other day at Clarissa's and noticed some cool displays in the Beau Luxe window—these sweet little cards with flowers on them."

"The floramancy cards?"

I pause. "Flora-what?"

"Floramancy." She throws her long, caramel-streaked hair over her shoulder. "Renée ordered them the other day —customers *love* the look of them. Apparently, they're like tarot cards. I don't know much about that, I kind of stopped listening, but the art is pretty. I can see why people use them to decorate."

I nod slowly. Elly's into the whole tarot-tea-leaf-what's-it reading on her TikTok channel. A nicely-printed flower card would be perfect for her.

"Sweet. Well, you know that Luke and Eleanor's wedding is next weekend, right?"

"I do." Gemma's smile tightens slightly. "Not that I got an invite."

My body stiffens. *Way to put your foot in it, Ivy.*

"I see," I squeak. I assumed Elly had invited her. "Never mind, sorry."

"No worries." Gemma shakes her head, still smiling. "So you want some flower cards?"

"That's really okay."

"No, go on," she urges. "I'd love to hear what you're thinking."

I shift on my feet. Awkward moments like this are *not* my specialty. The words spill out in a rush. "I'm looking for something borrowed for Eleanor, and she's all about tiger lilies these days, so I wondered if you had one of those flower cards with a tiger lily on it." I hold up my hands. "But I can find something else."

Gemma purses her lips. "Hmm, I don't remember seeing a tiger lily card, sorry."

It was a long shot anyway. And I must be close to out of time now. James is going to win.

I open my mouth to tell her not to worry about it when her eyes suddenly light up. "Ooh! I'm not sure if you've heard, but I've just started selling origami on Etsy. I can make her something."

She turns away to rifle through her things, and I check my watch.

One minute and thirty-three second.

Adrenaline courses through my veins and I glance behind me for James. Not here yet.

Gemma stands, holding a small stack of papers. "Pick a color, and I'll make her a flower. I've never done tiger lilies before, but I'm sure I can figure it out."

My brow wrinkles. "Are you sure?"

"Absolutely. And if it needs to be borrowed, you can just give it back to me after the wedding." She winks. "No harm, no foul."

I press my lips into a smile. I'm running out of time, and ideas. This'll have to do. "Thank you, Gemma."

"My pleasure. And maybe in exchange, you can get the word out around the Inn about my business."

I agree, happy to help out a fellow businesswoman in

Mirror Valley. I select a paper in a burnt orange color and Gemma files it away.

As she's turning back towards me, her eyes land on a point behind my shoulder. "Is that... James Weston?"

I look behind me to where James is strolling through the crowd. He scans the stalls lazily, hands in his pockets. Even from here, I can see women checking him out—the older ladies beaming up at him without an ounce of shame, while girls my age literally stop and stare. I guess I can't blame them—he looks good in his jeans and polo shirt with that wicked grin of his.

I bet he's loving the attention.

At that moment, his tropical-ocean eyes land on mine. He doesn't look away, just smiles slowly, like I'm the only person in the entire market. I feel that smile all the way in the depths of my stomach.

I turn away quickly.

"He's coming over," Gemma says breathily. She adjusts her hair and tugs at her jumpsuit. Before I can register what's happening, she's crossed her arms so certain things *pop*.

I feel more than see James sidle up next to me. "Hey, Brooks."

"Hi, James!" Gemma exclaims brightly, cutting off any response from me. "Long time, no see!"

"It's been awhile," he agrees politely. "How are you, Gemma?"

"Good, good." She flips her long hair over her shoulder, then crosses her arms again. "It sure looks like we've all grown up... you, especially."

Wow.

I cast a glance between her and James. See James's eyes drop down her body.

My jaw clenches involuntarily and a flame lights in my

stomach. Then, James looks at me again, and the cool sparkle in his eyes dulls the fire. "I'm here to get Ivy. Have everything you need?"

In the corner of my eye, I see Gemma deflate. "Oh, right." She sounds bored. "You two, like, finally together?"

I turn to her in confusion. "What? No. No way. What do you mean 'finally?'"

"There were rumors around school. People used to place bets."

James and I share a glance. He looks as shocked as I feel. "Bets on what?"

"On whether you two were secretly dating."

I shake my head vehemently. "What? Nooo, you don't understand. James and I are not a thing. Never a thing. We can't stand each other."

"Really," Gemma says, a little too eagerly for my taste. She looks at James again and smiles like she's a lioness in the jungle assessing a particularly tasty gazelle.

No, not a gazelle. A lion. A hot lion with too many soccer muscles and a chin dimple.

My stomach hardens, and I lose control of my mouth. "Yeah. He's insufferable. Too tall, and his hair is all squidgy and weird to touch. All he ever talks about is soccer." *Stop talking, Ivy!* "And he's probably a bad kisser."

Finally—*finally*—I manage to stop my motor mouth. My cheeks are flaming hot. Like, Dorito level.

Luckily, Gemma doesn't appear to have heard a word, and she gazes at James dreamily. I can't bring myself to look at him—I don't have an explanation for what came over me. It was like some deep, primal instinct was telling me to keep talking, keep going. Even though I was sabotaging a potential date for him. Even though I was digging a hole and throwing myself into it.

Yoga breath in, yoga breath out, I tell myself, closing my eyes.

When I reopen them, I feel calmer. I look at Gemma again and smile. "I'm kidding. James is great. Such a wonderful *friend*. I'll leave you to it!"

And with that graceful recovery, I turn on my heel and stagger away.

I'm Ivy Brooks, and I've lost my mind.

I wander to the stalls on the other side of the market in some kind of shock. But I find myself looking back to see what happens. Just to make sure I didn't mess things up for James and Gemma.

I tuck myself behind a stall, pretending to check out what's on sale, even as my eyes are fixed on the two of them. Gemma is flinging her hair around so violently, I'm surprised she doesn't hurt her neck. And James? He's laughing, the sound rich and genuine. I can imagine the way his eyes are lighting up, the way he's looking at her like she's the only person in the world...

My stomach does a weird little squeezing thing, and I force myself to look away.

All of a sudden, I realize what I'm feeling.

Am I *jealous*?

No. There's no way. I have no reason to feel jealous. And jealous of what exactly? Because I certainly can't be jealous of Gemma spending time with James. Of James turning that wicked, flirty, teasing smile on her. Right?

Although, I was wondering earlier whether I hadn't seen him around the last couple days because he was off with someone... Charlotte with the big hair, I assumed. Now, would he start dating Gemma?

James and Gemma. Jamma... or Gems.

Daisy would approve.

"Find something you like, Brooks?"

"Agh!" I stagger sideways, bumping into the stall and almost knocking the table over.

James chuckles. "Sorry. I saw you staring and thought you might be ready to go."

"I wasn't staring," I stutter. Thinking fast, I pick up a random object on the table and hold it towards his face. "I was just debating whether I want to buy this..."

I trail off as I register what I'm holding.

Oh, no.

James's lips twitch. "Pack of adult diapers?"

I open my mouth, but nothing comes out.

It's too late. I can either claim these eco-conscious, washable adult diapers as my own, or admit that I was creeping on the two of them and feeling a certain kind of way about it. We all know which is the less embarrassing of the two.

"Right. That's right." I clear my throat. "Adult diapers. Because... you just never know when you might need them..."

Oh, sweet heavens. Kill me now.

James cocks an eyebrow. "I see. I was thinking that you might be planning some joke bachelor gift for Luke."

Cowbells. That's good.

"You gonna get that?" a voice asks behind me.

I whirl around and, to my horror, the shop owner is staring at me expectantly.

"These?" I squeak.

"Yeah," James piles on, glee in his eyes. "You need them, right?"

My mouth is dry as the desert. This is the single most embarrassing thing I've ever experienced in my life. I'm half-expecting Cam or Zac Efron (my shameless celeb crush) to walk by and see me cuddling my stupid pack of diapers.

I know that, logically, there's no reason for me to be embarrassed. Lots of women use diapers for a variety of reasons—heck, I might use them someday if I'm pregnant, and there's nothing wrong with that. But James has a way of making things worse... Just like he did the day he started our feud.

James holds my gaze for a long, long moment. I wait for him to make some stupid joke, or laugh at me, or something.

Instead, he winks, grabs the diapers, and hands them to the shop owner proudly. "I'll get these, thanks. You know how things are as you get older—body changes and all that."

He laughs, which makes the shop owner laugh too, and they speak for a minute about the joys of incontinence. James pays for the diapers, then turns to me again, holding the pack under his arm. "You ready now?"

My body whirs back to life and I cough. "Ung. Yeah."

We start walking through the market and back towards the parking lot. I'm filled with all kinds of emotions—confusion at what I was feeling earlier, leftover mortification from the diaper debacle. And something like gratitude for James for not giving me a hard time, for not playing into my embarrassment.

I'm about to say thank you when I notice James and Gemma share a wave. I instantly feel bad for saying such mean things about him.

"I'm sorry." I stare at my feet. "You know, for what I said earlier."

"That I was a bad kisser? Don't worry about it, Brooks. It'd be hard to believe that anyway."

Something inside me seems to break apart and I chuckle. "Well, sorry. I didn't mean it."

"I know." James shoots me a smile. "So did you complete your part of the mission?"

"I found a blue tea cozy, and Gemma's making Elly a

135

paper flower thing for her something borrowed. What about you?"

"Got Elly a headband from a shop Luke recommended. She uses them for her makeup videos, apparently."

"And for your something old?"

James cocks an eyebrow and lifts the diapers.

I punch him in the arm. Try not to think about how firm the muscles are beneath my fingers. "That so doesn't count."

James chuckles. "When I paid for the headband, I got an old penny back so I was thinking of giving it to her for her something old. *And* it might count as a sixpence in her shoe. I'll have to ask Mum about that."

"Well done. I'd say our mission is accomplished." Without thinking, I hold up my fist and he bumps it. I force myself to add, "and on top of that, you might've picked up a date."

"Maybe." James shrugs, and I breathe through the weird feeling that comes up at his response. He taps the diapers under his arm. "Our next mission is only just beginning, though. What are we going to do with these for Luke's bachelor party tomorrow night?"

"I might have an idea..."

James and I are still talking when we reach our cars in the parking lot, and we continue talking even as the lot empties. I don't realize how much time has passed until my teeth clack together. James's eyes drop to my mouth and he looks concerned. "You're cold, Brooks. I shouldn't have kept you out this long."

I shake my head. "We should head out anyway. Big day tomorrow."

James smiles that slow grin of his. "Right. I'll see you tomorrow."

I get into my car, start the engine, and blast the heat.

Meanwhile, James starts up Betsy, and waves as he pulls out of his spot.

I sit in the lot a while longer, running my fingers across the diapers—James left them with me. My bout of jealousy earlier bothers me. Really bothers me. I don't have a reason or an explanation for it, but it has to be rooted in how things are changing with us. James has been my enemy for years, but now, because of this wedding, we have to act like we're friends.

Sometimes, I can almost believe that we *could* be friends...

I shake my head, rejecting the thought. We're not friends, we're enemies, and as soon as Luke's wedding is over, we won't have to hide that fact anymore. And I will no longer have to feel any of these weird, confusing, inexplicable feelings towards him.

I place the diapers in the passenger seat, put the car in gear, and go back to the Inn.

17

JAMES

The evening of Luke's bachelor party is everything I love most about the start of summer.

The breeze carries the smells of freshly-cut grass and barbecue, putting me right back to the bonfires and yard parties we had growing up. Crickets chirp, and I remember the days when Luke and I used to trick Ivy and Daisy into thinking that they were fireflies.

It's especially hard *not* to appreciate this time of year in the garden of the Brookrose. I never thought I'd be one of those guys who cares about plants and stuff, but here I am, looking out over the garden like it's a freaking work of art.

Just hand me a shovel and call me "Alan Titchmarsh" (my dad loves gardening. All the better when the gardener is a British TV personality... Who gets famous from gardening anyway?)

I breathe in deeply and close my eyes, allowing myself to enjoy the moment.

"Hey, bro, good to see you!" A heavy hand lands on my shoulder and tries to pivot me around.

Brad Norman was a teammate of mine on our school team. He also got a soccer scholarship and went off to college, though he dropped out two years in and came back to Mirror Valley. He's since gotten married and now works as a barber in town.

As Brad and I catch up, it's clear that he's basically the exact same person he was in high school—loud, enthusiastic, red-faced, and exuding party-boy vibes.

"Come on, I heard Cassidy brought a Guzzler. Let's get this party started!" He whoops.

I follow him towards the crowd gathered by the gazebo. I've used one of those beer guzzler helmets a total of once in my life, and that was more than enough. But, I'm not against watching the guys from my old team make fools of themselves while wearing said helmets.

There's a sudden burst of static across the garden, quickly followed by music. Brad whoops again and plunges into the crowd of guys, taking his rightful place among the Dude Crew. I hold back and take a sip of my beer.

"Wow. Was not expecting this turn-out."

I look at Luke, who's appeared next to me. His lips are pursed and he's staring at the crowd wearily.

"What are you talking about, bro?" I put on a thick drawl. "It's your bachelor party, dude. Last chance for freedom. Yeah."

Luke snorts and rolls his eyes. "I never understood that."
"What?"

"The whole 'end of freedom' thing. Isn't marriage just the beginning?"

I wrinkle my brow. I hadn't thought much about it. "You think?"

"Yeah. If you love someone, you'd think that committing to them would be the most liberating experience. To love them openly and freely, and be able to announce it to the world."

I'm silent for a long moment, pondering Luke's words.

Yeah, that all sounds great. Perfect, actually. But perfect for people who aren't me—some of us aren't meant to get that sort of freedom in their lifetimes.

I shake off the sudden pang that accompanies that thought, and sling my arm around Luke's shoulders, dragging him into a headlock. "You're supposed to be having fun, mate!"

Luke jostles to get away.

"Boys, boys, boys."

I drop my arm, and Luke and I turn around with matching guilty expressions.

Daisy's got her hands on her hips. "You guys are up to no good."

I point at Luke. "It *is* this guy's bachelor party."

"This seems a little wild for you, Luke." Daisy shoots him a teasing smile. "I was thinking that you'd opt for a game night, or watching baseball at McGarry's. Something low-key."

Daisy's right. That's definitely more his speed.

"This was Lenore's idea." Luke shrugs. "She didn't think it was fair that she got to have a big blow-out, and she wanted me to have a party too. Looks like she called every guy on our old team to come to the Inn." He peers around the garden. "Speaking of, isn't my sister supposed to be here?"

My heart involuntarily squeezes and I also look around for her. Scanning the crowd of guys, the few guests who are scuttling back inside.

Finally, I see her.

She's standing across the garden, talking to some guy by one of the speakers. She's got her hair in a bun, and her face looks sunkissed and fresh. She's wearing jean shorts that highlight her tan legs, and a black top that hugs her body and floats out gracefully at the same time.

She gestures to the speaker and laughs. The guy laughs too, and even from here, I can see how he's sizing her up. Taking in her sweet grin, her laugh, her gorgeous curves. He puffs out his chest a bit more, runs a hand through his hair to pop his bicep.

I go to take a step forward. I need to get over there and...

What, exactly? I can't and shouldn't do anything.

"Ugh. Is Chett flirting with Ivy?" Luke wrinkles his nose. "The guy got engaged, like, two days ago. Let's get over there."

Thank you, Luke.

It's everything I can do not to lead the charge over to Ivy and Chett. As we approach, Chett seems to realize that he's the target of Luke's glare, and he high-tails it away.

Ivy turns to us with a chuckle. "Thanks, guys. I helped Chett with the speaker and he was droning on about how he only ever hires people to help with that stuff now that he's made it with crypto, etc. etc."

She rolls her eyes. Ivy's got a solid BS-detector—best of luck to the guy who tries to pull the wool over her eyes.

At that moment, a huge "WHOOOP" goes up at the gazebo. Ivy cringes and glances towards the Brookrose. She's probably not loving this sort of atmosphere for her sweet family inn, and I suddenly feel upset that Elly didn't think to run this party past her before sending over the Dude Crew.

Even Luke looks a bit uncomfortable, shifting from foot to foot. And Daisy... well, Daisy's always smiling, but her smile is tighter than usual.

Which means that it's high time for a bachelor party intervention.

"How about we do something fun. Got any games, Brooks?"

She purses her lips. "We do, but I'm worried the guys'll want to get involved and break something."

Like clockwork, another raucous cheer goes up from the gazebo.

My eyes land on something next to the pile of clothes, drinks and food that the guys dropped unceremoniously on the grass. I jog over and pick up the soccer ball, twirling it on my finger like you would a basketball. "Anyone up for a game just the four of us?"

That seems to lift everyone's spirits.

We walk to a large rectangular patch of grass away from the Inn and gazebo, and ditch our shoes before joining together at the center of the "field."

"Here's the teams," I call out. "Daisy and Luke will go together, and I'll go with Br—"

"No way." Luke crosses his arms. "You and Ivy are *not* going together, you're going to rip each others' heads off before the game even starts. I'll go with Ivy, you go with Daisy."

I glance at Ivy just as she looks at me, and a thread of understanding passes between us. He's probably right.

Luke and I haul over heavy potted plants for the goal posts, and we mark the midline by placing our shoes on either side of the field. Meanwhile, Ivy goes back to the Inn and returns with a big, lumpy bag.

She catches my eye and nods once, and I know exactly what she's got. She hands me the bag before standing next to Luke and Daisy.

"Okay, this is a pretty high-stakes game," I say gravely. "Ready for the rules?"

"Let's do this," Daisy cheers.

"We're going to play five mini-matches total. Each match will go to whichever team gets three goals first. And we're going to be playing for the honor of *not* collecting these bad boys..."

I open Ivy's bag and whip out one white piece of fabric with a flourish.

Luke snorts. "Is that...?"

"A diaper? Yeah. And whenever your team loses a match, you'll each have to wear one of these on your person. There's ten diapers, so we'll play five matches."

"How exactly are we meant to wear multiple diapers?" Daisy asks.

"You'll have to be creative," Ivy volunteers. "So start thinking up ideas now. You *don't* want to know what happens if a diaper falls off during the next match."

Daisy lifts a brow and her eyes dart between Ivy and me. "Did you guys plan this?"

"Nope." Ivy shakes her head. "Of course not."

Daisy doesn't look convinced. I throw the ball on the ground to start the game and veer safely away from anymore questions.

What Ivy said isn't *technically* a lie. Last night, we simply agreed that we'd find a way to make the losers of a game wear the diapers creatively on their person. That was the extent of *that* discussion, at least...

But if either of us was to mention it, we might end up saying that we hung out at the market and actually got along. That we chatted in the parking lot afterwards for what could've been hours. I can't speak for her, but I enjoyed myself. More than I'd care to admit.

And I don't know how anyone else could understand that because *I* don't even understand what's happening between us these days.

The four of us throw ourselves into the first mini-match. I dribble the ball across the field, shoot, and Ivy blocks the shot. Luke dribbles back across, passes it to Ivy, who then shoots high, and Daisy deflects the goal with her hands.

"Yeah, that's how it's done!" she whoops.

With each shot, one side cheers while the other groans. And with every penalty, there are boos and laughter.

I have a hard time not focusing on Ivy. She might have all the grace of a newborn ostrich when she's flirting with someone, but she's quick on her feet playing soccer. She feints left and right, dribbles the ball, even does the occasional trick kick with her tongue sticking out the side of her mouth in concentration. Her hair's fallen out of the bun, and it hangs around her shoulders, and her laughter fills the air.

Finally, we're down to the final goal in the first game. The sides are tied, and it all comes down to this shot.

Daisy throws the ball from the sidelines, and Luke manages to jump in front of me and take control of the ball. He dribbles it downfield, but Daisy blocks him. He passes to Ivy, who rushes forward. Daisy and Luke are blocking each other at the side of the field, which means that it's just Ivy and me.

She starts to dribble the ball, coming right for me. I watch her, register her feet dancing along the grass, the smile on her lips. It's distracting, but I don't let my mind go there.

I wait as she gets closer, muscles tense.

"Hope you're ready to lose, diaper-boy," she sings.

"Not today, Brooks. But you're gonna look cute with a diaper on your head."

"Bah! Don't be so cocky. This might be soccer, but I have a trick or two up my sleeve."

"I don't know this 'soccer' you speak of. I thought we could *only* refer to it as 'football.'"

This has the desired effect and Ivy stands for a moment,

glaring at me.

I use the opportunity to steal the ball, spinning around her before making my way back towards the goal posts.

"No fair!" she squawks, sprinting after me. "You distracted me."

I laugh as she whips out in front of me, blocking my path. "I don't know what you're talking about."

"Fine," she says, frustrated, and I think I'm home free... Until she gathers her hair back up into a ponytail. The whole action takes about two seconds, but it makes me stop in my tracks anyway.

Too late, I see the glee in her eyes. She steals the ball and cackles. "Too slow!"

I take off after her. Wrap my arms around her waist and throw her over my shoulder.

"What are you doing?!" she squeals, clawing at my back. "This is so illegal!"

I twirl her around in a circle. "Say you're sorry."

"For what?"

"For distracting me."

"I didn't distract you. If anything, you distracted me! This is worth like 200 penalties."

She's still wriggling around, and I place her back on her feet. Her face is red and her lips are pressed together in a grim line. Her eyes are sparking, and the setting sun highlights the flecks of yellow near her pupils. Her hair's messy from being upside down, and a couple strands hang in front of her face. She puffs out a frustrated exhale in an attempt to blow them away.

Even though we're both sweaty from running around and covered in grass stains, I don't think I've ever seen someone so beautiful. Before I can stop myself, I tuck the bothersome strands of hair tenderly behind her ears.

The anger in her eyes disappears as my fingers graze her

skin. We're both holding our breaths.

"You guys okay?" Luke calls and I drop my hand. Step away from Ivy.

"Yeah, all good!" I say, my voice slightly off. "Bad play. Let's do it again."

Luke and Daisy are both staring at us, Daisy looking inexplicably excited. And Luke? He's got his arms crossed, an unreadable expression on his face.

All at once, I realize how that must've looked. I swallow thickly and collect the ball, resolving to behave myself for the rest of the night.

We're wrapping up the fifth and final match when the Dude Crew finally clues into the fact that we're playing soccer in the garden. By this point, the guys are pretty drunk and the likelihood of the soccer ball ending up in the lobby via the glass doors seems high, so we decide to call it.

The four of us return to the gazebo, where the guys move onto some game involving a ping-pong ball. The gazebo is far enough from the Inn for me to feel comfortable about the odds of the small ball ending up anywhere near the building. Still, as we take a seat on a picnic blanket near the party, both Ivy and I sit facing the Inn.

"We should give the final two diapers to the team with the most penalties," Ivy says before taking a long sip of her iced tea. She's propped up on her elbows, laying across the blanket with one diaper on her head, and the other hanging loosely around her neck like a cape.

"Disagree," Daisy counters. She's placed her diapers on either arm, like water wings. Smart. "I think we should give them to the team that was losing."

"There's no way that I'm ending up with the extra diapers tonight," Luke says. "I'm pulling my 'bachelor party' card."

"So that leaves..." Ivy grins at me wickedly.

"What? You want me to take *both* of the remaining diapers? No way."

"Come on. With four diapers, you can finally finish your crown."

I adjust the crown I'd so skilfully crafted using my two diapers. "I like my crown very much as it is, thank you."

We all cheers, cracking up. A happy silence settles over us.

"Thanks for the party, guys," Luke says. "I appreciate it."

"We didn't do this." I gesture to the pack of guys cheering in the gazebo. "This is courtesy of your future Mrs."

"Not them." Luke's smile doesn't reach his eyes. "This. Playing soccer and hanging out is the perfect bachelor party, the perfect way to spend my last days in Mirror Valley before Lenore and I move to San Fran."

Daisy pats Luke's shoulder while Ivy squeezes his knee. I take a sip of Gatorade, considering his words. Over the last few days, I've been caught up in Mirror Valley. There were times when I could believe that I was a kid again—seeing Luke every day, having Daisy's bubbly personality around. And of course, arguing and competing with Ivy.

Life marches on, people move forward, change is inevitable. But I never realized how much I miss my home-town, miss how things used to be. In Mirror Valley, time passes slowly, each moment rich and meaningful. A far cry from my nonstop life in Denver, where minutes and hours are lost to being busy.

I'd like to capture this moment—sitting here with close

friends and the girl who was my enemy but now makes me feel things I've never felt before.

On Saturday, Luke will be married and moving away. Next Monday, I'll be starting my new job. What about Ivy? What does she see for herself?

I look at her as she fiddles with the picnic blanket. My eyes linger for a moment before I look away.

Don't go there, Weston.

At that moment, Daisy lifts her glass again. "Cheers to the next adventure."

"To the next adventure," Luke and I both say.

Ivy's quiet. She slurps through to the end of her drink, and then clears her throat. "I'm, uh... going to get another."

She makes her way across the garden, towards the cooler she'd placed outside the Inn. She rifles inside it, and right then, the doors open and the guy with the baby face steps out onto the porch. She stands abruptly to greet him, then tucks her hair behind both ears. He says something that makes her laugh, and I shift uncomfortably.

What on earth is he saying that's making her laugh like that?

I don't even realize my fists are clenching until my knuckles start to hurt. I release them, but my eyes stay on the man and Ivy.

I watch as Ivy lifts a foot, looks like she's about to cross it in front of the other. But she freezes. Puts her foot down. Stands with her feet apart in a sort of power pose.

No more pretzling.

I wonder whether our conversation the other day got her thinking. And if so, I'm happy I helped.

Really. I am.

If only I could get over this urge to interfere. I have no reason to feel this way—get so bothered to see Ivy flirt with someone. Clearly, she likes this guy, and there's nothing I can or should do about it but sit back and give her space to be happy.

"Looks like Ivy's been waylaid," Daisy says. "Doing okay there, James?"

I tear my eyes away from the flirtation. "Absolutely. Why wouldn't I be?"

She smiles innocently. "Just checking."

I crack my knuckles and turn away so I don't have to see what's happening on the porch.

Meanwhile, Luke's brow furrows. "Hmm, that Cam guy again," he says quietly.

That's right. Cam.

"So they've dated?" I ask.

"I don't think so, but she's been into him for a while." Luke shrugs. "I don't know him all that well myself, but our conversation the other day got me thinking, and you're right. It doesn't matter what I think. Ivy's an adult, she should date whoever she wants to date. And from what I've heard, Cam's a good guy. Super smart."

I nod, glance their way again. "I could see that."

"Yeah, he moved here a couple years ago, started a cleaning company, and it's taken off. He looks harmless enough. Cam's probably one of the better matches for Ivy in Mirror Valley."

"That's great." The words taste like cement.

But Luke's right—Ivy needs to be with someone good. Someone who would be there for her and support her. Someone who matches her on an intellectual level and makes her think. Someone who doesn't drive her up the wall every chance he gets.

And if Luke is happy for Ivy to date this Cam guy, I could be happy for her too.

Promise. I'll get there.

18

IVY

Cam Harris is talking to me.

He's standing with his arms crossed and chest puffed out, smiling down at me in a supremely cute way. His blond hair is slicked back—literally not a strand out of place—and those dimples are out in full force. His dress shirt is tucked in, all prim and proper. He looks the perfect gentleman.

The other thing I like is the way his dark eyes are lasering into mine. Sure, I've been trying to match his eye contact and therefore haven't blinked in the past minute and a half. And yes, my contacts are drying out so badly my eyes are burning like the fiery depths of the sun.

But it's all worth it. Because Cam Harris is talking to me, and I haven't fallen into a bush yet.

"I could go on and on about the comics, but I don't think we have enough time for that tonight." He chuckles that short laugh of his. "Tell me about you, Ivy. What do you like to do? When you're not working, obviously."

"Me?" I squeak. Resist the urge to twist my arms around themselves. "I like to read too. I've never read any comic books, but maybe I could get into it."

"If only it was as simple as just diving right in. You're lucky you know me—I can tell you exactly where to start, guide you through your comic book education."

I press my lips together in a smile. "That'd be great."

"I had you pegged as a reader."

"Really?" I look down in what I hope is a flirty way, but it's mostly to give my eyes a break.

"Yeah. You've got a look about you. Maybe it's the glasses."

He laughs and my expression falters slightly—I was hoping for this observation to come out of something a little deeper. But I'll take it. He probably didn't mean it the way I took it. "Right."

"Aside from comics, I don't read much for fun. There are so many educational books and podcasts and documentaries out there to improve yourself, both at work and in life. I'm into autobiographies these days. Reading about these inspiring men..."

Cam goes on, and I find my mind wandering but I snap myself back to the moment. What am I doing? This is exactly what I've wanted for months.

Though it has been a while since I said anything...

Oh, gosh. Is James right? Does Cam not care what I have to say?

I shove the thought away. Nope, James is just in my head, a place he has no right to be.

"My personal hero usually shocks people," Cam is saying as I zero back in on his story. He's gazing at me with some intensity, thankfully unaware of my misbehaving thoughts. "But if I tell you who it is, I'll have to kill you."

Oh, I recognize that line!

So I do what every girl does in movies and books when a guy says that, and I giggle. "You can trust me," I say.

"Glad to hear it." Cam leans in closer, and I realize that

the overpowering spicy, musky scent I've been smelling for the past ten minutes and attributed to the gaggle of guys in the gazebo is actually coming from him.

Eek, not the smell I envisioned for Cam. Maybe he over-sprayed his cologne today. It happens.

He's also taken another step towards me so that his chest is at my eye level and he's peering down at me. My head is tilted back and my neck is starting to ache. I'm not used to this—even James usually bends a little to make this easier for me.

"My personal hero has to be... my dad."

Oh, that's very cute. "Your dad?"

"Cliché, right?" Cam smiles in a way that I think is meant to be adorably vulnerable, but looks almost boastful. I stow that thought away—it's just the lighting now that the sun's set. "He's the best. Whenever I think about Clear Reflections or the future, I wonder what he would do. I picture myself being like him when I get older. So in a way, maybe my personal hero is my future self."

He laughs loudly.

I kind of get it... I look up to my grandparents, and have often dreamed of following in their footsteps. Fall in love, get married, run the Brookrose with the love of my life. Would I say that my idealized future self is my personal hero? Probably not. Cam likely didn't mean for it to sound so arrogant.

I continue smiling as he launches into another topic. It occurs to me that there are a ton of things that I'd love to talk to him about—work stuff, our favorite movies, fun trivia. But my heart isn't in it right now. This is my brother's bachelor party; I shouldn't spend it flirting with Cam.

I take a small step away and rub my neck, inhale a subtle breath of fresh air. "I should get back to my brother and friends, but this was fun. And thanks for dropping by to check on everything."

Cam nods, places his hands on his hips. "Anything I can do to help, and to keep Clear Reflections shining forward. And Ivy, I meant what I said the other day about going for a drink. Just let me know when and I'll be there."

"Sure, Cam. Sounds great." I give him wave, and then stride off towards the picnic blanket. As I walk away, I look over my shoulder, attempting a flirtatious grin, but Cam's already walking off, typing on his phone.

I hurry back to the blanket, where Luke, Daisy and James are chatting.

"How'd it go with Cam?" Daisy asks.

I blush as I sit down. I notice that James has moved—he's sitting turned away from me. He picks at a spot on the blanket, like he's avoiding my eyes. For some reason, this bothers me.

"It went okay." I turn back to Daisy. "It was... good talking to him."

"You just let me know if he steps out of line, sis," Luke grumbles jokingly, cracking his knuckles. "I'll be here."

I roll my eyes. "You're ridiculous. Cam's a good guy."

"So everyone says," James mutters.

I frown. "What'd you say?"

At that moment, the guys in the gazebo break into cheers. I almost forgot the bachelor party was happening over there. I check my watch. The sun has set, it's after 8pm, and it's high time we shut this party down. Or move it elsewhere.

I look at my brother apologetically. "Luke, would you—?"

"Tell these guys to get going?" he finishes my sentence. "I'm on it."

"If you want, we can head into town with everyone. Go to a bar and all that stuff."

I don't really want to do "all that stuff." My idea of a perfect ending to this night is a review of the books for tomorrow, checking in with the night manager, running through my wedding to-do list one more time, and then curling up in bed for a dreamless sleep. But this is Luke's bachelor party and I'll rally if that's what he wants.

Luke shakes his head. "Nope. Not into that. I'm gonna send these guys home and head home myself." He stands and wipes the front of his jeans. "Wish me luck!"

Daisy stands next to him. "I'll come. Two is better than one, and I want another iced tea anyway."

Daisy and Luke stride off to break up the party, leaving James and me alone. James has taken off his diaper crown and, horrified, I realize that I was flirting with Cam adorned in my own diaper gear.

I squeak as I tear the diaper off my head.

James raises an eyebrow. "What?"

"Ohmygosh," I say, mortified. "I was talking to Cam while wearing my *diapers*."

James snorts. "That's kinda hilarious."

"What?"

"That's funny." James smiles a warm smile that I feel all the way in my toes. "Don't you think?"

"I guess..."

He shakes his head. "Sometimes you gotta laugh at yourself, Brooks."

"Easy for you to say."

"What do you mean?"

"I mean that it makes sense for you to laugh at yourself," I say smugly. "Because you're a clown."

Instead of seeming the least bit bothered by my stellar burn—okay, it was mediocre at best, but I'm working with old material here—James is smiling. He even looks smug himself, which is *not* the expected reaction.

"What?" I ask. "Why are you smiling like that?"

"I didn't expect you to go there."

"Where?"

"You know, go with the *super* obvious comeback. Come on, Brooks, I handed you that on a silver platter." James chuckles. "I thought you might be a little more skillful."

My nostrils flare and I cross my arms. "So you're making fun of me for *not* offending you."

"Exactly."

"You're a sucker for punishment, Weston."

"You have to admit that wasn't your best work."

I press my lips together, frustrated. Then, throw up my hands. "Fine. I know. That was lame."

Suddenly, something starts churning in my belly. Some strange, unexpected, uncalled-for feeling. It rises in me like bubbles through water, moving up my chest, to my throat. I can't stop it, I have to open my mouth.

And I'm laughing. A real, deep, genuine belly laugh. The sound surprises me, which makes me laugh all the more.

"It was so lame," I manage, hiccuping.

James is staring at me, clearly amused by my apparent descent into insanity. "It was, but I'll forgive you."

And then, the strangest thing happens—James starts laughing with me, and we're cracking up like two idiots on a picnic blanket. But it actually feels... good. Really good to take some of the pressure off. Even for something so small, even for just a moment.

We eventually calm down and I wipe the tears from my eyes. I pull my legs up to my chest and start absentmindedly massaging my calves and ankles—I haven't played soccer in years, and I'll probably be sore tomorrow.

I don't think much of it until I see James's eyes drop to my bare legs. His gaze locks in on the movement of my hands, and an intensity passes through his gaze. Something focused, and urgent.

When his eyes meet mine again, the intensity is still there. My breath catches.

The air between us changes, and now, I notice something. An energy—tangible, strong, and electric. I force myself to keep breathing, even though my whole body feels charged up.

James looks away. Goes back to picking at the blanket. "That Cam guy seems nice," he says quietly, and there's something in his tone that I recognize but can't name.

"Yeah. He is."

"I was wrong. It sounds like he would be a good match for you."

"I think so." I scramble for something else to say. "He... reads, which is cool."

James nods at the blanket. "That's good. It's good you guys have that in common."

"We do." I refrain from telling James that the only books we've discussed so far are comic books and autobiographies. There's plenty of time for more book discussions with Cam. "That's important to me."

"As it should be. You should be with someone who treats you well. Who agrees with you and shares your interests."

My brow furrows. Something in his words doesn't sit quite right. "Yeah. I mean, we don't have to agree on *everything*. It's kind of nice when you can carry on a discussion with someone. When they show you different ways of thinking. When you challenge each other..." I hear how that sounds and I backtrack. "Within reason. I think the key is finding someone who supports you, but still makes life an adventure."

"Definitely. To be with someone who makes even the most mundane, boring things fun. Like, shopping. Or running errands."

He glances at me then and something indecipherable passes between us. I'm leaning in slightly, or maybe he's leaning in. I couldn't tell you because literally all I can focus on right now are his eyes. Those oceanic depths that feel at once inviting and safe, and wickedly full of mystery.

I manage to nod. "I agree."

Memories of the market last night suddenly flash before my eyes—how much I enjoyed myself, how James and I got along. Even though it was just a boring wedding errand.

Surely, he isn't thinking the same thing. Maybe he was referring to Gemma.

I swallow audibly. Because now I know how I recognized the tone in James's voice before. It was the same tone in my voice last night.

Was James... jealous?

The thought kickstarts my heart into overdrive, and suddenly my entire body heats up. And not in a mortified-embarrassment kind of way, but in a new and unfamiliar way. A nice way.

James is close now. So close that his breath plays on my lips, and his achingly attractive smell of sandalwood surrounds me. "Hey, Brooks?" he whispers.

"Yeah?"

"Do you think you could ever date someone who drives you nuts?"

My breath catches. "I... I don't know."

"Because I think I could."

Our faces are inches away, his eyes locked on mine. And then, they drop to my lips. Just for a second.

The small action is enough to send my brain out the window. What happens next feels like the most natural, easy thing in the world. Like it's meant to be.

But, in the time between now and then, something occurs to me.

This is James. Can you really forget what happened that day?

The thought is like the shock of an ice cube sliding down your back—something teenage James did to me a couple times, by the way—and I'm suddenly sucked out of the trance. I sit back, drop my gaze, try to situate myself in the moment as all of my thoughts and anxieties and fears slam back into my body in a mad rush.

James doesn't move, but his expression is guarded as he assesses me. "You okay?"

"I'm fine," I say way too quickly, the words tumbling over themselves. I'm out of sorts—I could almost believe that my iced tea was spiked, but I know it wasn't. This is all us. This is all James.

James. The guy who single-handedly ruined my dating life in school. The flirt who could go out with literally anyone he wants, and knows it. The jerk who's going to return to Denver right after the wedding.

But here he is, and he's looking at me with a tenderness I don't recognize, and that scares the pants off me. And all I can think is... is any of this real? Is this how he made Gemma feel? And Charlotte? Am I another woman on his long list of flirtations?

Well, no sir. If I'm on anyone's list, it's Cam's.

Or he's on mine. Whatever.

I shake myself off, mind racing sickeningly fast as I grasp for some way to do damage control. Must exit this situation STAT.

"I was thinking that it's been awhile since I dated someone," I throw out haphazardly. "Cam asked me out, so I think I'll go."

James's expression doesn't shift, but I swear his eyes darken. "You want to go out with Cam?"

"Yup. I think we'll have an amazing time," I blab on. Like any of this nonsense is going to save me from the fact that, a few seconds ago, I almost might've kissed James.

"That's great." James nods slowly. "I'm happy for you."

"And I'm happy for you. And Gemma." I quickly add, "or Charlotte. Or whoever."

He bites his lip and my traitor fingers want to reach out and touch that lip. "Thanks, Brooks. Awfully nice of you to be so concerned. Maybe I'll ask one of them out this weekend."

"Great. You should do that."

"I will."

"And maybe I'll go out with Cam this weekend too."

"You should."

"In fact, maybe we should go out together." *What?!*

SOS, this is not a drill. This is an embarrassingly horrible overcorrection.

Now James's expression changes. He looks... amused. "You want to go out together?"

"Yeah, the four of us." My mouth is still talking even though my brain is begging it to stop. "You, Gemma, Cam and me."

James's smile is growing wider by the second. "A double date?"

"Sure." Then—a testament to how far gone I am—I whack him in the shoulder. "A double date with all of us. Just need to find a good night to do it."

"Isn't Elly's bachelorette coming up?" James offers innocently. "So we should probably do it tomorrow night, don't you think?"

Oh, goodness. No.

That's way too soon. That leaves me very little time to make up an excuse and re-damage-control my way out of this situation. But I can't say no, can I? I can't turn back now. James would catch on to what that means in a heartbeat.

"Let's do it," I say.

"Perfect."

Then, unexpectedly, James raises a fist.

I frown at his proffered hand, and then, even more unexpectedly, bump my fist to his.

19

___

IVY

I've always considered myself to be a reasonably intelligent person. Between graduating at the top of my class during my degree, and the random trivia facts I've memorized over the years, I thought that, if nothing else, I had that going for me.

My insane double date suggestion has thrown that entire belief into question.

What was I thinking? I haven't even regular dated in years, forget about having another couple tag along. And that other couple happens to be a girl I barely know from school, and the guy I used to hate but now suddenly have random urges to make out with a little bit. And it will also be my first date with Cam.

Imagine telling that story to our grandchildren—"hey kids, the first time I went out with your grandpa, the guy I used to feud with in high school happened to be there too."

Fantastic.

I was expecting-slash-hoping that Cam would be busy this evening, but when I told him about the double date, he said he was free. According to James, Gemma is also free. And he booked us a table for four at La Vita Dolce, the best and only Italian restaurant in Mirror Valley. *The* classic first date and anniversary spot, also known for their Tuesday sundae bar that's especially popular with kids.

How I wish this was Tuesday so I could drown my sorrows in bowls of chocolate salted caramel ice cream.

I check my watch—it's 5:05pm, which means that Cam is officially late. He was meant to pick me up so we could meet James and Gemma by 5:20pm. Why so early? Good question, but I'm hoping it bodes well for a quick ending to the night.

I smooth down my dress before taking a seat on the couch. It's one of my cuter ones—cream with a lace bodice and cap sleeves. I always imagined I'd wear this dress on a date, though never in my wildest dreams would I have thought it'd be going on *this* particular date.

I try to think positive, tell myself that it'll be fine. I've been too nervous and dejected to eat much today, so I'll be busy scarfing down spaghetti. As long as we don't linger, I should be back here by a very reasonable 7pm.

Finally, there's a knock on my door and I race to open it. But I stop myself, take a breath, try to make it seem like I wasn't literally perched on the edge of the couch already wearing my jacket, shoes and purse.

I paste on an easy, breezy smile and open the door.

"Hey, pretty lady," Cam says.

I blink, unsure how I feel about the term of endearment. "Hey... Cam. You ready?"

"Definitely. And look at this." He moves his hand from behind his back to present a single yellow rose. "I got this for you."

"Oh!" The gesture catches me by surprise. I take it gently, smiling. "That's so kind of you. Thank you."

"Of course."

162

I take a small step out the door, but he doesn't move. "Uh... We should probably go?"

"Agreed, we don't want to be late." Then, he drops his voice to a stage whisper, like he doesn't want the empty hallway to overhear. "But you'll want to put that flower in some water first."

"Oh, yes! One moment."

I leave the door open as I scuttle back into my apartment, palms already sweating. It's minute one of our date and I'm already showing how over my head and awkward I feel.

I bustle around, looking for a vase, but no luck. In the end, I grab a tall water glass, fill it, and place the rose on the sill next to my orchids.

"Let's head out," I say with a smile.

Cam turns on his heel and walks out of the building ahead of me. I ignore the niggling voice that wonders why he isn't saying anything about being late. It's no big deal—he brought me a flower after all. And it means less time spent with James and Gemma.

As I follow Cam, I assess his khaki shorts and T-shirt. A far cry from his usual outfit, and much more casual than what I'm wearing.

I tug at the hem of my dress, feeling a little self-conscious about our mismatched outfits. Then, I remember what James said last night about laughing at myself. I exhale and try to relax, removing all judgment of myself and Cam from my mind.

We stroll through the streets of Mirror Valley, and Cam talks while I walk in a distracted silence. He's going on about the meaning behind yellow roses and how they once symbolized greed and jealousy, and a part of me is fine not to be contributing to the conversation.

I chalk up my reticence to my deep desire not to be

going on this date. If it was just Cam and me, we'd be talking and laughing nonstop. We'd be getting to know each other, learning about each others' childhoods, the whole nine yards. It's just that I don't want to be doing this.

James and Gemma are waiting for us on the sidewalk between La Vita Dolce and the movie theater. Gemma has her arm intertwined with James's and is staring up at him adoringly. Meanwhile, he shoots her what I could only describe as a polite smile.

I have to admit, she looks adorable in a trendy shirt dress that goes to her midthigh. James is wearing a fitted white shirt and olive green chinos. His hair is that perfect amount of tousled and he's wearing sunglasses that make him look like a Hollywood star. He's gorgeous, and I have to remind myself to keep walking and not ogle at him.

I wrap my arm around Cam's in an effort to imitate Gemma and James, but Cam removes his arm from my grip, and instead, wraps it around my shoulder. He tugs me close, and I force myself to let him even though I'm drowning in that same musky cologne he had on yesterday. Does he always wear so much of it?

Too late to wonder about that now. James and Gemma have spotted us and are waving us over.

James's gaze focuses in on Cam's arm around my shoulder. A shadow crosses his expression, and his jaw clenches. I smile brightly, pretending this is all fine and good, even as I try to subtly wriggle sideways out of Cam's grip.

The way James raises an eyebrow makes me wonder if I'm being all that subtle after all.

"Ivyyy," Gemma sings. She detaches herself from James and runs towards me, arms out.

"Hey, Gemma," I respond automatically. We aren't close enough to be hugging, but apparently, we're breaking all the rules tonight. Behind her, James and Cam shake hands. "You look great."

"So do youuuu," she drawls before returning to James's side. She wraps her arm around his again, bringing him close.

I'm slightly gratified to see that James doesn't lean in. Instead, he looks at me. "Hey, Brooks. You're looking fresh."

"Thanks." I give him a saccharine smile. Is "fresh" a compliment?

"Actually." Gemma scopes out my dress and her brow twitches. "You guys kind of look like you came together. And your date and I match, Ivy." She giggles, then extends her hand towards Cam. "I'm Gemma."

"Cam." His eyes linger on her a second too long. "Nice to meet you."

I purse my lips and look away. Straight into James's gaze, as it turns out. His smirk widens and his eyes drop slowly, approvingly, down my body. It's not like we *planned* this.

"Ready for dinner?" I ask quickly, wanting this evening to be over already.

"I had some thoughts on that," James says. "I was thinking we could check out that new action movie first. There's a showing that'll let out right before our reservation time. Gemma's keen to see it if you guys are."

I narrow my eyes at James. The last thing I want to do is extend this date by another two hours.

"Absolutely!" Cam unfortunately says before I can respond. "I've been wanting to see that one. Let's do it."

There's a flash of something resembling irritation in James's eyes, but then he looks at me. "What do you say, Brooks?"

All three of them are staring at me. I can't exactly say no.

As we walk into the theater, Cam tells us about the comic book that the movie is based on. Slight agitation niggles at me, and I eventually tune him out. Until, to the surprise of everyone in our little group, Gemma joins in. She, too, is into comic books.

After getting our tickets (Cam paid for his, I paid for mine, James paid for both his and Gemma's, but who's keeping score?), we file into the darkened auditorium and find seats. Cam goes first, and I sit next to him, with James on my other side, and finally, Gemma. Cam takes out his phone and starts typing. I try not to fixate on it—I'm sure this double date is uncomfortable for him too.

"Gemma, you want snacks?" James whispers as the ads start.

"Maybe some peanut butter cups? I love the chocolate coating." Gemma giggles at full volume.

I sneak a glance at Cam, but he doesn't look up from his phone. I feel bad for tuning him out earlier, and I decide to be kinder. I lean towards him. "Would you like some snacks?"

"Get what you want. I'm okay, thanks." Cam shoots me a quick smile. "Have to answer this work text before the movie starts."

He turns back to his phone.

Then, "want something, Brooks?"

I clench my jaw. Okay, so I'm hungry and the thought of food is super tempting right now. But, I won't let James have this. Ideally, my date would be offering to get us snacks, but I'm not going to give James the satisfaction. I'll wait until he gets back, then get myself something at the snack bar after.

"No, thanks," I say brightly.

Unfortunately, my stomach chooses that exact moment

to make a very loud grumble. I shift in my seat, hoping the movement disguises the sound.

By the time James gets back, the movie's started and Cam is leaning so far forward in his seat that the people behind us are uttering hushed complaints. I've asked him to sit back a couple times, and have now given up.

James takes his seat and his familiar sandalwood smell surrounds me again. He hands something to Gemma, then sits back and places his arm next to mine on the armrest. His forearm grazes against me—warm and firm—and the sensation makes my breath catch.

We sit there with our arms pressed together, and though I wish I could say it was uncomfortable, my misguided heart is loving being this close to him.

He tilts his head towards me. "Popcorn?"

He holds out the bag and I breathe in the sweet, toasted smell. My stomach grumbles again, thankfully during an on-screen explosion. "What kind?"

"Kettle."

Ugh, my favorite. I frown at him. "I thought you hated kettle corn."

James's eyes meet mine. "I can tolerate it. Help yourself, Brooks."

Something in his voice triggers me. There's that tenderness again, a caring I've never noticed in him before. A lump forms in my throat as a wave of something like gratitude travels the length of my body. Did he remember that I love kettle corn?

Did he get it for me so that I wouldn't have to get it myself?

The thought completely trips me up. I'm not used to someone looking out for me like this... Least of all James Weston.

I shoot to a stand. "Have to pee," I whisper as an excuse before dashing out.

I lock myself in a bathroom stall, and call Daisy.

"Hey, girl."

"Dais..." I trail off, unsure what exactly I'm feeling right now.

"Ivy? Aren't you supposed to be on the double date? Do you need an out? If so, I can make a pretty convincing outraged guest. 'You promised you'd give me *two* pillow chocolates, you no-good ninny!'"

"It's not that."

Daisy is silent for a long moment. When she speaks again, her voice is serious. "Talk to me. What's going on?"

"He got popcorn."

"Who? Cam?"

"James."

"And we don't like that because..." Daisy trails off and I can hear the frown in her voice. "We hate popcorn? No, that's not right. You love your kettle corn."

"I know. He knows."

"Okay. So we're sad because James got kettle corn and... didn't want to share with you?"

"But he *did* want to share with me."

Daisy is silent again. "You gotta help me out here."

"It's just... he just..." I breathe, though my chest feels heavy. "He got kettle corn even though he hates it. And he offered it to me."

"So he got you kettle corn?"

"I guess so."

"That's nice of him." Now, Daisy's smiling. "Did you say thank you?"

"No, I don't..." I clear my throat, take another breath through the bizarre wave of emotion currently taking hold in me. "I don't know what to think, Dais. I don't know what

168

I'm feeling. I'm angry with him all the time, and I kind of want to rip his head off, but I also want him to kiss me and wrap his arms around me again. And I don't know what to do with all of these feelings."

My voice is weak as I finish the sentence. Daisy's silent again for a moment. Then, she sighs. "Have you ever considered *why* you feel all these things for James?"

"What?" I hiccup.

Oh, great. I'm crying. That'll be good for the makeup.

"Like... maybe you feel all these things because something deeper lies beneath it. And maybe you're scared."

"Scared of what?"

"You tell me. Maybe it's time you faced your feelings instead of covering them up with anger. I've seen the way you look at him, Iv, and I've seen the way he looks at you. This isn't just high school bickering anymore. You have to dig deeper."

My breath is shallow again. Whatever Daisy's saying, whatever the implications are... it terrifies me. "What if I can't?" I ask, my voice a whisper. "What if it all ends badly?"

"What if it doesn't? You've got to stop running sometime, you've got to face this."

I squeeze my eyes shut again, try to calm my racing heart.

"Listen, I'm not saying you have to do this right now," Daisy says gently. "Just... think about it. Maybe everything you want is waiting for you on the other side of a little faith and bravery. And in the meantime, I'm here for you."

I lean my head against the wall of the stall. "I'm not sure."

"Trust me. And do your yoga breaths."

I bark out a laugh. "You know I spend half my yoga sessions distracted and writing down to-dos for the Inn."

"Breathe in, breathe out..."

I follow Daisy's soothing voice and take my breaths. After a few minutes, we hang up, and I leave the stall. I'm not sure what I'm expecting when I look in the mirror, but all I can say is that I look remarkably like a wet racoon. That'll teach me to try smoky eyes.

I clean myself up quickly, reapply some mascara and lip gloss. I love Daisy, but whatever she was alluding to on the phone... It's not so simple. It's never going to be so simple. And now's not the time to think about it.

With my head held high, I open the door to the bathroom and stride out.

Run immediately into James.

I bounce backwards, take a huge step away from him. "Woah."

"Hey, Brooks." He smiles easily. "That took awhile."

My nostrils flare. "How long were you lingering outside the bathroom, weirdo?"

James does a goofy face that actually, annoyingly, makes him even cuter than normal. "Does it bother you?"

"I think it would bother a lot of people."

"The movie had some technical issues, so we had to leave. I sent Cam and Gemma on to the restaurant to see if they could get our table now instead of later."

Embarrassment claws at my insides. "Were you all waiting long?"

"Not too long." James shrugs. "I told them you had stomach issues and they went off quickly after that."

I sock James in the shoulder. "You're such a jerk."

"All in good fun, Brooks."

20

JAMES

I'm pretty sure the movie theater workers think I'm a creep.

Yup, the one at the cash register keeps looking at me. And the one at the popcorn machine is full-on glaring. I stare right back at them over Ivy's head.

The technical issues started soon after she ran out of the room. I made a joke that the entire production was hinging on Ivy, and Gemma stared at me blankly like she had no idea what I was talking about.

We waited in the theater lobby for a few minutes, but Gemma was getting impatient and Cam wouldn't look up from his phone for longer than twenty seconds. Don't get me wrong, Gemma's a nice girl, but we don't have all that much to say to each other.

At a certain point, Cam glanced at the bathroom and had the audacity to roll his eyes, like waiting for Ivy was a massive inconvenience. I mentioned that maybe she wasn't well, and he sighed impatiently.

Nice.

And that doesn't even cover the fact that he didn't check with her about seeing the movie, and didn't offer to get her snacks even though her stomach was roaring louder than the explosions in the film.

I might be biased, but it's getting hard for me to believe that he's a "good guy," as everyone keeps saying.

Finally, I insisted that Gemma and Cam go on to the restaurant, and that's when I began pacing in front of the bathroom. I was starting to worry about Ivy, was wondering if she was okay. I was half-tempted to pop my head in and ask, but I don't particularly want to be known around Mirror Valley as a grade-A lurker and restroom peeper. Unfortunately, no other women were around, so I couldn't ask them to check on her. I decided to stay close, just in case.

Hence why the theater people think I'm a creep. I saw the relief on their faces when Ivy finally walked out and spoke to me.

Now, as she checks for something in her purse, I take the opportunity to look at her. She doesn't seem ill or anything, but her lips are slightly puffy and... are her eyes glassy?

She starts to walk towards the doors, but I take her arm. "Hey, you okay?"

"I'm fine."

"You sure? Because we don't have to do this."

A shadow crosses her face and I get the distinct sense that whatever is bothering her doesn't have to do with our bizarro double date. In fact, with the way she's avoiding my eyes, I could believe...

Is she upset because of me?

"Did I do something?" I ask.

"What? No. Well, nothing more than usual." She barks out a laugh and turns away, yanking her arm of out my grip. "Shall we get to La Vita Dolce? Hopefully Cam and Gemma have a table."

Ivy strides towards the door and I follow her outside. As we're passing the restaurant window, she stops, peering inside. I stand next to her, all too aware of her.

When we were sitting together last night at Luke's bachelor party, the air filled with Ivy's shampoo and the heady sound of her laugh, every logical part of me was telling me not to go there. That I was in dangerous territory. And yet, I couldn't stop.

There are so many reasons why I can't fall for Ivy Brooks. Luke is one of them. He's my best friend, we've been through so much over the years. I would never do anything to risk our friendship. I definitely wouldn't risk it for a girl.

But Ivy's not just a girl.

I've tried to keep that mental box of mine locked up tight over the years—tried not to think of her. But the lock is coming loose, and it's getting harder and harder to convince myself that I'm not feeling what I'm feeling for Ivy.

Which is why I couldn't put my heart into this date with Gemma even if I wanted to. Ivy's the one I want to spend my time with.

Last night, it seemed like she might feel the same way. But then, she pulled away and insisted on this double date, and I wondered if this was another challenge—a way for her to see what this is between us.

Ivy's face creases as she stares into the restaurant and I wonder what she's thinking. Does she not want to go in? Are we done with this particular challenge? Is she ready to call it quits?

"Brooks?" I ask.

Ivy looks up at me, her green eyes boring into mine. And for a split second, I think that she might give in, might decide to leave. Go do something together. But the next moment, she shrugs. "We better get in there."

"Whatever makes you happy."

Ivy's silent for a moment, her eyes searching my face. But then, she steps away and I follow her lead.

We're about to walk inside when my phone rings—that familiar ringtone again. I go to answer, but I hesitate. Look at her.

Her eyebrows are raised. "You wanna get that?"

"I should."

"I'll let Cam and Gemma know. Maybe say you're the one with the bathroom issues this time."

With a wink, she walks through the door.

I shake my head as I answer the call. "Hey, Martin."

"James. How are you, man?"

I run my fingers through my hair. It feels like I spoke to Martin this morning, but thinking back, it had to be a few days ago. It might be the longest we've gone without speaking—and the longest I've gone without working—since I started on his team. "Busier than expected with wedding prep, actually. What're you doing working on a weekend?"

"I wanted to touch base with you before we go into next week." I hear Martin typing in the background. "Xavier's got the team assembled and wants to get started."

My brow furrows. "Already? These projects usually take months to start up."

"They do, but Xavier's got the investors all excited and they want us to get going right away."

I shift on my feet. "The wedding's in just a few days..."

"I get it, but you do see the difficult position we're in, don't you?" Martin inhales, and I notice the typing has stopped. "Tell you what—why don't we start moving forward over here, and we'll do a full write-up for you to review when you're back. Then you can take it from there."

I bite the inside of my cheek. My automatic response

would've once been that I'd be there. But I'm starting to realize that work isn't everything.

My eyes land on Ivy inside the restaurant. She's got her nose in the menu and is tugging at her hair. I take a deep breath, and decide to let go. "Sure. Go ahead, and I'll pick it up next week."

"Fantastic! And not to give too much away, but I think you'll be very happy with our first steps. It should hit home how much success you could have in this role, get you jazzed."

"Uh, awesome. Thanks. I'm looking forward to hearing more."

"Chat with you soon."

With that, Martin hangs up and I stand in the street for a moment. I've never turned down an opportunity like this, never said no to work. Especially after just getting a promotion. But I made the right decision, I can feel it.

I paste a smile on my face, and head into the restaurant to finish off the weirdest date of my life.

21

IVY

When I wake up on Monday morning, I already know that it's going to be a bad day.

For one thing, it's May 15—the anniversary of my parents' deaths. Which is never easy.

On top of that, everything that can go wrong *is* going wrong. It isn't just that my phone wasn't properly plugged in overnight and died before my alarm could go off. It's the guest in Room 20 who comes flying into the lobby at check-out complaining about bed bugs (it was literally one spider on her dresser across the room), and the chef running out of eggs (eggs!) in the middle of breakfast service.

I had to run out to the shop, and of course, my car wouldn't start, so I had to take the rickety, creaky old bike we stow away behind the Inn for emergencies. And the air is full of dust this time of year, so my pants and blouse were covered in a thick coat of dirt by the time I got back.

The one piece of good news is that I *finally* brought a spare suit to work. It costs nothing to be prepared—even if that preparation consists of a tweed skirt and a white blouse with a high neckline reminiscent of the Victorian era.

Reminder to self to bring a cuter suit to work. Preferably one from this century.

Tonight, Luke, my grandparents and I will have dinner together to remember my parents, followed by a visit to the cemetery. And today, my goal, as it always is on the anniversary of their deaths, is just to soldier through and get to the end. Preferably without fixating on what happened before they left for a day trip in the mountains almost twenty years ago, never to return.

Luke said he planned his wedding to happen around May 15 on purpose—he wanted to bring an element of joy to this time of year, and he thought this was a way to honor and celebrate them.

But the last thing I want to be doing on my lunch break, today of all days, is standing on a podium at Belle's Bridal for an emergency dress fitting.

Late last night, Elly suddenly decided that I should have the same dress as her bridal party, even if I don't stand with them at the ceremony—with her two bridesmaids and maid of honor, I didn't make the cut.

So, per her request, I am now standing in a dark green dress with off-the-shoulder sleeves that would be cute if I wasn't squeezed to within an inch of my life to fit into it. It must be five sizes too small, but Elly insists it looks perfect.

Belle's also has a makeup artist and hair stylist on hand, so we've gone the full nine yards. My smoky eyes are giving me wet-raccoon flashbacks from the movie theater, and my hair is in this painfully tight chignon that makes it feel like my scalp is ripping off every time I so much as raise an eyebrow.

"Turn around," Elly commands from where she's assessing me next to the oh-so-flattering shop mirrors.

"Okay," I mumble. I've discovered that if I don't enunciate too much, my hair won't hurt. "One sec, just gotta get my balance."

I'm wearing sky-high silver stilettos with sparkles all over them and laces tying up my calves. As I turn carefully on the podium, I make a mental note that, on the big day, I should try to stand next to something in case I spontaneously fall over. Even without flirting, there's a very real chance I will be going down in these shoes at some point.

"Looks great," Elly says. "So lucky that Belle ordered an extra dress. You can have this one."

"Actually," Belle tinkles from the front of the shop. "You put down an order for four dresses instead of three. But don't worry, these things happen."

Ah, the truth comes out. This isn't a way for Elly to make me feel included in the wedding—she just wants me to cover the cost of the extra dress.

I press my lips together in a thin smile. Literally everything hurts right now, and my bank account will soon be joining the mix.

"You look fantastic, Iv." Luke steps forward. Frowns. "Are you... breathing?"

"I'm fine," I say on an exhale. Shallow breaths are the trick.

Luke looks at his fiancée. "Babe, I don't think Ivy's comfortable. Are you sure we can't take the dress out or anything?"

"No time for that. The measurements on this dress are the same as Francesca's, and Ivy and Franscesa are about the same size, don't you think?"

Uhm... *No!*

I frown, seriously considering whether Elly might've lost her vision. Even Luke looks concerned. Fransesca is a tiny, petite, pixie-fairy sort of woman. My hips and thighs are about twice the size of hers. Scratch that—confirmed to be twice the size of hers, if this dress is any indication.

They both turn back to me, and their eyes rake over my body in a supremely analytical way that makes me want to duck and hide behind one of Belle's absurdly plush loungers.

"Do you really think it's too small, Lukey?" Elly asks, staring at me like I'm a frog she's dissecting in science class. "I'm going to ask Ana and Francesca."

Before I can say anything, she takes out her phone and starts snapping photos. My cheeks heat and I try to cover myself up. "Uh, Lenore? I'm not sure I'm very comfortable with you doing th—"

"Okay, sent." She types furiously on her phone.

A moment later, there's a text back. She snorts and looks at me, her eyes skating over my body again. She giggles, and types on her phone.

The whole thing is making me super self-conscious and I look at Luke with pleading eyes. He turns to Elly. "Babe, that's enough. I don't think Ivy wants you taking photos of her. And if she isn't comfortable in the dress, she doesn't have to wear it, right?"

Elly lifts a brow and sighs. "Whatever. I just thought it'd be nice if she wore it. Francesca doesn't want to pay for two dresses, and I'll never fit into that. So who else is going to wear it?"

Someone who's a comfortable size two? I want to say, but I don't have the oxygen.

"Can I change?" I finally manage.

Elly waves a hand. "Sure. We'll figure something out."

With a grateful nod, I try to walk across the podium, but the dress is like plastic wrap around my legs. Plus, with these shoes, I might as well be teetering precariously on those vertical slabs of wood at the playground. I suddenly feel a kinship to stilt-walking people everywhere.

I eventually give up attempting to walk and I sink down and lean back, crouching into a sitting position so as to not tear the dress. Having the butt rip is just what I need right now.

I half-scoot, half-shuffle to the edge of the platform and try to swing my legs around to get at the laces on my ankles. Luke and Elly are at the front of the shop speaking to Belle. I don't think they're seeing me struggle, and that's probably for the best.

I actively suppress my grunts as I wriggle around like a flopping fish, trying to reach the laces on my shoes. No dice —there's literally no more give in this dress. All I want right now is to be in my regular clothes, taking air into my body, without my head feeling like it's ripping in two.

I try again, and there's no holding back the grunts now.

I'm wheezing and panting, but I'm almost touching the laces on my right shoe...

Just about there...

"Brooks?"

Suddenly, James is standing right above me, smirking at me.

"What're you doing?" he asks, amused.

"Trying... to... get the... shoes," I wheeze again as I finally take hold of the laces on my right shoe. I tug hard.

Cowbells. They're tied in a double knot.

I give up with a frustrated grunt. Lie flat on the podium with my eyes clenched shut, angry tears gathering at the corners.

This is fine. I'm fine. I'll just die here.

Suddenly, a hand grazes my ankle. "Maybe I can help."

"I've got it," I say without moving.

"I don't think you do."

James touches my ankle again and alarm floods my body. I reach back in my brain—did I shave my legs recently? I come to the sad realization that it's been a few days, and the last thing I want is James feeling up my prickly legs. "Can you get Luke or Elly?"

"They're busy with Belle. Arguing about an extra dress or something."

"This would be the one," I wheeze again.

I've never been so attractive in my life.

"Let me help you, Brooks." James says again, his voice firm and commanding this time.

I finally open an eye and peek up at him. To his credit, he's staring at my face and not my legs, looking resolved. Clearly, he's not going to take no for an answer. Once again, he's helping me whether I like it or not.

"I didn't shave my legs," I confess, my voice small.

James's eyebrows raise for a half-second, and then he laughs. The sound is surprisingly comforting. "I couldn't care less about that. The hairier the better."

"Okay, weirdo." I squeeze my eyes shut and a fresh wave of pain stabs through my scalp. I just want to be comfortable again, even if it means having James judge my legs. "Fine."

"Thank you," he says. Which is weird, as I should be thanking him.

My eyes are closed, my focus on breathing without tearing the dress, when James picks up my right ankle. His hands are warm and strong, even as they gently grasp my foot. I feel every action of his fingers as he undoes the double knot—why, oh why, did Belle do a double knot on these shoes?

His hands skim the tender skin on my ankle bones as he unwinds the laces down my calf. It almost tickles, but the feeling is more complex than that—instead of making me want to laugh, it makes my heart skitter. He slides the shoe off and holds my foot for a moment. It's everything I can do not to look up at him, wonder what he's thinking.

He places my right foot on his knees and repeats the action with my left. The whole thing is unexpectedly intimate, and I don't know what to do with myself. I scramble for a conversation topic.

"So, what're you doing here anyway?" I venture. "You're not getting fitted for a dress, are you?"

James snorts. "Luke asked if I could meet him and Elly here to check the suits one last time. I think he wanted a second opinion on the..."

He goes on but I'm no longer listening. Because he removed my left shoe and is now absentmindedly rubbing my feet. He massages into my arches, and man, it feels *good*. He carefully rubs into the tender spots and stretches my foot left and right. I've never had a foot massage before, but I have a feeling this is better than most.

"Anyway, I decided work could wait, and here I am," James finishes.

"Unggg," is all I can offer in response.

James chuckles, pauses his work on my feet. "You okay?"

"How do you know how to do this?"

"Soccer, Brooks. In college, we had physios who did foot massages. I picked up a few things."

"Cool," I mumble, then lay back down as he digs into my arches again.

I let my mind wander. It should be weird that James is doing this—especially after our double date a couple nights ago that could easily make it into the Hall of Fame for most awkward dates.

After the action movie debacle, the dinner at La Vita Dolce was no better. It started with Gemma asking if the

Serengeti is named after a type of pasta (it's not), and finished with her and Cam speaking nonstop about their love of comics, which morphed into discussions of their favorite crafting past-times when Gemma gave me the origami flower she'd made for Elly.

The most unexpected parts of the evening, though, were the moments in between the stretches of Gemma and Cam. When I'd catch James watching me and we'd share eye contact. When he offered me a napkin after I dropped some spaghetti and our fingers touched. When, at the end of the night, he politely hugged me goodbye and I didn't want to let go.

Each of those individual seconds felt far more intense and charged than anything with Cam. And if James's small, secret smiles my way were any indication—along with the fact that he and Gemma barely spoke the entire night—they weren't a good match either.

And now, here we are, me lying prostrate across a platform at a bridal shop, barely able to breathe, while he works literal wonders on my feet.

"What the..." I hear Luke somewhere behind me. "Ivy, you okay?!"

James places my feet on the ground and I'm brought back to the moment.

"I'm fine," I wheeze. "Everything hurts."

Luke appears in my field of vision, looking at me with an eyebrow raised. James also pops into view, and they both stare down at me. I suddenly get an uncomfortable understanding of what it must've been like to be one of the slugs they used to pick up in the garden.

Luke looks at James. "On three?"

"On three."

I frown as they each grab one of my arms. "What're you—?"

They hoist me up and stand me upright. The sudden rush of blood out of my head makes me dizzy, and I topple sideways into James's chest. He holds me for a second as my body regains its equilibrium. Too soon, he lets me go.

"Get changed, and I'll get you back to the Brookrose," he says. Then, he looks at Luke. "Everything work out with Belle?"

"Yup. Lenore's getting the dress at a discount, and Belle will call if anyone wants to buy it off her."

"Awesome, we can walk out together. But in the meantime..." He spins me gently on my feet and leads me to the dressing room. "I'll wait for you here, Brooks."

22

JAMES

"Ugh. Unzip already," Ivy grumbles from behind the curtain of her dressing room.

"Doing okay in there?" I ask from the seating area, where I'm leafing through a magazine about ties. Who knew that a person who collects ties is called a Grabatologist? Ivy, probably. "I'm hearing an awful lot of whinging."

"'Whinging.'" Ivy wheezes out a laugh. "You're so British."

I roll my eyes, though she can't see it.

A second later, there's a "yes!!"

After more grunting, grumbling, and muttered British slang I don't even recognize, the curtain finally opens. Ivy stumbles out wearing a skirt and a white blouse that looks like it's from another time period. Her makeup is smudged, the dark around her eyes making her irises look extra green. Her hair is still pulled back and she tugs at the strands.

"Let's get back to the Inn," she mutters.

"You sure you want to go back to work?"

She pulls at her hair again, blinking and moving her face around weirdly. Then, she throws her purse over her shoulder. "Yes."

She marches towards the door and I give Luke a wave as I follow her. I make a mental note to catch up with him later.

This errand at the bridal shop isn't the only reason I'm here. May 15 is a hard day for Luke, and I bet it isn't easy for Ivy either. I used to mark the date in my calendar, make sure to call Luke. Now that I'm in town, it seemed right that I should make myself available in case either of them needs anything.

Judging by Ivy's horizontal gymnastics in the shop, she definitely needed help. When I walked in, I thought her wriggling and grunting was some sort of weird joke she was playing, until I saw her frustrated expression.

Whose idea was it for her to squeeze into a teeny dress with zero give while wearing the world's most complicated shoes? Sounds like a lot of pain and effort to me, especially when Ivy's beautiful just as she is.

I catch up with her outside, where she's standing on the sidewalk with her arms crossed. "Where's the car?" she grumbles impatiently.

I try to lighten the mood a little. "Demanding today, aren't we, Brooks?"

"Don't test me, *Weston*. I need to get back to work." She rifles through her purse, then mutters something so quietly, I barely hear. "I just need to get through today."

The teasing mood is knocked right out of me. Today is harder for her than she's letting on.

I reflexively place a hand on her elbow and she freezes, examining it like it's an alien tentacle. She trails her gaze up my arm and to my face, and when she meets my eyes, her expression falters for a moment. She looks so exhausted, so weary all of a sudden.

I react instantly, moving forward to wrap her in a hug. "Ivy?"

The voice shocks me and Ivy steps away to peek over my shoulder. "Grams!"

She darts past me and right into her grandmother's arms. I watch from a distance as Ivy's grandparents wrap her in a hug.

"What're you doing here?" Ivy asks. "Aren't we doing dinner later?"

"Of course, sweetie." Grandma Maggie assesses her in that special maternal way.

Maggie is like the ranch mom from a TV show—she's tough as nails but with the sweetest heart, wears jeans and vests over plaid shirts, and her long white hair is always pulled back in a neat bun. Her light eyes sparkle, and her tan face has smile lines that tell the story of a long, fulfilling life.

Ivy's grandpa Richard is like the carbon-copy male version of his wife, complete with a plaid shirt, jeans, and a cowboy hat. Plus, he has a mustache that would impress Sam Elliott.

"We're grabbing a few things for dinner, and I remembered the dress fitting," Maggie says. "We thought we'd pop by in case you were around."

Richard's green eyes—the same color as Ivy's—suddenly land on me. "Is that James Weston?"

Maggie's eyes widen and she swoops forward to wrap me in a hug. "It's so good to see you, Jamie! Darlene mentioned you were in town for the wedding, and we were wondering when we'd bump into you. You're looking well, dear boy." She steps away, holding tight to my hands as her eyes drop down my body. "Very well. My goodness, you've turned into quite the handsome young man."

I chuckle, my cheeks warm. "Thank you, Maggie."

"He was always a good-looking chap," Richard booms as he shakes my hand heartily. "Strong, too. Remember the forts he and Luke used to build in the garden? Chopped the wood themselves and everything."

Maggie wraps an arm around Ivy's shoulders. "Where's your brother?"

"At Belle's, he'll be out in a minute. I was just about to go back to the Inn."

I could swear that a shadow crosses Maggie's face and she glances at Richard. "Right, of course." She looks at her granddaughter again, and if I didn't know better, I'd say that her bright smile is forced. "Well, no rush. Val's got it under control, I'm sure."

"Val's great, but I need to get back."

"I understand, but don't work yourself too hard, dear. We don't want you to be burdened with the Brookrose."

Ivy's brow wrinkles for a moment. "The Brookrose isn't a burden. It's our family business."

This time, the look Maggie gives Richard is unmistakable. A bad feeling swirls in my stomach.

Ivy clearly saw the look too, because her face darkens. "What was that?"

Maggie and Richard look at each other again.

"We shouldn't do this today," Maggie whispers to him.

"Do what?" Ivy asks.

At that moment, the door to Belle's Bridal opens, and Elly and Luke walk out. "Grams, Pops! What're you doing here?"

Maggie wraps Luke in a hug, then goes in to hug Elly. Even from here, the hug looks a little awkward.

"Hang on," Ivy interrupts. "What were you about to say?"

Richard looks at Maggie again, who bites her lip. "Should we tell them?" he asks. "We have to talk about it soon anyway."

188

Luke looks between his grandparents. "Talk about what?"

"Let's discuss it later." Maggie shakes her head. "Today's hard enough as it is."

Elly wraps her arm around Luke's and squeezes tight. He pats her hand, and I'm thankful that Luke has someone who cares about him like that. Meanwhile, Ivy's frozen on the sidewalk, her eyes laser focused on her grandparents. I step closer to her, fighting the urge to wrap my arm around her.

"What is it?" Ivy's voice is carefully calm. "If it's something to do with the Inn, I need to know."

"So does Luke," Elly pipes in.

I glance at him and he shakes his head once. He hasn't told her about wanting to give up his ownership.

Maggie presses her lips together. Then, finally, she deflates. "We got an offer."

I feel more than see Ivy startle next to me. "An offer?"

Richard wraps his arm around Maggie's shoulders and holds her close. Just like I wish I could do with Ivy. "Yes. Someone wants to buy the Inn."

"What?" The word comes from Luke's mouth like after a blow to the chest.

Ivy's face has gone white. "The Inn's for sale?"

"It isn't—wasn't."

"So what're you saying?"

"A company reached out and made us an offer," Maggie explains, her brows drawn together in a frown like she's trying to make sense of Ivy's reaction. "We said no, but they just kept coming back with higher and higher numbers. And now... well, they're offering a lot of money."

"How much?" Elly asks.

"If we say yes..." Richard looks at his wife. "Our family will be set up for a long, long time."

"But our family's fine," Ivy says.

"Of course we're fine, dear." Maggie grabs her hands. "But this would change everything. You won't be stuck in Mirror Valley anymore, you can do whatever you'd like. Maybe get a job with a hotel that uses software from this century. And Luke, this would set you, Lenore, and your future kids up for years to come. You'll be starting your life together on the right foot. You're thinking of giving up your share of ownership anyway—"

Maggie cuts herself off. She said too much.

"You are?" Ivy turns to her brother with wide eyes.

But Luke's facing Elly, guilt written across his face. Elly's arms are crossed, her mouth turned down in a sneer. "You want to give up your ownership? And you didn't think to tell me?"

"I'm sorry, babe, I was going to bring it up soon. I'm only thinking about it—it doesn't seem fair to Ivy that I keep my share, but then move away."

Ivy opens her mouth to say something, but holds back. Everyone watches Elly as she considers the news, and I wonder how she's going to react. From everything Luke's told me, Elly's pretty attached to the Brookrose...

Her brow clears, and she shrugs. "Luke should keep his ownership until the sale. That's all that matters."

Or she's attached to the money. But now's not the time to get into that.

"Do you really want to sell?" I ask Maggie and Richard. "The Brookrose is a staple of this town, I can't imagine anyone else running it."

"We're not sure. Obviously, we want to speak with Luke and Ivy about it first."

"It's where we grew up," Ivy says, and now, I can't stop myself—I reach out and my fingers graze her wrist. She looks up at me and her eyes are carefully guarded. Masking something.

Richard shakes his head definitively. "Let's drop this for now. We haven't made any decisions, and we don't know what's going to happen. Today's a tough enough day, so there's no need to put any more stress on ourselves. This can wait until after Luke and Lenore are married."

Maggie places both hands on Ivy's face. The gesture is kind and motherly, and I'm so glad she did it. "Listen to me, sweetie. There's no way this is happening overnight, so don't worry about it." Ivy gives her a small smile, and Maggie looks at Luke next. "Are you going to be okay?"

Luke squeezes Elly's hand. "We'll be fine."

"Okay. We'll see you tonight then."

After giving everyone a final round of hugs, Maggie and Richard walk off towards the center of town, holding hands.

Luke turns to Elly, tugs his fingers through his hair. "I'm so sorry, I should've talked to you about the whole ownership thing earlier. I just didn't want to put any more on your plate right before the wedding."

"It's okay, I know you meant well. And just think, when the Inn sells, we'll be set for life. We can do whatever we want."

"*If* the Inn sells," Luke says off-hand. Then, he takes out his phone and taps through to what I'm sure is his Notes app. "Speaking of the wedding, there's a few things I should get done today. You're still busy with the bachelorette, babe?"

Classic Luke—whenever anything big happens, he ignores it. Goes right back to his usual routine.

"Definitely," Elly responds, sighing like she's carrying the weight of the world. "I can't believe it's already happening tomorrow. There's still so much to do."

"I get it. I'll get started then." Luke's eyes land on Ivy.

"It's going to be okay, Iv. Grams and Pops haven't sold yet, and it *is* our decision. We won't do anything that'll hurt our family."

"Of course," Ivy says with that same small smile. But this time, I see the cracks in her expression—the corners of her mouth pulling down, the sadness hidden behind her eyes.

"Good." Luke wraps her in a hug, then looks at me. "You've still got Betsy, right? Ivy rode over on that old trick bike we used to ride, can you take her back to the Brookrose?"

I understand why he's asking—that bike was on its last legs fifteen years ago. "Happy to."

As Elly and Luke walk away, I turn to Ivy. Her arms are crossed and she's staring down the road. At first glance, it looks like she's lost in thought, but I have a feeling there's a lot more happening beneath the surface.

Her jaw twitches like she's cold, and I want to wrap my arms around her, tell her everything's going to be okay. But I'm not sure where we stand, and I don't want to make her more uncomfortable.

I pick up the old bike and place it in the truck bed, and when I return to Ivy's side, she still hasn't moved. I take her hand, and my touch seems to shock her. Her fingers are ice cold, and she stares at our hands, then meets my gaze.

Her eyes are glazed over, and it's everything I can do not to pick her up and place her in the car. I just know that I need to get her off the street.

I lead her back to Betsy and put her on the bench seat before going around to the driver's side.

23

———

IVY

When I was eight, my family took a trip to Disneyland.

I was so excited, I couldn't sleep the entire week leading up to it. Once we got there, Mom and I split from Dad and Luke. Luke was nine and wanted to go on the "big kid" rides, whereas I wanted to spend all day every day on the spinning strawberries and eating my weight in cotton candy and corn dogs.

On our last day, I decided that I wanted to try a big kid ride too. Just like Luke.

He took me to the scariest ride in the park.

The ride was based on some TV show involving a hotel. On the ride, you get into this elevator, they strap you in, play a video, and then... the ground drops from beneath you.

Suddenly, I was hurtling through thin air in the dark.

I froze. Couldn't scream, couldn't even make a sound.

How I feel right now is similar to that—like the ground's opened up and I'm free-falling into nothing.

In the recesses of my mind, I know that my body is safely and firmly on the earth—literally strapped into my brother's truck. And yet, my muscles are tense, hot and cold waves are rushing across my skin, and I feel frozen in place again.

"Brooks? You okay?"

I'm trapped in my memory at Disneyland. That was the year before my parents passed away.

And now, their only legacy—the place I've always called home—might disappear too.

"Brooks?"

A hand lands on my shoulder, goes behind my neck, and the gentle touch brings me back to life. I paste on an automatic grin. "What? I'm fine."

"Really." Unfortunately, James sounds the polar opposite of convinced.

I grit my teeth, force myself to look at him with a reassuring expression. "Yes, everything is a-okay. Why do you keep asking me that?"

"Because you look like someone just told you they lost your clipboard." The teasing tone in his voice is immediately followed by a grimace. "Sorry, bad joke. Tried to lighten the mood."

"Why? There's nothing to lighten. I'm fine, James. Let's just get back to... the Brookrose."

Despite my insistence and my very convincing act, James doesn't put the keys in the ignition. He doesn't turn on the car, or even turn away from me. It's like he's staring right through me, seeing the ache in my heart that I'm trying so, so hard to hide right now.

"You don't seem fine, Brooks," he says simply. "I wouldn't be."

Suddenly, I can't keep up the facade anymore.

My shoulders sag and I collapse back against the seat.

Two big, firm arms circle around me, one hand undoing the seatbelt, while the other pulls me close. I don't even realize how cold I am until the warmth wraps around me. Reflexively, I cuddle in, curling up on the bench seat.

We sit there for a long while as everything I've been trying to suppress comes to a head. All of the little stresses that have piled up today, the memory of my final moments with my parents, the thought of my family's inn being sold to some big company.

The tears fall and I'm probably soaking James's shirt, but I can't bring myself to care.

Eventually, James starts the car, keeping one arm firm around me. "Let's get out of here."

"I need to get back..." I exhale heavily, tugging at my hair. It still hurts, and it'll take me some time, a slew of mirrors, and careful, doctor-like precision to untangle this mess without twisting the strands into an untameable rat's nest.

"I'm not taking you to the Inn, Brooks."

"What?" I ask blearily.

"Trust me."

I literally don't have it in me to fight, so I just shrug and close my eyes. My spinning head feels heavy, and I try to focus on my breaths. The gentle hum of the motor lulls me to something resembling a trance as James drives to goodness-knows-where.

Finally, the car stops and the engine cuts. I open my eyes, frown. "What're we doing here?"

"This is your apartment building, right?"

"Well, yeah... how do you know that?"

James lifts an eyebrow and there's something so familiar and comforting in the teasing movement. "I have my sources."

I'm too stressed and emotionally wrung-out to ask what those sources might be. "Why are we here, James?"

"This is your house."

I let out a dry laugh. "I know that. But I don't want to be here."

"I want to be here."

"Why?"

James bites his bottom lip, then faces me head on. His expression is dead serious.

"Because you're stubborn and independent and will always insist that you can take care of yourself. But I want to take care of you too."

Before I can react, he gets out of the car, comes around to my side and opens the passenger door. He holds out an arm like I'm a senior citizen who can't be trusted to walk without a cane.

Honestly, at this point, maybe I can't. So I take it, refusing to think about what this could mean.

James and I walk up the pathway to my apartment building. I feel a brief panic that I left laundry hanging around or I didn't take out the garbage or something, but when we get inside, I'm relieved to see that it's neat.

Actually, more sparse than neat. I tend to spend a lot of time at the Inn anyway, but with the wedding coming up, I've barely been back the last couple weeks. The couch pillows are perfectly plumped, the table has a light layer of dust on the surface, and my orchids are looking pretty limp. I wonder if Gary the spider is still around.

James called this my house, and he's correct. My apartment is my house, not my home.

The Brookrose is my home.

The thought makes me stagger, and I'm grateful that I'm holding onto James's arm. He places me on the couch and then putters around my kitchen for a moment, starting the kettle and grabbing a couple mugs. "You still drink tea, right?"

"Is the sky blue?" I shoot back and James smirks at me

over his shoulder. I shrug apologetically. "Sorry. Yeah. I love tea."

"Good."

James opens cupboards, closes them again. Does something that sounds suspiciously like chopping.

"What're you doing?" I ask.

"What's it look like? I'm making you food. It's past lunchtime and you're probably hungry. I know I am." He sighs. "This isn't easy, by the way—when was the last time you went to the store?"

I shift on the couch. "I don't know... I usually eat at the Inn. I'm a baker not a cook, remember?"

"Right. I'll see what I can scrounge together."

James continues moving around my kitchen, humming under his breath. It's an entirely foreign concept to have a man—let alone a man like James—moving around my apartment. Making me food.

It's not the worst thing to ever happen.

The kettle boils and James pours out a couple mugs of tea. He walks back to the couch with the mugs, and a plate of apple slices and shortbread cookies. I bought the cookies a couple months ago, put them in my cupboard, and promptly forgot about them.

"Are those still good?" I ask sheepishly.

James picks one up, sniffs it, then bites into it. His nose wrinkles. "Gross. No, these are terrible." He moves the plate away from me. "Disgusting. Actually, I better spare you from eating them."

A laugh bubbles out of me. "Nice try, jerk."

I swipe a cookie and pop the whole thing in my mouth. It's delicious. I have a soft spot for shortbread cookies, and Darlene recommended these from a bakery near town ages ago. I eat another one, and another.

Finally, the plate is empty and I sit back on the couch, tugging at my hair absentmindedly.

"So." James rubs his hands on his knees. "You want to talk about it?"

For a few moments—for that fleeting amount of time that James was in my kitchen and then scarfing down cookies with me—I managed to forget the sadness clawing at my chest. "Not really."

"Okay," he says, and I wait. Wait for him to probe deeper, to ask questions I don't want to answer, maybe to make a joke about how stupid I look with my smeared makeup.

Instead, he sits back next to me. Close enough that our arms press together. I find myself curling into his side, leaning on him, just a little. He puts an arm around me, and we sit in silence. Like this is completely normal.

"Why do you keep doing that?" James suddenly asks.

"Doing what?"

"Touching your hair, twisting your face. Is this some newfangled face yoga or something?"

I didn't even realize I was doing it. From this day forward, I will never, ever take for granted how nice it feels to have your hair down. I will also never again get my hair done at Belle's.

I know I should just take out the stupid bun. Spend the requisite hour removing all the bobby pins, washing my hair, brushing it out. But I actually feel okay here under James's arm for now.

"It hurts," I eventually say.

To my surprise, James chuckles. "Where's your bathroom?"

His hand envelops mine and he leads me down the tiny hallway to my even tinier bathroom. James looks like a literal giant standing next to the sink.

He points to the bathtub. "Sit."

I follow his command and sit on the edge of the tub. He comes around behind me and his hands graze my hair. In the mirror, I see his perplexed frown and I snort. "You okay?"

"What happened here?" he asks, staring at the bun in wonder. "What's with all these pins? And is this... a net?"

I can't help but laugh. "The joys of being a woman."

"This is just... Why?"

"I don't know. To do something different? To feel beautiful?"

James catches my eyes in the mirror. "You're already beautiful, Brooks. You know that, right?"

I blink in surprise. He must be delusional, or we're not seeing the same thing right now. Because I am a sight for sore eyes—my dark makeup is streaked down my face from when I was crying in the truck, and my nose is Rudolph-red. My lips are puffy, and with my hair tied back, I look bald. Which is not a good look for me.

James's fingers begin to work in my hair, taking out the bobby pins one by one. He's careful, slow, and patient. I watch him in the mirror—the furrow in his brow, the way he bites that gorgeous lower lip when he isn't sure what to do next. Watch the small smirk of victory when he figures it out. His big hands are gentle, never pulling or tugging.

My hair begins to fall around my shoulders, and my entire head seems to cry out with relief. I close my eyes and let it happen, let James's fingers work their magic. Let myself succumb to him taking care of me.

Finally, my hair is free. When I open my eyes and meet his gaze, those turquoise depths draw me in—like staring into clear ocean water.

But I can't stop looking at his lips, that chin dimple that I'd love to touch...

Suddenly, I'm standing, and his hand wraps around mine again, turning me to face him. I stare into those eyes that seem so endless, and James lifts a hand. His fingers graze my shoulder as he pushes my hair back.

A million goosebumps rise on my skin.

Ringgggg!

The noise wrenches us out of the moment and James takes his phone out of his pocket. He checks the screen and takes a small step back.

"It's Luke."

"Oh..." I also step away, hit the bathtub but manage to keep my balance. "You should answer it."

"You sure?"

"Absolutely." I say this a little too eagerly. Like we have something to hide.

Which we don't.

James takes the call. "Hey."

I hear the muffled voice on the other end of the line and James glances at me. "I am." Another few words. "Okay, sure. Whatever Eleanor wants."

I hear Luke's "it's Lenore."

After another couple moments, James hangs up. "Your brother wants to know if Daisy can go to Elly's bachelorette tomorrow."

"I'll ask her." I frown. "Weird that he called you about it."

"He said he tried to reach you, but your phone's off."

Right. I didn't get a chance to fully charge it this morning, and it ran out of juice again when I was at the bridal shop. "Why does he care if Daisy's at the bachelorette?"

"It's Elly. She wants Daisy there, if she's free."

"Random." I exhale, but mentally thank Elly for this unexpected kindness. I have to admit that I've been dreading going to the bachelorette alone with her and her

200

college friends. If Daisy can come, at least we can be awkward wallflowers together.

I run my fingers through my hair, closing my eyes at the wonderful sensation. When I open them, James is looking at me, smiling this funny little smile. That tenderness is in his eyes again.

I ignore the warmth in my cheeks. "I might take your advice and lie low this afternoon. I don't think I'm in a good state to be at the Inn after all."

"Good idea." He's silent for a beat, then runs his fingers through his hair. I watch his arm move as if in slow motion, fighting the urge to follow his fingers with mine. "Is there anything you usually do today?"

"What do you mean?"

"Well. I know you and Luke have dinner with your grandparents later, and then you visit the cemetery together. Luke also usually goes to the Brookrose and gets flowers for the graves. So what about you?"

I tilt my head, surprised by his question. But I'm even more surprised to be giving him an honest answer. "I... I like to watch old movies."

"Old movies?"

"The classics. When I was little, Mom and I would put them on while baking or eating cookies or doing crafts or something. Luke and Dad always started off complaining about the movie choice, but then they'd join us. Those are some of my favorite memories—it doesn't matter what the movie was, we'd all sit together, laugh and talk and joke... It was our family time. So I like to put on a couple classic movies today as a way to remember them."

"If you want company, I'd be happy to join you."

"You'd want to watch an old movie? Fair warning, I tend to watch the romantic ones."

"Yeah. Only if you want."

Ohmygosh. I do.

I've never had the option *not* to do this alone. But I like the idea of having someone here to celebrate and remember with me. Someone who knew my parents too.

A shy smile plays on my lips as we head back into the living room. James sits on the couch while I turn on the TV and put on one of my mom's favorites—*Casablanca*. James pats the spot next to him and I sink down, letting him wrap me in his arms.

I don't know what's happening right now—why I'm letting James be here, why I'm letting him witness this. But as he holds me close and the movie starts, it occurs to me that I don't care. I'll care tomorrow, and the next day, and the next.

For right now, this is exactly what I didn't know I needed.

24

IVY

Elly's bachelorette party/retreat/getaway/whatever-she's-calling-it-now starts off with a bang. And I mean that literally.

During our two-hour class at Mirror Valley's yoga center, Elly and her friends spend most of the time taking photos of themselves doing handstands and complicated leg-twisting poses that they inevitably fall out of. The poor instructor, Mr. Wilhelm—who also doubles as our town's physio and high school gym teacher—looks like he wants to tear his already-thinning hair out.

Between Elly and her friends squealing at the photos in their matching yoga outfits, and Mr. Wilhelm's continual, agitated reminders to "stay with the breath," it's a pretty entertaining morning.

Daisy and I relegate ourselves to the back of the room and watch the events unfold at a safe distance from the flailing arms and legs. It's far from your usual slow-paced and relaxing yoga class, but Elly's glowing with happiness.

I try to stay focused as best I can and not let my mind wander. Though I can't help but think of a promise I made to a certain someone about a yoga-off...

What would James think of this class? I imagine his amusement, his cheeky smirk.

The thought makes me smile. Quickly followed by a dose of self-chiding that I let my mind return to him. Or to my couch, where we sat for hours yesterday, watching movies. James ordered us pizza for a late lunch and we talked, ate, and remembered my parents. It was not the worst way that I've spent the day.

When it was time to meet my grandparents and Luke for dinner, a part of me was almost disappointed. But James drove me over before heading to his own parents' place for dinner. We texted sporadically through the evening and this morning. And yes, maybe I want to check my phone to see if he texted back.

I bring my thoughts back to my mat, remember that yoga is a *practice*. It's not meant to be perfect... which, admittedly, does brush up against every single instinct of mine.

"Can you take it again?" Elly whines as she frowns at Ana's phone screen. "My leg looks weird."

There's a loud kerfuffle as Francesca, Leona and Elly gather together, posing with their arms around each other. At the front of the room, poor Mr. Wilhelm sighs tiredly.

Meanwhile, Daisy and I sit cross-legged with our hands in prayer position. Daisy rolls her eyes at me and I shake my head in agreement. Thank goodness my best friend is here.

"Ladies, let's return to our mats," Mr. Wilhelm says with an impatient twinge. "We'll be moving into downward dog..."

I close my eyes and try to focus.

Breathe in. Breathe out.

Don't think about James.

By the time the yoga class comes to an end, I've had to

redirect my thoughts away from James a total of twenty-six times. Twenty-six!

Elly and her friends roll up their yoga mats and snap a couple more photos. They give Mr. Wilhelm a wave as they walk out the door and he shakes his head again, looking like he's aged years in the past couple of hours.

"Bye, Mr. Wilhelm!" Daisy says brightly. "Thanks for a great class."

"I don't know about *great*," he grumbles.

"Bachelorettes," I chime in with a forced laugh. "You know how it is."

He scutters off, still muttering. "I'm too old for this."

Daisy and I walk outside to find Elly and the girls on the sidewalk, silent and staring intently at their phone screens. Elly glances at us. "Posting photos on social. Need to make sure we're documenting *every* moment today."

"It's going to be great," Ana squeals and wraps her arms around Elly. "Now, to the spa!"

The girls walk down the street with their arms linked, and Daisy and I hurry along behind them.

"What's Luke up to today?" Daisy asks.

"I think he's hanging out with James. Most of the wedding prep is done, so it's basically smooth sailing to the rehearsal dinner."

"Your brother is nothing if not prepared."

"Seriously. He's got to be one of the most consistent people I know. All about that status quo."

Status quo like... not having his best friend cuddle his little sister on the couch for hours?

I grimace at the intrusive thought. I have a feeling that Luke would *not* appreciate that particular change. He's always been protective of me—I can't imagine what he'd think about James and me.

But then again, what exactly *are* we? Nothing. Nothing's happened and nothing *can* happen. Even if we could somehow move past our complicated history and get Luke on board, he's still going back to Denver next week. Back to his home.

Annoyingly, even those logical conclusions can't stop me thinking about him. The way he made me food, how right it felt to be wrapped in his arms, the sincerity in his voice when he said he wanted to take care of me...

"Whatcha thinking?" Daisy asks. When I look at her, she's smirking.

"Nothing," I say quickly.

"You're blushing."

"Am not."

"You so are! Is it Cam? Or James?"

I shake my head. "Nope, we're not doing this."

Daisy laughs, then her expression goes serious, her blue eyes intent. "Have you thought about our conversation the other day?"

"Hm? What? I don't know what you're talking about."

Luckily, at that very moment, we reach the Alpenglow Spa and Elly claps her hands. "Ladies, I've booked out the spa for the afternoon and we have three hours, so go nuts! Get a massage, facials, whatever. And remember, we're going out tonight, so for *some* of you, I'd recommend spending time at the hair and nail stations."

Elly stares pointedly at Daisy and me, and we look at each other with matching wide-eyed expressions. Like her passive-aggressive comment went over our heads.

We step inside and it's clear that the rest of our group has done their homework. Ana and Leona sign up for a seaweed body wrap, while Elly goes for a peach mud mask and facial. Francesca is pulled away for her lavender foot and calf massage.

Meanwhile, Daisy and I browse at the service menu blankly.

"That's a lot of options," I mutter.

Daisy drops the sheet. "You're not off the hook, Iv. What's happening with you and James?"

"Oh, would you look at that? There's a discount on eyebrow threading, whatever that is."

"It's where they use strings to do your eyebrows." Daisy's impatient now. "You're not getting out of this."

"And I bet this..." I squint at the page. "Margarita-lime body mask would be... refreshing."

Daisy opens her mouth, then my words register. She grimaces as she rubs her arms. "And stingy."

"Hello, hello." Heather, the kindly, middle-aged receptionist, returns to the front desk. In recent weeks, Heather and I have worked together on spa packages for Brookrose guests. This was another initiative I was excited to tell my grandparents about, another way to prove myself. I try not to consider whether those packages will still happen if the Inn sells. "What would you ladies like?"

Before I can say anything, Daisy raises a hand. "Couple's massage!"

I raise a hand. "Actually—"

"Just the two of us!" Daisy cuts me off, then leans towards Heather. "It's a great time for girl talk."

Heather agrees wholeheartedly, and the two chatter while she leads us to the back of the spa. Apparently, Heather isn't too concerned about my quasi-kidnapping— Daisy is dragging me along behind her rather aggressively for someone going for a massage.

Minutes later, I'm in my tank top and athletic shorts, lying flat on my belly and frowning through the face hole of a massage table. The heady smells of incense and essential oils fill my lungs, and the harp music playing through the speakers is kind of mesmerizing.

Against my better judgment, my jaw unclenches and I start to relax.

Until Daisy settles onto the table next to mine.

"Okay, spill!" she insists in a whisper.

"The massage therapists will be in soon. Can't we talk about this after?"

"Nope. Now. You can't expect to call me from a bathroom stall, whining about James getting you popcorn, and then not talk about it."

I press up onto my elbows. "Girl talk in the spa. What are we, the Kardashians?"

"As if." Daisy tsks. "Go on."

I sigh heavily and lie back on the table, placing my face into the hole. "I don't know what you want me to say, Dais," I start. I'm suddenly glad to be staring at the ground—I don't want to have to face or explain my expression right now. "I'm confused."

"About what?"

"I think I... like him," I admit in a whisper. The confession dances on the air in front of me for a moment, then dissipates like smoke. "But it's nothing. Just a crush. It'll go away as soon as he leaves."

"Do you really believe that?"

"I have to. There's no alternative."

"I've got an alternative for you." Daisy's table squeaks as she shifts on her elbows. I pop my head up to look at her, and she's staring at me earnestly, her blue eyes even bigger than usual. "What if you and James have been *obsessed* with each other since high school?"

"Excuse me?"

"Come on. I've waited years and years and *years* for you to come around to this, and I think it's finally happening.

You and James are so into each other, you don't even know what to do with yourselves."

My cheeks are flaming red. "We are not."

"Think about it. Your entire feud in high school was basically trying to prevent each other from dating other people."

"It didn't go *that* far. They were just harmless little pranks to make the other look bad. James went on to date many of the girls anyway, so no harm, no foul. And he's the one who started it."

"Right." Daisy nods slowly. "Because he embarrassed you in front of Willie Myers."

A bad taste fills my mouth as I remember that day.

Yeah, I knew Gemma Myers's younger brother because I had a crush on him, a big crush. Willie— though I preferred William—was exactly the kind of guy I was looking for. He was the skater boy, I was the nerdy girl. We were a match made in heaven. And it didn't hurt that I was totally into Prince William at the time.

But right when I was about to make my move, right when I thought we might finally be together... James got involved.

"Iv, that was high school," Daisy says, bringing me back to the moment. "Things are different now."

"Not different enough."

"Don't you believe that people can change?"

I want to say no, pull the whole "no to say no" childish thing. But I find myself hesitating.

I'd like to think that I've changed over the years— become more mature and grown up. With the exception of my behavior around James, I try to be a fully-functioning, serious adult most days. The kind of adult who's a good sister and granddaughter, the kind of adult who can take over her family's inn and build on a legacy when her parents never had the chance.

If I didn't believe that people could change, would that mean that I never changed?

"I guess... I do," I acquiesce. "But this is different, Dais. What he did—"

Daisy waves her hand. "Tell me, though. Is there even a sliver of a chance that you don't know the full story?"

I open my mouth, but nothing comes out. I *know* the full story, know exactly what happened that day. I told James my deepest secret—that I had a crush on Willie Myers—and less than four hours later, he proceeded to mortally embarrass me in front of Willie at the skate park.

There was no coming back from that. Willie and I never dated, or even said much to each other, after that day. What more could there be to the story?

But did I talk to James about it? Technically, no. I never asked him what would possess him to do such a thing. I just assumed that he was a boy becoming a jerk of a teenager, and then he went on to become a jerk of a man.

It's been a few moments since I spoke and Daisy looks more smug than ever. "Thought so."

"I don't know what you're trying to prove."

"That we live in a world where people can be better. Where they can try again. Why not give James that chance? Especially given how much he obviously cares about you."

My stomach dips dangerously as I consider how sweet he was yesterday. "Even if there *was* something there, even if something *could* happen, it's not a good time. Luke's about to get married, and James is going back to Denver. Plus, with the whole Inn issue—"

"Inn issue?"

I hold my breath. Bow my head. "My grandparents are thinking of selling the Brookrose."

"No way," Daisy whispers, shock crossing her face. She reaches out and places a hand on my arm. "That's awful, Iv. Is there a specific buyer?"

"Yeah, some big company in Denver. My grandparents didn't really want to talk about it."

"I can't believe this..."

"Me neither." I shake my head. "It's my fault, though. I should've talked to them directly about what I wanted instead of planning all these secret initiatives. Now, it might be too late. The offer is really good, apparently, and I think they're seriously considering it." I pause for a moment. "James was there when I found out. He was very sweet about it all."

Daisy's eyebrows raise a touch, but thankfully, she keeps her mouth shut about the James of it all. "I'm really sorry. So you think they'll take it?"

"Hard to say. They want to talk to Luke and me about it, of course, but not until after the wedding. Which makes sense."

"So there's time. I'm sure they'd want to know how dedicated you are to running the place. Just stay positive."

At that moment, the door opens and Daisy gives me one last reassuring smile. Then, she lies down, and turns her head towards her massage therapist. "Hey there! Not sure if you do toe massages, but I did a spin class yesterday and my foot cramped right up. Like, bird claw level. Have you seen that movie..."

I lie back on the table. Sometimes, I wish that I could be as positive as Daisy.

I may not have Daisy's positive spirit, but I can tell you one thing I'm positive about:

I do *not* belong on social media.

TikTok, Instagram, Snapchat... Whatever it is, I'm not on it and I shouldn't be. I'm like a geriatric with thumbs instead of fingers when it comes to taking "aesthetic" videos, and the thought of posting photos of myself gives me levels of stress akin to what I felt in Fran's photo studio.

I'm so in admiration of women who can post these gorgeous, brazen photos of themselves on social media—with or without makeup, showing off a cute outfit or being upfront about their post-meal bloating. I wish I could be that brave.

So how I've ended up being Elly's photographer for the evening is beyond me.

"Try the Rose filter!" she barks as she leans back against the faded vinyl booth, pursing her lips and looking off to the side.

"What's the Rose filter?" I mutter to Daisy in a panic.

"How am I supposed to know?" She sounds just as alarmed. She fiddles with something on Ana's phone, then says, "oh wait, try looking under—"

"Ivy? You got it?" Elly asks.

"One sec!"

She sighs, clearly ticked off by my lack of iPhone know-how. I look around desperately for Leona, Francesca, someone to give me guidance. But the three girls are across the bar, posing for Daisy's photo.

It's now abundantly clear why Elly wanted Daisy along for the bachelorette—another photographer for her and her friends.

Unfortunately, the joke's on them. Daisy and I are clueless with this stuff.

I snap a photo with one eye shut, hoping I've magically summoned this "Rose filter" she's talking about.

"Let me take a look." Elly walks briskly to my side and leans in to check the photo. I cross my fingers, but unfortunately, she grimaces. "Hmm. Ivy, I thought you said you were good at this."

I screw up my mouth. "Did I?"

She ignores me. Sighs deeply. "I'll have to do a *ton* of editing on this, but let's move on. I'm going to reapply my mascara and we can take some photos by the bar. This time, you should stand by the door."

With that, she swishes off to the restroom. The other girls follow close behind, praising Elly for her choice of venue for their night out.

I never realized before just how "retro-chic" and "dive-bar-cool" McGarry's Pub is, but apparently, it's exactly right for TikTok and Instagram. Leona even went on a rant about how her followers are "hungry for vintage, small-town content."

Daisy and I collapse into the vinyl booth and I take a long slurp of my Diet Coke. The girls' drinks are sitting untouched, condensation running down the sides.

"She's putting us to work, huh?" Daisy jokes.

"This wasn't what I was expecting when Elly said we were going to McGarry's for a night out. I was thinking, like, trivia or charades. Bachelorette party games, that kinda thing."

"What? You're not enjoying being unofficial paparazzi?" Daisy deadpans.

I take another long sip of my drink, gazing towards the pool tables wistfully.

A few minutes later, the girls come out of the restroom with their makeup freshly touched-up. As promised, Ana's cousin from LA did their makeup after we got back from the spa (her smoky eyes are above and beyond anything I could've done in my wildest dreams).

The girls then changed into their outfits, which they had apparently coordinated. Elly's long, white boho dress with a lace overlay flows delicately to the ground, and her bangles and long necklaces clack together musically as she walks. Her bridesmaids are wearing matching baby pink satin dresses, looking less boho, more formal.

If I didn't know better, I'd say the wedding was happening right here, right now, in the midst of McGarry's Pub. Minus the groom.

If Elly's bachelorette dress is this extravagant, I wonder what her wedding gown looks like. I haven't seen it yet; she wants it to be a big surprise on the big day.

But while the girls look ready to strut down the aisle, Daisy and I are wearing reasonable little black dresses, and that is perfectly fine with me. Except when my thighs are pressed against the vinyl too long.

I shift on the seat, unsticking my legs.

"Eeeeee!" Elly suddenly shrieks, rushing towards the door of the bar.

Fran and her "just a friend" Raymond have walked into McGarry's. Fran's sporting her denim jacket and a loud purple skirt, while Raymond's dressed in zip-off khakis and a beige shirt. Somehow, they look perfect together, though Fran insists she would never date the sweet older man.

"Madame Francoise, good to see you!" Elly gushes, grabbing the woman's arm and pulling her towards the bar. "You're a godsend. I've been trying to get a decent photo in here, but am lacking a good photographer. Would you mind?"

She shoves her phone into Fran's hands before the woman can respond. Fran sighs and waves Raymond on.

"Okay, darlin'. But Ray and I have a reservation and you know how I get on McGarry's baked potato night."

Elly doesn't even bother to look towards Daisy and me, just gathers her friends under her arms while Fran snaps photos. After a minute, Elly assesses her phone screen, then smiles as she hurriedly types something.

"Looks like you might be out of a job." Daisy chuckles.

"Fine by me. It's honestly better for Elly to have Fran take the photos. I'm the worst at this."

Daisy taps her chin. "What if we suggest a game? Change things up a bit?"

"It's worth a try."

During the next photo break, I wave the girls over. Fran shoots me a grateful wink, then skitters off towards Raymond and her beloved baked potato.

"Ladies, Daisy and I were thinking of playing a party game! What do you think?"

Francesca wrinkles her nose. "We didn't plan anything like that."

"That's okay." I think fast. "I've got one in mind. Have you played fishbowl?"

"What's that?" Leona asks, sliding gracefully into the booth.

I grab my clipboard out of my bag and remove a blank page, which I start tearing into strips. "We each write a word on one of these papers—maybe something related to the wedding, or Luke and Lenore—then put them into a hat or a bowl. Each of us needs to pick one of the papers, describe what's on it, and the others guess what it could be. We then play another round where we act out the words, then a final round where we guess based on a single descriptor."

Elly lifts a brow. "So... charades?"

"Kind of," I say, getting into the groove. "We can even

215

up the ante. Like, if you lose a round, you need to do a dare in the pub. What do you think?"

I gaze at them, excited. Daisy's on board, but the rest of the girls seem unsure.

"It's just not what I envisioned for the night." Elly sniffs, no longer paying attention. She's gazing around the bar and her face suddenly lights up. "Ooh! Let's take a photo by the jukebox. I'm sure Fran won't mind."

With that, the group runs off.

"We tried," Daisy says.

"I genuinely don't think they'd notice if we left."

"So why don't you?"

The deep, familiar voice shocks me, and I whip around to see James standing next to our booth. He's smiling cheekily, his eyes bright as they lock with mine.

"James?" I croak. I've thought about him so much today, I'm not even sure this is real. "What are you doing here?"

"I'm meant to meet with some of the Dude Crew tonight." He looks around with a slight grimace.

"You don't want to?" I ask.

"It's not that I don't want to..." James trails off, looks like he might say something else. Then, thinks better of it. He shakes his head with a dry chuckle. "Yeah. No. I don't want to."

"I get that," I say, staring at Elly and her friends as they gather around the jukebox.

"So what do you say?" James asks. "Want to get out of here?"

"I definitely do!" Daisy cuts in, scooching out of the booth and grabbing her purse. I follow her and stand next to James shyly.

He looks good tonight. Like, *really* good. He's wearing a black Henley with dark jeans, and his hair's damp. His cheeks are slightly rosy, and he shaved recently, making his chin dimple look especially adorable.

It looks like he just got out of the shower... Not like he's come to meet with a group of guys for a night of pool.

"Let's say bye!" Daisy beelines towards the girls. James and I follow her through the bar, and he stays close behind me, placing a gentle hand on my back when someone jostles into me. I'm hyper aware of how my body is sparking being this close to him.

As we approach, Leona's eyes lock on James and her jaw drops. Ana's face goes slack as well. I peek up at James but his expression is neutral—he seems oblivious to their reactions.

Their eyes then drop to his hand where it rests on my back. Ana's face turns into a slight sneer, while I could swear Leona nods approvingly. This is very weird for me—I have a lot of life experience being the invisible wallflower, not the woman with the gorgeous man on her arm.

Francesca mutters something to Elly, who turns towards us with wide eyes. "James! I wasn't expecting to see you here." Then, to my surprise and slight irritation, she looks annoyed. "Did Luke send you?"

James stiffens, clearly catching the edge in her voice too. "No, I'm here to meet with the guys from the soccer team. But I think I'm going to bail."

Ana elbows Elly rather aggressively and Elly clears her throat. "Sorry. Ana, Leona, this is James Weston. He's the best man."

Is it just me or is her tone boastful? It's like she's proud to show off such a hot member of her wedding party or something.

"Nice to meet you." James's tone is clipped.

"Anyway," Daisy says. "James was just leaving and Ivy and I were thinking we'd go with him."

"Is that okay?" I ask Elly. I don't want to ruffle any feathers at her bachelorette.

"Sure. We have Fran now, so the photos are covered." She laughs this high-pitched giggle that sounds false to my ears.

"Oh. Great." I try to ignore my relief. "I hope you ladies have fun tonight."

Elly gives us a wave, then turns back to her friends.

James, Daisy and I make our way out of McGarry's, and right before the door shuts, I look back. The little group is giggling and looking at their phones, talking animatedly. Poor Fran is hiding behind her menu a few steps away. I have a feeling she's not off the hook yet.

I clench my jaw, suddenly sad. This is Luke's future wife, my future sister-in-law, and I can't even get along with her for an evening. There has to be a way that we can be friends. Maybe their move to San Fran will somehow make this easier.

As soon as we step outside, Daisy yawns loudly. "What a *night*, I'm exhausted. I'm going to head home right now. James, would you be a dear and take this one back to her apartment? You know where it is, right? I just... I can't right now."

She slumps dramatically, like she's so tired she can't even stand. She's laying it on a little thick given that it's barely past 8pm.

Then, to my horror, she winks at me so obviously that there's no way James didn't see it.

Excuse me while I plan her murder.

"It would be my pleasure." I can hear the laughter in James's voice, and I glance at him. His eyes are on me, sending an unexpected wave of shivers across my skin.

"Great. See you later!"

With that, Daisy runs off down the street.

James chuckles. "That was subtle."

"Yeah. Daisy's more the type of person to shove the thing you've been ignoring right in your face until you can no longer avoid it."

"And what is it you're avoiding?"

I peer up at him for a moment. In the warm glow of the streetlights, I see his wicked smile, the gleam in his eyes. He knows *exactly* what I'm ignoring. He probably somehow knows that I spent the day thinking of him.

But I'm not giving in that easy. "Wouldn't you like to know."

James chuckles and shakes his head. When he speaks again, his voice is sincere. "You look beautiful tonight, by the way."

His eyes don't leave mine—it's like he doesn't even have to see what I'm wearing to know. His compliment makes my breath catch.

Then, he holds out an arm with that adorable smirk. "Shall I walk you home, milady?"

There's something about the slight English accent, the way he's holding out his arm like we're in a period drama. This whole situation feels ridiculous, and I shouldn't be sucked into it. Up until a few days ago, James was my nemesis, the person I swore I'd never trust.

But Daisy made a good point. Maybe James has changed.

And maybe, being a bit ridiculous isn't the worst thing.

I take his arm. "You may, kind sir."

James's smile melts down my walls a little more, and we set off towards my apartment.

25

JAMES

I can't stop looking at Ivy.

And it's not because she looks so beautiful tonight that I almost wish I could spot her at McGarry's all over again. It's bigger than that, more complex than anything I've ever felt.

It's like, with every time I see her, I fall for her a little more.

I seem to no longer care about the fact that she's my best friend's little sister. Or that, until recently, we were enemies. I've been crossing a lot of my previous boundaries —going to her apartment and taking care of her, showing up at McGarry's tonight...

To me, she's simply Ivy—this sweet, intelligent, unbelievably strong woman that I haven't been able to get out of my head.

And now, here we are, strolling down Main Street together with our arms linked and she's chewing on that full bottom lip of hers.

"So, what were you *really* doing at McGarry's?" she asks.

I let out a surprised laugh. "How'd you know?"

"It was too convenient. I didn't see any of the guys there, and the freshly-showered hair was suspicious."

"You got me."

"Can't get much past me."

"Shouldn't have even tried."

Ivy grasps the sleeve of my shirt. "How many of these Henleys do you own, anyway?"

"If you want to see me with my shirt off, Brooks, you just have to ask." I smirk at her.

She responds by poking me aggressively in the ribs. I laugh and throw an arm around her shoulder. Then, I notice something. "You don't smell like coconuts."

Ivy stares up at me, bemused. "You know what my shampoo smells like?"

"A guy notices when a girl smells good."

"Are you saying I smell bad?" Her lips twitch.

"Not at all. You just smell more like... mango or something."

Ivy snorts. "I had a mango lime hair mask thing at the spa this afternoon. And for your information, my shampoo is called Coconut Dream. It's my favorite."

"That explains it," I mutter.

"Explains what?"

"Well, I always thought you kinda smelled like sexy coconuts."

Ivy comes to a full stop. She stares at me for a long moment, then keels over with laughter. "I'm sorry, what did you say?"

"Sexy coconuts," I repeat self-consciously. "What?"

"Nothing, nothing," Ivy sputters. "I've just... never heard that before. Is it a compliment?"

I smile at her question and come back towards her. "Definitely."

Ivy wipes a tear of laughter from her eyes. "So you weren't stalking me tonight, then?"

"Stalking you? Why would I do that?"

"I don't know, isn't it your thing? Making sure I'm okay and all that?"

"I guess it is my thing." I chuckle. "And look at this, I'm even walking you home."

"No thanks to Daisy."

"Actually, it is thanks to Daisy," I confess. "She texted me fifteen minutes ago saying that you both needed an out." Then, I add, "she's also the reason I knew where your apartment was yesterday."

Ivy nods. "That checks out."

We fall into a comfortable silence as we walk along the deserted road towards her apartment building. It's a calm night, and the air is fresh and dry. The only thing that would make this better is if I was holding her hand. I want to reach out, but I hold back.

Yesterday was emotional, but it was also eye-opening for me. In more ways than one. We spent hours together on the couch in her apartment—talking, laughing, eating, watching classic movies. That was an education, and I can now say I'm a shameless fan of Humphrey Bogart.

But all I can think is that I want more time with her, I can't get enough. Is she feeling the same way?

I set my jaw, making a decision. "Hey, I—"

"Do you—"

Ivy and I shut our mouths at the same time. She bites her lip shyly. "You go first," she says.

I take a breath in. We've reached her building now, so I turn to face her. "Brooks, I've been thinking a lot about our conversation at the bachelor party."

She raises a brow. "Which one?"

Her eyes betray her—she knows which conversation I'm

talking about. But I'll play. "The one where I asked you if you could date someone who drives you nuts."

Ivy inhales sharply, a quick little breath. "Right."

"I never got your answer."

"Sure you did."

"Nope." I shake my head adamantly. "I'd remember."

"And you don't?" Now, Ivy takes a small step forward. I pause, unable to ignore the almost overpowering urge to wrap my arms around her, pull her against me. "I seem to remember you asked me that question, and then you leaned in... like this."

Ivy takes another step, so our bodies are almost touching. She stands on her tiptoes and places her hands lightly on my chest.

She tilts her head up so her sweet breath grazes my lips. My heartbeat spikes.

Wow.

I swallow audibly. "Yeah. I remember that."

Ivy grins, then she steps away. I have to keep from staggering forward, and I try to regain my composure. Her eyes are dancing—she's clearly amused to see just how under her spell I am.

Before I can stop myself, I'm stepping forward and wrapping her in my arms. She laughs and tries to fight me off, then relaxes into me.

"Go out with me," I say in a playful growl.

"Out where?" she giggles.

"I've got a couple ideas. If you seriously want to do this."

Ivy takes a big breath, steps slightly out of my arms to look at me. I see a battle raging in her eyes, and I wonder what she's going to say. Finally, her brow clears. "I do."

Those two words make my heart ache in the best way. A stupid smile plasters itself on my face. "Can you trust me? Leave the details to me? I want to do this for you, Brooks."

Ivy's face is carefully composed as she looks at me dead on. Then, her eyes drop to somewhere near my mouth and she slowly, slowly raises her pinky finger.

Presses it to my chin dimple.

It's so bizarre and weird and quirky and cute that I almost burst into laughter. But there's something loaded in the depths of her eyes, so I don't.

"Okay," she whispers.

26

IVY

James: Today's the day, Brooks.

I spend way too much time staring at James's text message. It's been a couple days since he asked me out, and he finally sent me this text this morning.

I keep waiting for him to show up unexpectedly at the front desk. Or show up anywhere. Over the last days, he's become a ghost. The one time I walked by his room on a totally separate and unrelated errand—which, by the way, I managed to complete while *barely* slowing down near his door—he didn't seem to be there.

What is he up to?

And why is a part of me secretly thrilled to see what happens next?

This may come as a shock, but I've never been good with surprises. I have a vivid core memory of my sixth birthday party, when I walked into the Brookrose lobby only to have friends of mine launch out from behind couches, chairs and tables. I was so terrified, I burst into tears and was inconsolable for the rest of the evening.

At school, I became known as "scaredy-Ivy." Until Luke got involved.

When you're in first grade, you just don't mess with a boy in second grade.

I live my life according to plans and rules, and surprises pretty much defeat the purposes of those. And yet, I'm excited for whatever James has planned.

The day goes on as usual, and I throw myself into work. But as the sun begins to set and I haven't seen or heard anything else from James, I start to wonder if something's up. Did he forget? Did something go wrong with his plans? Or is this going to be a late-night kind of date—which I'm not sure I'm on board with?

I'm behind the front desk, taking notes on upcoming reservations while also actively ignoring my black phone screen, when a familiar figure walks through the door.

My brow wrinkles. "I wasn't expecting you to come by today."

Daisy smiles a weird little smile. "I just came to drop this off."

She places a garment bag on the desk. I frown at it, then look at her. "Is this for the wedding?"

"Open it."

I narrow my eyes, but do what she says. I slowly open the bag...

And there lies my cute lace dress. The one from the failed double date.

I look at Daisy in surprise. "What's this about? Do you want to borrow it? You definitely can, but I'd recommend you wear shorts underneath. My legs aren't quite as long as yours and if there's a wind—"

"Put it on," she orders.

"But—"

"Go on!"

When did she get to be so bossy?

I raise an eyebrow at her, but dutifully head to the

226

restroom. While I get changed, a warm, bubbly feeling starts to gather in my stomach—is James behind this?

When I return to the reception, I'm wearing the dress and I've pulled my hair into a half ponytail. Daisy's sitting on a stool behind the desk, a book open across her lap. She nods approvingly as I approach. "Don't you look cute. And you're right on time."

At that moment, a dark figure steps out from around the corner—James, wearing nice jeans and a light, fitted shirt. My stomach fills with butterflies as his turquoise gaze locks on mine and he walks towards me.

"Sorry if I'm late," he says quietly.

I have to smile. "Nope, this is perfect."

"And because we're doing this date thing right..." James trails off as he moves his hand from behind his back to hold out small bouquet of white roses. The same kind of rose I picked to show him what a boutonniere looked like.

My breath catches and I cradle the roses close to my chest, touched. I remember when Cam brought me the yellow rose for our date, but this... this is different.

"Okay, you two," Daisy orders. "Go on your date. I've got it here."

I look at her gratefully. "Are you sure? I can call Val and see if she can come in."

"It's her day off. I'll take charge here. How hard can it be to manage an inn?"

She winks at me teasingly and I laugh. "Okay. Thanks, Dais."

"My pleasure. *Anything* to get you two together already."

With a satisfied sigh, Daisy returns to her book.

James and I share a look, then he gestures towards the French doors. "After you."

We walk outside and I stop in my tracks.

The garden is transformed. Fairy lights are strung up between the willow trees, casting a warm glow over the plants. Small tables with various odds and ends are set up along the green walkways.

I frown. "What is this?"

"This is our first date," James says with a sweet, vulnerable smile. "I know you're busy, but I wanted to do this right, so I figured we could have a speed date, of sorts."

I shake my head slowly. "This is..."

"I know, it's kind of lame. I wanted to do more but—"

"Incredible." I remember to take a breath. "Where do we start?"

James's face lights up. He takes my hand and leads me towards a corner of the garden. "Over here, at the popcorn station."

Two bags of freshly-popped popcorn are laid across a garden table. James passes me a bag of kettle corn and then opens his own bag of salted popcorn. We start to walk through the garden together, going from one "station" to the next. Board games (to bring out our competitive sides), buckets with iced tea and my favorite chai from Morning Bell (in to-go mugs), a soccer ball (for obvious reasons), and a dessert table with salted caramel treats (how did he remember that?)

And the music? A mix of Beyoncé, ABBA, and hit songs from our teen years.

"How did you do all this?" I ask, mesmerized, as we walk past the gazebo—strung with more fairy lights and cute paper snowflakes.

"I can't take all the credit. Daisy was all too happy to help."

I've spent years in this garden, exploring every nook and cranny. Playing on the grass, digging in the dirt, throwing pebbles into the creek. But James has somehow made the garden into something fresh and new. Made it into an adventure. Who *does* that?

We stroll around for a while, munching on popcorn and stopping to play the occasional board game. And we talk. The conversation is so easy, so pleasant. I'm not in my head, and I think that may be one of the things I like most about spending time with James—I don't have to force myself to think of conversation topics or try to *be* any way.

He knows me already. Better than most people, I'd argue. He knows the ugly, mean, catty side of me, and for some reason, he wants to know me better anyway.

"How're you feeling about the potential sale?" James asks as we're walking along the creek.

I let out a shaky exhale. It's a heavy subject—not really first date talk, from what I've heard—but I kind of like that we're breaking this rule. Talking about something deeper.

"I don't know what to feel," I say slowly. "All I've wanted for so long is to manage the Brookrose, and I have so many ideas for it. But it feels like I'm in a limbo state right now—I want to tell my grandparents how much I want to do this, but it's a bad time with the wedding coming up. I just... I really wanted to prove myself, and I thought that getting the Inn on the wedding circuit would be a good way to do that."

"That's what the magazine feature thing is about?"

I glance at him, surprised. "You know about that?"

"Luke mentioned it. Sounds like a great idea, Brooks."

"The Brookrose is *perfect* for it. The Colorado Rockies Wedding Review is the biggest wedding magazine in our area. Wedding shows from LA have come out here based on features in the Review. If we got the Brookrose in there, it could be life-changing for the Inn."

"Are you still thinking of applying?"

"Well, if my grandparents sell, it won't be up to us anymore."

"There's no harm in trying. Sometimes you gotta give it a shot and deal with the consequences later."

"Is that what we're doing here?" I shoot him a sideways glance. "On this date?"

James laughs. "What can I say. I go for what I want."

His words make me blush and I bite my lip shyly. "In any case, I don't have much to apply with at this point. Just a few prep photos that Fran took of the Inn a couple days ago, and about eleven drafts of a description."

"You should send me what you've got, Brooks. I might know someone who can help."

"I don't want to waste anyone's time."

"It's not wasted time. If I can help, I want to."

How on earth does he have so much faith in people all the time? Faith in *me*? "Thanks, James." I smile at him, then before I can think about it, I slip my hand in his. His large palm is warm and solid against mine. "Enough about me and my Brookrose woes. Tell me about your job."

"Well... I got promoted a few days ago."

I stop abruptly. "That's so exciting! Why didn't you mention it?"

"It's not a big deal." He runs his other hand through his hair. I could swear a shadow crosses his expression, but the next moment, it's gone.

"Tell me about it," I coax. "What's the new position?"

"I'm the Director of Marketing Strategy and Optimization."

I stare at him blankly. "I'm sorry, what?"

James chuckles. "I'm basically overseeing our marketing and corporate strategy departments."

I nod. My Hospitality Management degree only lightly

touched on marketing. A thought occurs to me. "So you're good at the whole social media thing."

"Nope," James says immediately. "I'm leaving that to the younger generation. I've got a few people on my team fresh out of school and they're up to speed with all things social, thankfully."

I can't help but laugh. "So you think you'll stay in Denver for awhile?" I ask, my voice carefully neutral.

Okay, fine. I'm fishing for information.

Can you blame me? I don't like surprises, remember? And the best way to avoid a bad surprise is to get the details upfront.

A small frown wrinkles James's brow. He's holding tight to my hand, and it's hard to ignore how comfortably our fingers intertwine. It sounds dumb and cliché but it really does feel like our hands are supposed to fit like this. How could such a simple gesture contain so many layers?

"I'm not sure," he says. "I'm pretty happy in Denver, but I wouldn't call it home. I've briefly thought about moving back to England, but it's far away from my family."

"I've thought of moving to England too."

"You have?"

"Well, yeah." I chuckle. "I might've hated you growing up, but you didn't sour me on the whole country. I don't think I'd do it, though. Mirror Valley is my home, it's always been my home."

James stops walking but doesn't drop my hand. "You're lucky to know that, Brooks."

Something in his voice beckons me to look at him then, and I stop walking too.

His eyes travel over my face slowly, as if he's memorizing me or something. I shyly grab his other hand, so we're facing each other. The fairy lights make him look even more ethereal—I swear, no one should be this handsome. I can't stop looking at him, but he can't seem to stop looking at me either.

A summer breeze caresses my face and blows my dress around my legs. Standing here, the two of us, the world feels at peace. I feel at peace.

"Hey, Brooks?" James asks, his voice low.

"Yeah?"

"What would you say if I wanted to kiss you?"

My heartbeat spikes as my eyes drop to mouth—his gorgeous mouth that has been on my mind far more than I'd care to admit. "Hypothetically?"

"For research purposes."

I smile, bite my lower lip. There's a flash in James's gaze and his lips part. My heart is racing, banging against my ribcage, like the force of it could push me against him. "I'd say that maybe I want to kiss you too," I breathe.

James's chest rises and his eyes take on a new intensity. He lifts my right hand and kisses the sensitive skin on the inside of my wrist. Then, he places my palm against his chest so I feel his heartbeat beneath my fingers.

I step closer. His fingers skim my cheek, leaving a trail of goosebumps as he tucks my hair behind my ear. I tilt my head into his touch. I might as well be Ingrid Bergman looking at her Humphrey Bogart.

He wraps his arms around me and pulls me against him.

My entire body is warm, vibrating. The world melts away, and it's just James and me again.

Finally, he dips his head low, and his lips brush against mine softly. Once, twice. Feather-light but my breath goes ragged.

He pulls me closer and I tilt my head to deepen the kiss. It's unlike anything I've ever experienced, and it's nothing like I would've expected from James. There's nothing rushed or fast-paced about it. Instead, this kiss is slow, and tender, and deliciously patient.

It's like we both know this is the start of something so much bigger, so much more intense, and we have time. We don't need to hurry, and I don't want to...

"Ivy!"

The voice falls on us like a bucket of cold water and James and I spring apart.

Daisy's waving at us from the porch of the Inn frantically. "Luke's here. He's about to come outside!"

James and I take another huge step away from each other. Right as the doors open and my older brother appears behind Daisy.

"There you are!" he calls out. He registers James and me looking more than a little ruffled. "What're you doing?"

My mouth has gone dry. I feel like I have whiplash from the events of the past twenty seconds.

Luckily, James doesn't have that problem. "Ivy and I were arguing over this game of Scrabble," he says smoothly, pointing at the table next to us.

To my relief, Luke crosses his arms. "Of course you were." Then, his eyes skate down my body. "What's with the dress?"

"Oh..." I look down, thinking fast. "I spilled something earlier and had this dress on hand."

"Pretty fancy for work." Luke raises an eyebrow, then tilts his head towards the door. "Should we get inside? I want to go over some stuff for the rehearsal dinner."

"Let's do it!" Daisy cheers, grabbing my arm and dragging me towards the Inn.

As we walk inside, I can't help but peek over my shoulder at James and Luke. Luke's saying something, waving his hands around, but James catches my eye. He gives me that wicked grin of his, and winks. I have to look away to hide my blush.

A moment later, my phone buzzes. My heart begins to pound when I see who it's from.

James: Here's looking at you, Brooks.

Casablanca.

Yup. Things just got a whole lot more complicated.

27

JAMES

We might have a problem.

Because I kissed Ivy Brooks last night, and it was by far and away the best kiss I've had in my life.

Normally, I approach dating with the same rational, logical perspective that I do my job, or soccer. Yeah, closet romantic over here...

My date with Ivy was something different. It wasn't anything extravagant or Hollywood-worthy. It was a walk in the park, with some food that I brought for us. Hardly anything special on the surface of things, and yet, it was perfect. A lot of things feel perfect with Ivy, I'm realizing.

Whatever I'm feeling for her goes way past enemies, friendship, whatever you want to call it. It's like I want to know her, learn everything about her. I want to do every boring, mundane wedding errand with her. I want to protect her, and be there for her.

It's weird to be having these feelings—I decided long ago that I was a lost cause, destined to become the fun uncle to Jake and Jesse's kids. Now, I'm catching myself thinking about my own hypothetical children, my own hypothetical home.

A home that I wonder if Ivy would like too...

"Slow down," I mutter to myself. "It was one date. One kiss."

I snap my computer closed. I canceled my flight back to Denver for Saturday evening—I'll reschedule it later. I need more time here. More time with Ivy.

There's one thing I need to talk to her about. Something about our feud that I probably should've addressed before we kissed.

I guess you could say that I don't have the best discipline when I *do* know what I want. And the truth is, I think I've wanted to be with Ivy much longer than I let myself admit. If I'd opened that mental lockbox of mine sooner, would I have seen that I was always crazy about her?

Maybe Daisy and Gemma and those high school rumors were right.

But all of this is a very big problem because Luke has no idea about any of it. And while I wish I could say that I regret what happened, I don't. I do think that Ivy and I should take a breather until we can talk to him. I need to hold off on kissing until after the wedding, as hard as that might be.

I grab my dinner jacket and rush out of my room. I only have a few minutes to get to Morning Ball Cafe for Luke and Elly's rehearsal dinner.

I walk briskly towards the reception and stop abruptly to see a familiar figure bent over the desk. "Brooks? What're you still doing here? I thought you'd be at the cafe by now."

Ivy looks at me, slightly frantic. "I was there all day helping Val, Ethan and Luke decorate for tonight. But I had to get back here to change, and then I was reviewing the books and noticed there was an issue with a guest, and—"

"She won't leave." Tony, a friend of Maggie and

Richard's who sometimes helps at the Brookrose, suddenly appears from the back office. "I've told her to go about fifteen times."

"I just need to make sure I'm not forgetting anything—"

"You're not," Tony grumbles, his hands on his sizable hips. He's all but tapping his foot impatiently. Not that this is unusual—Tony is our resident lovable grump. "Everything's under control. And your grandparents are gonna give me an earful if you're any later for Luke's party."

I walk up to Ivy and lay my hand on top of hers where she grips the reservation book with white knuckles. "Brooks, it's going to be okay. Tony's got this. And Luke and Elly are expecting us."

Ivy blinks, then nods slowly. "Okay. You're right."

I bring her around the desk. "Betsy's just outside. I'll drive."

"Okay." Ivy looks at Tony. "Thanks, I'll see you later."

"Hallelujah!" Tony cheers.

We head outside and get into the truck, squeezing onto the bench seat. But as I start the car and pull out of the parking lot, Ivy still seems stressed and preoccupied. She smoothes down her skirt self-consciously. "Ugh, I shouldn't have worn this. It's too casual," she mutters.

I take her hand again and squeeze it. "You look beautiful, Brooks."

"You didn't even look at me when you said that."

"I don't have to. You're beautiful every time I see you."

Ivy's face softens and she relaxes into the seat. "What about when I'm wearing a shirt with a huge coffee stain on it?"

"Beautiful."

"And when I'm raccoony with crazy hair?"

"Even more beautiful."

Ivy laughs that real belly laugh that makes my chest squeeze in the best way. She shakes her head. "You're full of it, Weston."

I bring her hand towards my mouth and kiss the inside of her wrist. She shivers and when I glance at her, she's looking at me with such intensity, I almost pull over and drag her into my lap to kiss her again.

"So we should talk about this," I say instead.

"About what?"

"About the fact that I want to kiss you again, but we're headed to Luke's rehearsal dinner."

"Right... Luke." Ivy faces the road again.

"Yeah, I don't think he'd be thrilled with me spontaneously planting one on you."

"I can't see him liking that either," Ivy says, frowning.

"What should we do?"

"Well, the wedding's in, like, three days. We could pretend we're still enemies for three more days, right?"

"I guess I can act like I hate you. I've had years of practice."

Ivy punches my shoulder with a giggle. Then, she bites her lip thoughtfully as she gazes down the road. A wave of heat expands down my body and I have to look away.

"But if I can't kiss you again until after the wedding, I have conditions."

"What kinds of conditions?"

"For one thing, you need to stop doing that."

Ivy frowns. "Doing what?"

"Biting your lip," I say, my voice low. "It's driving me crazy."

Ivy raises her eyebrows, then teases that lower lip with her teeth once more. I shake my head, fighting the urge to stop the car. Seeing my reaction, Ivy laughs again.

"Okay, condition two," I continue. "No high ponytails."

"What do you have against high ponytails?"

"They're like a man's kryptonite. Don't know why, that's just the way it is."

Ivy rolls her eyes. "Anything else?"

"I think that's it for now."

"Okay, nemesis. Happy to hate you for another couple days," Ivy says, raising her fist. I press mine firmly against hers.

I thought of a third condition.

Ivy should not, under any circumstances, no matter what, be so insanely adorable when she's giving me a hard time.

Why have I never noticed this before?

We spent the dinner portion of the evening playing perfect enemies. We lobbed insults back and forth, shot each other death glares from across the room. She even booed quietly during my speech. I never realized how pink her cheeks get when she spits out something she believes might offend me. Never noticed the glow in her eyes when she thinks up a good jab.

By the time dinner's over, I'm all too pleased with our performance.

"It's a good thing you're so tall, James," Ivy says now as we stand next to a square of space that people are making into an dancefloor. Ethan's even dimmed the lights and raised the volume on the speakers. "We might need someone to take aerial shots at the wedding."

I give her a wide smile. "Whatever makes Luke and Lenore happy."

Luke, standing next to us, rolls his eyes. "Please. Keep me out of whatever you guys are arguing about now."

"Lukey, where's the dairy-free gelato?" Elly appears next to him. "It's not on the dessert menu for tonight and Francesca just went vegan."

Luke frowns. "I thought you said she was vegetarian? None of our guests noted that they were vegan so I didn't order any vegan options."

Elly sighs. "Oh, Lukey. You should've run it past me."

"I tried, babe. Remember? We had to finalize the rehearsal dinner menu with Ethan by Monday night."

"You mean the day before my bachelorette? You know how snowed under I was. I couldn't have anything distracting me."

Doesn't that prove Luke's point?

I wait for Luke to say something, to stand up for himself.

His jaw clenches for a moment, but then, he smiles, though it doesn't reach his eyes. "I should've found a way to tell you. My mistake."

"Well, next time, talk to me first. Now I have to find the girls. Our followers are going *crazy* over Mirror Valley. It's the right time for us to move to San Fran, babe. Capitalize on all this buzz."

Elly blows Luke a kiss, then flits off across the rapidly-filling dancefloor. She waves at people as she glides through the crowd, her long, filmy purple dress trailing behind her. Luke stares after her with his jaw set.

"I swear..." he mutters. Then, he shakes his head, seems to come back to himself. "It's just the wedding stress," he says aloud to a question neither Ivy nor I asked. "This'll pass."

Ivy glances at me and I give a little nod. Time to distract Luke.

"Ready to hit the dancefloor?" Ivy says brightly. "We've got some time before Ethan and Val lay out the desserts. Actually, it looks like they're having a great time themselves."

I follow her gaze to where Ethan and Val are swaying back and forth in the middle of the crowd. It's an upbeat song, but they're dancing slowly, lost in their own world. Ethan bends his head to say something to Val, and she laughs, swatting him on the arm. They're adorable.

"Excuse me."

The voice surprises me, and we turn to see Elly's cousin Rodney staring at us. Staring at Ivy.

"Would you like to dance?" he asks.

My gaze swings to Ivy, whose mouth pops open. "Me?"

"You don't have a date tonight, right?"

Ivy's eyes shoot to meet mine for a half-second, then she shakes her head jerkily.

A strange feeling rises up through my chest. I'd like to step in, say something, but for obvious reasons, I can't. Rodney's waiting, Ivy looks lost, and Luke is standing between all of us with his eyebrows raised.

"I..." Ivy trails off. Then, she shrugs. "I have no reason to say no."

Rodney seems satisfied with that answer, and he grabs her hand. Drags her into the crowd. I watch them go with a bitter taste in my mouth. He takes her to a spot across the dancefloor, then faces her. Takes her hands and starts twisting his hips around, not quite on the beat.

"I should see if I can find that ice cream," Luke mumbles.

I'm distracted. "What was that?"

"I'm gonna call Mirror Grocery. See if they have dairy-free ice cream I can pick up."

I pull my gaze back to him. "I'll do it. It's your rehearsal dinner, you should be enjoying yourself."

"Don't worry about it." Luke shakes his head. "A walk to the store sounds good right about now anyway."

Before I can say anything, he's walking away, tugging his hand through hair and dialing a number on his phone.

I turn back towards Ivy and Rodney.

Oh, great. Now, he's got his hands on her hips and is jerking her rather violently back and forth like they're on a see-saw.

Not to be over-dramatic, but this is torture. Normally, I think I'd be enjoying this—seeing Rodney throw Ivy around the dancefloor while her expression is caught somewhere between a polite smile and startled gazelle.

But this is bothering me more than I could've expected. Yes, I'm jealous, but it's something more than that. I want to be dancing this dance with Ivy—so many dances with Ivy. I want people to see that we're together, be able to show it to the world, just like Luke himself said a few days ago. I finally understand what he means.

Rodney begins to inch closer to Ivy, step by step, and she inches back in equal measure. It looks like they're doing a sort of wonky two-person conga line, headed straight for a collision with the drinks table.

I can't take it anymore. I walk across the dancefloor, and Ivy blinks up at me in surprise.

"Rod, mind if I cut in?" I ask, my eyes never leaving Ivy's.

He sputters for a moment, looking between the two of us. But I have a solid few inches on him, and I think he knows there's no point in arguing. He exhales deeply. "Fine."

"Thanks, mate."

Rodney ambles off and I take his place. Ivy relaxes into the dance, smiling up at me with her beautiful emerald eyes sparkling. "What are you doing?"

"Something that I've wanted to do with you for a very long time."

28

IVY

I used to think that James Weston was the kind of man who'd drop a girl if they were dancing together at the royal ball.

After last night, I can now confirm that I was wrong. James is a half-decent dancer.

According to him, his mom made him take lessons for prom when he was seventeen. After getting over my initial disbelief—and spewing out a few teasing comments and jokes—I had to hand it to Darlene. There's nothing quite as magical as dancing with a man who knows what he's doing.

It's yet another surprise, another side of James that's caught me unawares. For everything I think I know about him, for every assumption I've ever made, he finds a way to surprise me. And I have to say that I'm not hating what I'm seeing.

Actually, I think I'm liking it way, way too much.

I rifle through the papers on the front desk and find my phone. Dial a familiar number.

"Hello?" Daisy sings.

"Do you really believe that people can change?"

"Good morning to you." She giggles. "As to your question, I'd like to think so, yeah."

"Even if their natural instinct is to do one thing?"

"Especially then. I think that change comes from making conscious decisions. You can choose to do the same thing over and over, or you can choose to do something different."

"But what if doing something different feels terrifying?" I say with a squeak.

"I'd say that it's all the more important to do something that scares you. It's how you grow and learn." She pauses for a second. "And if this happens to be about James and you two dancing together last night, I'd say it louder."

"I just... I don't know how to do this. I've never felt this way before. I keep trying to put my walls up and it's like he blasts through all of them. I think I'm protected, but he finds a way around my defenses."

"James is good at that." I can hear Daisy's smile. "Think of how riled up he gets you. I've never seen you get so upset with anyone else."

"It's freaking me out. I feel like I'm falling for him way too hard. Whenever we're together, I manage to forget all of the things that'll pull us apart."

"Like what?"

"Like Denver," I burst out. "He's leaving right after the wedding. That gives us hardly any time to... what exactly? Commit to a relationship? Agree to do long distance? We've kissed a total of one time, and I'm already envisioning what it'd be like to spend my life with this man."

"He's not just 'some man.' You've known James since you were six. You guys have a weird, intense connection none of us can explain or understand." Daisy chuckles. "Ooh, maybe you can move with him? Or be there part-time?"

"I can't do that, Dais. I need to stay with the Brookrose, especially now. My grandparents won't talk about the sale until after the wedding, but the more I think about it, the more I've realized..." I trail off, mind racing.

"What?"

"Well, how could I convince them *not* to sell? My grandparents deserve a cushy, comfortable retirement after all they've been through and the years they put into the Brookrose. This sale will give them that."

"Who says they won't get it if you take over the Inn?"

I laugh dryly. "Thanks for believing in me, but that's a lot of pressure. If I failed and the Inn went downhill while I was managing it, I could never, ever forgive myself. They'd be taking a risk trusting me with it instead of accepting the offer, and I don't know if I can ask them to take that chance."

"Take a chance on you?" Daisy sings.

"Don't start with ABBA."

"Sorry. I feel like your grandparents would rather keep the Brookrose in the family than sell."

"I hope you're right. I'll get my thoughts together and talk to them about it after the wedding. I've stalled on the Wedding Review thing, anyway. Right now, the focus and attention needs to be on Luke and Lenore and making this a wonderful day for the both of them."

"Yeah. About that..."

There's a noise from the hallway next to the front desk and I look up as James rounds the corner. My heart skitters and I fight the urge to dive behind the front desk. I just don't know what to say to him. I don't know how I'm feeling.

Be brave, Ivy.

Nope. Can't do it.

I slide off my chair and slink behind the desk like I'm a

freaking caterpillar or something. "Sorry, Dais, gotta go," I whisper. "Chat later?"

"I'm around."

I hang up and sit on the floor with my arms wrapped around my knees. So much for being brave—for making the courageous choice. Instead, I'm curled into a ball behind the desk again, practically cowering.

I just need time to process, to figure out a plan of action. Then, I can face him.

"Brooks?" His voice is just above me, and I cross my fingers that he didn't see me hide.

Please, walk away. You don't want to see me like this...

"Hey, Brooks."

The voice comes from directly next to me, and I almost topple sideways. "Agh!"

James is sitting next to me with that teasing smirk that chases away all of my fears and anxieties. My stupid heart skips a beat.

"Whatcha doing?" he asks, like it's totally normal for us to be sitting on the ground, huddled up behind reception.

"I... thought I lost my contact," I offer.

"No, you didn't."

"No, I didn't."

"Talk to me, Brooks."

I try to keep it in. Really, I do. But my mouth has a mind of its own.

"What's there to say? We went on a date, and we kissed, and things are progressing, but I don't know what to make of all of this, and I don't know how you feel or how I feel or what's going to happen next." I blurt it all out in a single, anxiety-ridden exhale. I clench my eyes shut—my neuroticism isn't exactly my most attractive trait. "Sorry, that was a lot."

"It was." James chuckles. "But I like that about you. I

247

like that you're always thinking ahead and considering what might happen next. And I like when you tell me what's going on in that brilliant head of yours. It's one of my favorite things about you."

My heart softens at his compliment and I almost smile. Almost.

"See?" I say, exasperated. "You say stuff like that and I forget everything I was worried about. But these are valid concerns, James."

"I agree, they are. And the first thing you need to know is that I've canceled my flight to Denver on Saturday night."

I blink, surprised by this revelation. James takes his work so seriously. "You did?"

"Yeah, I wanted more time to..." He trails off, then exhales a deep breath. Runs his fingers through his hair a couple times, looking more serious than I've seen him in a long while. "Look, there's something I need to tell you. And I hope we're at a point now where you can believe me."

His mouth is pressed in a grim line. Whatever he's about to tell me is going to be big.

I hold my breath, my heartbeat like a drum in my ears.

"Do you remember back in high school, the day at the skate park?" he asks. "The day you told me about Willie?"

My mouth goes dry and my stomach turns to stone. I've been purposely pushing this memory to the back of my mind. Pushing away any reminder of the painful day when I realized James wasn't the person I thought he was.

My face must betray my reaction because James immediately looks pained. He shakes his head sadly. "You remember. I hate that. I'm sorry, Brooks."

I couldn't say anything, couldn't move if I wanted to. I stare down at my intertwined fingers around my knees.

"The first thing you need to know is that embarrassing

you was *never* my intention. Please believe me. I didn't want it to go that way."

"So what *did* you want?" I ask, the betrayal from long ago gathering in my temples.

"I wanted Willie to be taken down a peg or two."

I glance at him. "Why? You didn't even know Willie."

"I found out all I needed to know about him that day." His brow furrows, like he's trying to puzzle something together. "Okay. You might not believe this, but I had a crush on you, Brooks. Obviously, I couldn't do anything about it, couldn't even admit it to myself. You were Luke's little sister, totally off-limits. But I've realized recently that I liked you even then."

I blink, shocked. I want to look at him, ask him a million questions, but I can't bring myself to. James's voice is wary and tired, like he's been holding onto this for a long time.

"The thing is, tamping down feelings doesn't make them go away. It just... redirects them, and I channeled mine into looking out for you. So when you told me you liked Willie, I was happy for you—he seemed like a good kid."

He exhales slowly. "That day, when Gemma invited me, Luke and some of the guys from the team to hang out at the skate park with her 'board-obsessed brother,' I thought it'd be a good time to scope him out. You can imagine my surprise to see that he'd also invited some friends— including you and Daisy."

I did often wonder why James and Luke were at the skate park that day. Silly me, I thought that Willie invited Daisy and me to get to know me better. Instead, we showed up to a party.

"What you don't know is that, when you left to get some water, I went over to talk to Willie. To check him out, make sure he was solid. But I overheard he and his friends talking about—"

He cuts himself off and my curiosity peaks. I sneak a glance his way. "Talking about what?"

"Talking about how..." James runs his hands through his hair again. He says the next part in a rush. "Talking about how Willie was going to 'get with you' that night. They used a bunch of terms I didn't appreciate and won't be repeating. My first instinct was to punch him in the face, but then you came back and I knew how angry you'd be if I did that. So, I decided on another course of action—expose him for what he was so that you'd see the real him."

James takes a breath, and it's so silent, I can almost hear the bees buzzing in the garden outside.

"I saw the two of you talking and laughing and it set me against him all the more. I wanted to pull you aside, tell you what he said, but I wasn't sure you'd believe me. Then, Willie handed you his skateboard. He had his hands on your hips, showing you how to do it, and all I could think was that this was going according to *his* plan. And I hated that."

I remember that moment vividly, how thrilled I was to be spending time with Willie.

"Then, you fell." James swallows. "And I knew that was my chance. I walked up next to Willie and chuckled. I knew that he looked up to me, so I thought he'd laugh too, show his true colors so you could see what a snake he was. The problem is, he outdid himself. He laughed so loud, pointed at you instead of helping you. He called his friends over and they laughed too. And suddenly, everything was backwards. Because you were hurt and angry, and he was thinking he'd pulled something off in making you look bad."

"*You* tried to help," I say, my voice choked as I remember. "I pushed you away, I thought you were going to make it worse."

"I wanted to make it better, make it stop. But you were so angry, and you stormed away before I could say or do anything to fix it. The moment you left, I told everyone that if they ever gave you a hard time, I'd find them."

He sighs deeply, the noise full of regret. "Things changed after that anyway. I tried to find you and explain myself, tell you the whole story, but you were furious. Rightfully so. Next thing I knew, we were in this feud—a feud I never wanted to start. And I'm so sorry, Brooks. The last thing I wanted was to hurt you, and instead, I made everything a billion times worse."

My mind is in overdrive as I relive that day. Thinking Willie and I were getting along, the flirty looks when he was helping me skateboard. Was it all a lie? A pretense to "get with me" or whatever he'd told his friends?

In retrospect, I was so quick to brush off the way his grip sometimes made me uncomfortable, the weird, loaded looks he'd give his friends when he thought I wasn't looking...

Then, on top of that, the fall—one from which I've never managed to fully recover. James came over to laugh at me, and the shock of that betrayal hurt more than anything else. His chuckle made Willie laugh harder, made me the butt of a school-wide joke. Or so I believed.

Because, James makes a good point. No one ever mentioned the incident to me at school. Willie avoided my eyes in the hallway. When the time came to retaliate and I embarrassed James, I thought that maybe I'd redeemed myself in the eyes of my classmates.

James is looking at me. "I hope you believe me, Brooks. I hope you believe how sorry I am."

"I do... believe you."

And unbelievably, it's true.

As my mind skips back over everything we've been through—and everything that's happened between us recently—it actually makes *more* sense that James made a mistake while trying to help me than him being out-of-the-blue awful to me.

For years, I believed that James had taken my little confidence and used it to hurt me. Hurt me in the worst way—I was a perfectionist, even then, and having everyone laugh at my failure was painful. I never expected this, never considered that he might've done it in a misguided effort to help.

It doesn't excuse what he's done, but I feel a sense of relief in the understanding.

Daisy was right. I didn't know the full story.

"Uh, guys?"

James and I both startle back to the present.

"Y'all okay?" Val is staring down at us with an eyebrow raised. "You do realize that to work the front desk, you need to be standing behind it?"

"Sorry, Val," I say as James and I scramble to a stand. I brush off the front of my skirt, still reeling. "We were just... taking a break."

"It's about time I let you get back to it." James meets my eyes. "But call me, or come by if you need to talk. I'm here, Brooks."

29

JAMES

"I'm in the kitchen, Jamie!" Mum hollers as soon as I walk in the door of my parents' bungalow. "I hope you're hungry, there's lots of food tonight."

I hang up my coat and follow the delicious smells of roast beef and warm bread into the kitchen, where Mum's puttering about in her red checkered apron. I take a deep inhale, my stomach already growling. I haven't had a Sunday roast at home since I was in college.

"Did you see your father in the garden?" Mum asks as she stirs something on the stove. "The man's been tending to his crocuses all day. The sunburn is going to be... Ugh. I keep telling him to wear his hat, but the man is stubborn as a mule."

I give her a kiss on the cheek. "He sure loves his visor."

"That's all well and good for people who have hair. The amount of times I've had to rub aloe on the top of his head..." she trails off, tsking.

Dad's love for gardening has blossomed (excuse the pun) since he retired—he even entered some of his crocuses and dahlias into a contest last year in Denver. He came in second and is on a mission to win this year.

Maybe that's where I get my admiration for the Brookrose garden. Genetics.

"Smells great in here. How can I help?"

"I taught you well, my boy. Peel some carrots, would you?"

I dutifully take the peeler and get to work, and Mum chatters away as she checks on the roast in the oven. Mum makes the best roast—though we're having it on Friday seeing as Sunday will be hectic after the wedding.

And then, next week, I'll have to go back to Denver.

I've been shoving the thought further and further in my mind. I haven't checked in at work in days, and surprisingly, I haven't heard a word from Martin since he called to tell me they were going ahead with the campaign. I wonder vaguely how it's all coming along, then push away that thought too.

I want to be here, present, with my parents tonight. Being in the kitchen with Mum, chatting about life and the latest gossip in Mirror Valley... well, it feels right.

Feels like I want to do this more often.

"You should've heard Fran at the last city council meeting, going on about the wasps in her garden." Mum tsks again. "You'd think she'd want to take down the hive instead of 'respecting the circle of life' and getting stung every time she walks onto her back porch."

"I can go over and help her out. Between Raymond and I, we should be able to take it down and seal up any cracks."

"That'd be nice of you, Jamie." Then, Mum sighs dramatically and sweeps towards me. "It's so nice having you home. Everyone in town is talking about it."

"Really? I'd think this would be old news by now."

"Well, you are a *celebrity* in this town."

I chuckle. "Mum, it's been years since I played soccer. Surely the town has moved on."

"Maybe there isn't much to keep the rumor mill busy these days," Mum says as she places a plate of steaming Yorkshire puddings on the table. "Mirror Valley's been surprisingly uneventful lately. Not even Mrs. Perez has news to share. It's all on you, Jamie. And Ivy Brooks." Mum waggles her eyebrows.

"What about Ivy and me?" I ask carefully.

"Everyone's been talking about the two of you dancing together at the rehearsal dinner the other night. Now aren't you glad you took those lessons when you were seventeen? Said you were too tall to waltz."

"Mum—"

"Okay, okay. But is something going on with you two?"

At that moment, the back door opens and Dad lumbers into the kitchen. His khaki shorts, long socks, and linen shirt are covered in a layer of dirt, and his sunglasses are teetering down his nose.

"Dar, we've *got* to do something about those raccoons under the deck. They have cubs now and they're making a —James!" Dad booms my name, then takes four big steps over to me. "Good to see you, son. How're things with the wedding? Luke getting cold feet?"

Dad guffaws before Mum smacks him with her oven mitts. He wraps his arms around her waist. "Sorry, dear. You are an absolute delight, my feet are very warm."

"As they should be," Mum scolds teasingly, whacking Dad with the mitts once more for good measure. She turns on her bunny slipper and heads back to the oven. "You're right on time, Tom. I was just about to serve dinner."

Dad and I catch up about his "sure to be prize-winning" crocuses while Mum lays out the food. Mum and Dad banter and laugh, teasing each other. It's amazing to me that, even after all these years of marriage, they still clearly love each other. I don't think I've ever recognized what a feat that is.

I wonder if Ivy and I could be like that someday...

I give my head a little shake. What an irrational thought.

We haven't talked since I told her what really happened at the skate park yesterday. It was a heavy moment, but it was necessary. In order to have a future, you first need to heal the past.

And I want to see where things go with Ivy, which means that she needs to trust me. I wonder if she's any closer to that point now that she knows the truth, or if my revelation pushed her further away.

"Gravy?" Mum asks and I snap back to the moment.

"Absolutely." I take the bowl, still preoccupied. I notice Mum's mouth twitching. "What?"

"You went off on a daydream, didn't you?" She leans in with a wry smile. "Does this have anything to do with what we were talking about before?"

"What were you talking about?" Dad asks, mid-bite. "Ivy?"

I groan. "Not you too."

"Sorry, son. If you want to keep things private, don't be dancing with the girl for the entire town to see."

I purse my lips—I wasn't thinking straight when I did that. Luke was gone to the store at the time, but has he heard about this? As nervous as I am to tell him how I feel about his sister, him hearing about it through town gossip would be much worse.

The good news is that it's all just rumors for now. As soon as the wedding's over, Ivy and I can stop acting like enemies and tell him... what?

Well, I know what I want to tell him. I just hope Ivy wants the same.

"Here's the thing with Ivy—"

Mum drops the serving spoon and squeals. Loud enough to scare our under-the-deck raccoons. "I knew it!"

"No, no," I backtrack hastily. "There's nothing to tell. And even if there was, I can't do anything about it until after the wedding."

"So what's going on then?"

I shift on my seat. "I've... realized I might be falling for her."

"*Might* be? You've had it bad for the girl since school!"

I blink. "How did you know?"

Mum taps her nose. "A mother always knows. You two were fixated on each other. The entire town was waiting for you to get together. After you quit soccer, I dreamed that you would graduate from your program and come back here to settle down with her, but it never happened." Mum sighs. "You went to Denver instead."

"Now, Darlene," Dad says reasonably. "He built his career in Denver. He's the Director of Whatsits and Gadgets at that sunset company."

"Penumbra Hospitality." I don't bother to correct the job title.

"And we're very proud of you, son. We knew you were destined for great things."

"But if you *wanted* to move back here," Mum says as she serves herself another Yorkshire pudding. "It wouldn't be the worst thing in the world. There are plenty of places for you to work in town. Mirror Valley is very up and coming, you know."

"I'm pretty happy working with Penumbra," I say automatically. The words feel like a lie.

"That's all that matters, then. We just want you to be happy, Jamie. That's what you do when you love someone— you want them to be happy." Mum had taken Dad's hand

257

and they're gazing at each other lovingly. "Of course, you're not responsible for anyone's happiness but your own, but you're happy just seeing them happy. And you do what you can to help that happen."

I sit for a minute, mulling over her words. But I think I understand exactly what she means.

Then, I remember something. Something I've been meaning to do for the past few days, but haven't got around to doing.

I keep the thought in the back of my mind for the rest of dinner and dessert, soaking in every moment with my parents. I'll be back in Denver soon, and these dinners will, once again, be few and far between.

But before I go back, there are two more things I need to do.

So, as I'm leaving their yellow bungalow, I make a detour to grab something in the garage. Then, while I'm still parked in my parents' driveway, I place a call.

"Hey, it's James Weston. I'm wondering if you can help me with something..."

"What do you think, Ivy?"

Val's question jolts me back to life, and I scramble to straighten up from where I'm leaning over the front desk, staring blankly at the landscape painting on the opposite wall. She's looking at me expectantly and I feel bad for zoning out.

I've been doing that a lot since James told me about what happened at the skate park.

I hazard a guess, not wanting her to know that I was checked out. "Sure. That works for me."

Val's smile grows concerned. "So you want me to cancel the tiger lilies for the wedding?"

"What? No," I say with alarm. "We need the tiger lilies."

"Well, as I said, the ones at Clarissa's shop have started wilting. They must've gotten cold or something..." Val trails off.

"Cowbells," I mutter, rubbing my temples. This is just what we need the night before the wedding. "Do any of the florists in the next town over have some?"

"I'll give it a try, but they're probably closed as it's after

9pm. Ooh! I'll call my cousin—she's close friends with one of the shop owners in Summer Lakes and might be able to help."

Val picks up the phone and dials a number. I give my head a shake—I've been out of sorts all day. What James told me was a shock and I'm still processing it all. Thank goodness for Val—she's managed to stay on top of everything while I'm basically a semi-functional potato.

I sigh deeply, setting a mental reminder to bake her some peanut butter chocolate brownies as soon as possible. Then, I open the reservation book, vowing, once again, to get my head in the game.

At that moment, my phone buzzes.

I check the screen and it's none other than the person I haven't been able to stop thinking about.

James: Hey Brooks. I know it's late and you're working, but I'd love to show you something, if you have some time.

James: (To be very clear, this isn't a late-night-booty-call sort of text.)

I snort despite myself and bite my lip as I type out an answer.

Ivy: Thanks for clarifying. Wouldn't want to be getting the wrong idea.

James: Nah, those kind of texts are exclusively reserved for after 10:30pm. You're safe.

Ivy: I don't know about "safe" when it comes to you.

James: Hey now, I've kept you safe, haven't I?

I pause, my fingers hovering over the screen. I guess he has kept me safe... in his own weird, backwards way that was completely unclear to me. Because the question has been swirling in my head all day as I revisit my memories—

those times that I thought he was letting me down, was he trying to help?

Maybe the issue was never that James could or couldn't change, but that I wasn't open to seeing another side of the story. I was closed off from him for years, holding onto my grudge like it was a life preserver keeping me afloat.

James asked me recently whether I could trust him. I was nervous then, unsure what would happen if I gave up control. Especially to someone who I believed had wronged me so badly.

But, maybe, with James, it doesn't have to be like that. He's surprised me in so many ways, been there for me when I didn't even realize how much I needed it. Maybe it would be okay to trust him a little, believe that he has my back.

"Good news!" Val sings as she hangs up the phone. "Lawson's Blossoms in Summer Lakes has tiger lilies. They'll send them over first thing tomorrow... for a price."

"That's great! Luke's pulling out all the stops for this wedding so the price shouldn't be a problem, but I'll shoot him a message to let him know."

"Sounds good." Val sinks onto her chair. "Why don't you take off, Iv? You've worked overtime today."

"You sure?"

"Absolutely. Plus, I saw the way you were smiling before. James been texting you?"

I can't stop the blush. "Yeah... he wants to show me something."

"Well, what are you waiting for?" Val twinkles. "We have no late check-ins, and the flowers have been dealt with. It's going to be a quiet night, so go on. It's the least I can do after everything you did for Ethan and me."

I throw my arm around her, squeezing her to my side. Then, I type out a new message to James.

Ivy: Meet you outside in ten?

31

IVY

James pulls up exactly ten minutes later in Betsy. I slide onto the bench seat next to him and he looks at me with that adorable smirk, his tropical eyes bright and endless.

"No quips or jabs this evening?" he taunts.

"Not tonight." I relax into the seat and feeling calmer than I have in a long time. James's left hand grips the steering wheel and I reach for his right one. His palm is firm and warm against mine, and the heat spreads out through my body.

James turns towards the outskirts of town and drives into the darkness, ABBA playing quietly in the background. I have no idea what we're doing or where we're going, but I'm trusting James. I know that he's got me. I have no idea what might happen tomorrow, or the next day, or the next, but being with James is like learning to love each moment. Learning to be present.

Being with him is basically yoga.

Shut up, brain.

"I like this song," I say.

"Me too." I hear the smile in his voice. "It's got a good message, don't you think?"

Take a Chance on Me?" I squeeze his hand. "Guess so."

Eventually, we pull up in a parking lot that I've only visited again in those vivid, feverish dreams you get after eating too much chocolate ice cream right before bed. Bright lights flood the cement shapes, and I stiffen automatically.

James cuts the engine, his eyes scanning my profile. "What do you think, Brooks?"

I tear my eyes away from the windshield. "I think... well, I think that I trust you. And whatever we're doing here."

James gets the door for me, then goes around to the truck bed. I stand with my arms crossed, tense as I look around. Until the childish screams and laughter make me smile. It might be late, but it's a warm evening and kids are scattered across the skate park.

When James returns to my side, I burst into nervous laughter. "Noooo. No way."

James holds a skateboard—ancient and covered in stickers. He must've dug around at his parents' for ages to find it. "If I've learned one thing, it's that sometimes you gotta face your fears. I faced mine yesterday when I told you what happened here all those years ago, and tonight, you're going to face yours."

I stare at him skeptically, an eyebrow raised.

He chuckles. "Or, maybe I'll make a fool of myself on a skateboard and you can laugh at me."

"That's much better."

James takes my hand again, and we walk into the skate park. We find a flat section of pavement away from the hordes of children—probably too boring and easy for these little pros—and James sits me down on a bench clearly meant for a supervisory adult.

I do a wolf-whistle as he does a bow and gets on the skateboard.

Immediately falls off.

I laugh.

He tries again and, of course, succeeds. It isn't long before he's skating back and forth. James just has that handy body coordination I can't seem to master myself.

I lean back on my hands. I haven't even been near the skate park since high school. But as I watch the kids—girls and boys of all ages—do tricks and jumps through the park, I realize that maybe this place isn't anything to be scared of. After all, if a ten-year-old with pink knee pads and her red hair braided down her back can ride on a metal rail, I can, at the very least, sit here.

And maybe I, too, can face my fears.

Before I can talk myself out of it, I hop to a stand. "I'd like to try."

James hands me the skateboard and I tentatively get on. My heart is racing, but I feel more exhilarated than scared. I already know that James will catch me if I fall. Figuratively —and hopefully—literally.

He places his hands on my hips, and rolls me forward and backward across the cement. We probably look ridiculous, but I don't care.

For the first time, I'm not thinking about being perfect or doing everything right. I'm letting myself enjoy what's happening here and now—the breeze on my face as James launches me forward, the feeling of his big hands on my waist. My fingers clasp onto his, and I hold on tight. And every time I lose my balance, he helps me get it back.

After skating across the cement for awhile—and squealing every time I pick up speed—the adrenaline starts to wear off. I'm leaning into James, my body sagging against his.

Finally, he wraps his arms around my waist and picks me up off the skateboard. We return to the bench and sit together. The skate park is shutting down for the night, and all the kids have gone home. It's just the two of us here now, and we face the twinkling stars above the peaks.

"You were right," I say with a smile. "I needed that."

"Don't sound so surprised, Brooks," he murmurs, dragging me towards him.

I giggle as I relax, cuddled against him. When I speak again, my voice is serious. "Thank you for telling me the truth. Sadly, I think you made the right call—I probably wouldn't have believed you if you'd told me everything earlier. I'm sorry about that."

"It's okay, Brooks. Clearly, I've made mistakes too."

I glance up at him. "There's one thing I can't believe though."

"What's that?"

"You used to have a crush on me?"

James laughs. "I knew you'd ask about that." His voice is low in my ear. "I liked you. Not that I admitted it to myself at the time."

"That makes no sense," I breathe. I kick my legs out to release some weird, nervous energy that's building in me. "I thought you just saw me as Luke's sister."

"I did. But you became more than that, and that scared me. Luke was my best friend—sometimes he felt like my only true friend. I couldn't let myself go there with you."

I shake my head. "I used to like you too."

"I thought you were all about Willie."

"But before Willie, there was you." I blush. "Whenever I went to soccer games, no matter how much I tried not to, my eyes were on you." Fear claws at my insides as I tell him

265

the truth, but I don't want to be afraid anymore. It's time I faced it. "In fact, I think I still have an old soccer medal you once gave me as a joke. I couldn't get rid of it, even when I hated you most. I never thought you might feel the same way."

James pauses for a moment, seems to consider something. Then, he moves me slightly as he reaches for his wallet. "Maybe this'll prove it to you."

He rifles through for a moment and takes out a small stack of square, passport-sized photos. He hands them to me. There's a photo of his mom, his dad, his brothers, Luke and...

"What is this?" I ask, sitting straight as I hold up my horrendous yearbook photo from junior year. Braces, glasses, bad side bangs, bright blue eyeshadow. Oh, dear.

"Remember how livid you were about this picture? Well, I loved it. I thought you looked adorable. So, when everyone was trading yearbook pictures that year, I asked Luke for one of you. It still makes me smile."

"It should. Look at that hair."

James chuckles. "But look how cute you were."

My cheeks heat even more. "James, this is without a doubt one of the most unattractive periods of my life. You can't seriously mean that."

"I do, Brooks. I meant what I said the other day—you're always beautiful to me."

I stare at the photo. It's as well-worn and wrinkled as the others in James's wallet—he really has held onto this for years.

I still remember that day. It was another "everything goes wrong" kind of day. My hair was a disaster, I'd spilled orange juice on my preferred photo day outfit while trying to flirt with Willie (classic), and Pops sat on my glasses by accident that morning so they were lopsided.

But James held onto this memory—saw something in me I couldn't see in myself.

That nervous energy rises up through my chest and I cradle the photo. For every ache and pain in my heart that I've tried to hide and protect, James finds a way through. Shines a warm, loving light on all of it. He holds each insecure, scared part of me that he discovers with such tenderness.

I look at him, hoping that my eyes can convey what I'm feeling better than words. He meets my gaze with a similar intensity, and there's something moving in those turquoise depths that I can't identify, but that I feel in my core.

Goosebumps rise on my skin and I feel this sudden urgent, yearning need to be closer to him. To run my fingers through his hair, to feel his lips against mine. And given the way his eyes are boring into mine, I have a feeling he knows exactly what that's like.

"James?" My voice is so low I barely recognize it. "I know we agreed to wait until after the wedding, but do you think maybe we could break that rule? Just once?"

James leans forward slightly and I automatically tilt my body towards his. "We both know I have a hard time following certain rules."

I gulp, every nerve ending feeling like it's on fire. "I think I'd be okay with it this time."

I barely get the words out before I'm reaching for James. Or maybe he reaches for me.

All I know is that, suddenly, my fingers are tangled in his hair and his arms are clasped tight around my waist. Our bodies slam together, and his lips meet mine.

This kiss isn't like last time. It's hot and hungry and filled with years of emotions neither of us let ourselves feel or acknowledge. He tilts my head back and deepens the kiss

267

and I'm lightheaded from how much I want this. How I've wanted this for so long.

It occurs to me that *this* is what we should've been doing. What we've been fighting against instead of fighting for.

In some corner of my mind, it occurs to me that I never would've expected to be kissed like this in a skate park. And especially not by James Weston. But there's something so perfectly imperfect about this moment, and my mind is wonderfully calm as I lose myself in him.

And eventually, the heat gives way to something else—something much more tender. James releases my mouth to plant kisses along my jawline, down my neck. I close my eyes and relish every touch. He kisses the corners of my mouth and then his lips meet mine again, and I realize that if James is the only person I kiss for the rest of my life, that's all I would ever need.

Our journey has been filled with roadblocks and U-turns and crazy potholes, but I'd do it all over again if it means ending up here.

James and I stay on that bench for a long time, kissing and talking and laughing. Finally, when the night gets too cold and I start to shiver, we return to Betsy. My lips are swollen and sore, and James's hair is all mussed up in the best way.

We get into the car and James pulls me close again while we wait for it to heat up. He rests his chin on the top of my head.

"I think we broke that rule pretty effectively," I say.

"Do you regret it?" James asks.

I take a moment, then smile. "I don't. The wedding's tomorrow, so we can talk to Luke after."

I feel rather than see James nod. He hugs me tighter. "I hope you know how much you mean to me, Brooks."

"I do now. You'd have to be crazy about me to hold onto that photo all these years."

James laughs and I shut my eyes, feeling so happy in this moment.

When James speaks again, his voice is serious, his chest rumbling against my cheek. "I've been thinking... I want you to come to Denver."

Woah.

I sit up and away from him, stare at him straight on. "What?"

James's eyes widen and he backtracks. "No, no. Not, like, move there or anything. You have the Brookrose and want to stay in Mirror Valley. But I'd like for you to come visit. I want to show you around once everything dies down."

I open my mouth, unsure what to say.

Of course James is intending to go back to Denver— that's where his life is. His career and apartment are in Denver. Whatever *this* is between us, it's very fresh and new. I can't exactly expect him to drop his whole life to move back here. That would be irrational.

So why am I disappointed?

I shake off the feeling. James means so much to me, and his life is in Denver, so we will make it work. I want to see where things go with us. I feel so much more for him than I ever could've imagined feeling. So I'll do the distance thing —if that's what we need—and that means that I'll visit him in Denver every once in awhile.

I nod, shoving away any inkling of sadness. "I'd love to come see you."

James smiles the warmest smile. "That makes me so happy, Brooks."

I relax against his side, appeased. My heart feels so full right now. James and I can do this—we'll work it out, no matter what comes our way.

32

JAMES

The morning of Luke and Eleanor's wedding is perfect. It's like Ivy called in a favor for the most beautiful early summer day. The smell of flowers and freshly-cut grass wafts through the window of my room, waking me up.

I hop out of bed and get dressed quickly. Luke's probably already here, going through the garden with a fine-toothed comb or something to make sure everything's ready. I want to be around in case he needs anything.

And, okay. I can't wait to see Ivy.

Seriously. When did I become this person? What is this power she has over me?

Whatever it is, I don't want it to stop. I'd be happy to be under her spell for as long as she'll have me. After last night at the skate park, that kiss... I've never been so sure. I would do anything for her. Even—especially—move back to Mirror Valley.

It's why I asked her to come visit me in Denver. I want to experience it with her as a visitor instead of as a local before moving back here. Moving back home.

The thought brings a smile to my face. I can't wait to tell her as soon as I see her this morning.

The next step is to let Martin know that I'm resigning. I don't want to leave anyone in the lurch, so in a way, this promotion came at just the right time. I tied up a lot of loose ends in my old position while working here in Mirror Valley, and my new position technically hasn't started yet.

I'm surprised how easily I've been able to detach myself from Penumbra. I worked there for so long, the company was basically my family. My life.

But, I guess, when you know something as sure as I know how I feel about Ivy, everything changes. I want Ivy, want her for the rest of my life. And after last night, I know she's crazy about me too.

My eyes fall on my phone. Martin's been quiet, but it would be just my luck for him to call mid-ceremony, so I turn it off. It feels strangely liberating.

I assess my reflection in the mirror as I button up the top of my shirt and run my fingers through my hair. I remember how enthusiastically Ivy did the same last night, the way she pulled me towards her and held on like it was something she'd thought about doing for a long time...

Heat expands through my chest—that kiss is something I definitely want to repeat. Many times.

I lock the door to my room, drunk on happy thoughts of Ivy and eager to see her again.

"James? Is that you?"

The booming voice stops me in my tracks.

No. There's no way.

I turn around stiffly and almost keel over in surprise. When I speak, my voice is choked. "Martin. Xavier. What are you doing here?"

Martin's a big guy—the kind of guy who was a linebacker in college and still eats and lifts like he's eighteen.

He lumbers towards me and slaps me on the shoulder. "We came to disrupt your vacation!"

"Now, now, Martin." Xavier steps forward. He comes to Martin's shoulder and my collar bone, but he has the kind of presence that dominates a room. Maybe it's the steel gray eyes—they pierce right through you. It can be unnerving.

Xavier and I haven't spent a ton of time one-on-one—he's often on the road for work or basing himself out of some tropical destination for months on end. But he extends his hand toward me like we're buddies. "We were wondering if we might run into you. I'm not sure if you remember my nephew—Cameron Olsen? He worked for Penumbra years ago and lives here now."

The puzzle piece slides into place.

That's how I recognized Cam. He was on the sales team at Penumbra when I first started. He wasn't there long—I only saw him a couple of times, then never again. Guess he found his calling opening his cleaning company in Mirror Valley.

What are the chances that he'd be related to my boss's boss? Does this mean they're both here for a family vacation?

I register their perfectly-pressed suits and my brow furrows.

Doubt it.

"So you came to see Cameron," I say slowly.

Xavier's smile twitches. Just barely. "Cameron's gone on and on about his business and the town. Obviously, we've seen that Mirror Valley is growing in the industry, becoming the next up-and-coming destination. So when Cameron mentioned netting a contract with this lovely inn, I had a fun thought that maybe *this* was where you were staying, and Martin and I decided we'd take a trip out."

"Looks like we came at the right time," Martin adds. "Your buddy's wedding is today, huh?"

I swallow thickly, my mind still stuck on the fact that my two bosses are standing right in front of me when, five minutes ago, I was thinking about how I'm going to quit. "That's right."

"We don't want to keep you," Xavier says, shifting his body away. "We know you're on vacation and the last thing we want to do is cramp your style. We'll catch up with you at the office on Monday, hm? It should be a *very* interesting meeting."

Then, Martin and Xavier exchange a look. A look that curdles my stomach.

The two men continue towards the deluxe rooms—they're staying at the Brookrose too—but I stay put, processing my shock and confusion.

Something isn't adding up. Xavier and Martin are two of the most intensely work-focused people I know. Seeing their hungry expressions, the look in their eyes as they glanced around the hallway of the Inn, I have a feeling I'm not getting the full story.

I take off towards the lobby to find Ivy—with a very different mindset than I had before.

33

IVY

I am not hiding.

I promise I'm not.

I'm just doing my due diligence, checking over Elly's bridal suite. Making sure she has everything she needs when she arrives this morning to get ready for her wedding.

I'm certainly not throwing myself into work in an effort to avoid the crushing self-induced pressure I'm feeling to make this wedding perfect. I'm also not avoiding the mildly annoying men in suits who keep wandering through the Inn and muttering to each other. I wondered whether they're here as secret shopper types, and the thought made me so anxious that I couldn't bear to hang around.

Plus, though I might've slowed my steamrolling towards getting the Brookrose in the Wedding Review, I'm not ready to give up yet. I need to make sure the photos are perfect, just in case the discussion with my grandparents goes in my direction. After everything I've seen from Fran, I trust her and her unexpected expertise, so I need to make sure everything looks photo-worthy.

With that, I fiddle once more with the tiger lilies next to

the vanity mirrors in the suite's spacious bathroom. Fran will be here soon to take photos of the bridal party getting ready. Luck is on my side with the weather today—the sun's hitting the room *just* right.

I'm mid-fiddle when James wanders back into my mind. For the first time in awhile, though, the thought doesn't make me feel better. In fact, I feel worse. Because thinking of James means thinking of him going back to Denver.

What's going to happen to us? He loves his job as much as I love mine—can we sustain a long distance relationship?

Things with James and I haven't gone according to any sort of plan. In no mental map of mine would we have followed this particular trajectory. I've loved that about us, but it also makes me unbearably nervous. Because what if James gets home to Denver—back to his regular life—and realizes that I don't fit?

As usual, my neurotic mind is fifteen steps ahead of any logical point. I'll feel better as soon as I talk to him about it, but that conversation will have to wait.

I spend another few minutes checking on the dresses in the corner closet, spritzing a little more perfume around the room, and filling the jug of water on the table (read: *not* hiding), before I head out the door. My heart is racing for some reason, and a part of me is relieved when I see Fran and my grandparents standing outside.

"Ivy!" Grams strides forward and wraps me in a hug, then pulls back to tuck a strand of hair behind my ear. "You look beautiful, sweetie."

"As do you," I say, my eyes dropping down her outfit. Grams is dressed in a lovely peach dress, and Pops is wearing a suit with the same color tie. His cowboy hat is perched on his head, and it looks like he put balm in his mustache. Next to them, Fran is dressed in a billowy red dress covered in rhinestones, and a gray blazer for that professional flair. "You all do!"

"Thanks, darlin'," Fran drawls, pressing her red lips towards me in an air-kiss. Then, her expression goes all business. "I've been walking around the property this morning, taking photos here and there. Are Lenore and the girls ready for their close-up?"

"Not yet. They should be here soon."

"Fabulous. Raymond knows he'll have to be patient today. That man always wants to make these big events all about him. I tell him, though, I always say—Ray, this isn't *about* you. And today, I'm right because... it's about *me*." She laughs grandly. "I'm only joking. Today's about dear Luke and Lenore."

"Absolutely," Grams chimes in, emotion coloring her voice. She puts her arm around me and squeezes me close. "We are just so, so proud of our babies. You and Lukey..." She trails off thickly, gazing at me. "Your parents would be so happy to see what strong, brave, wonderful people you two have become."

Brave? a voice asks in the back of my mind. I certainly haven't been feeling very brave today. But Grams's words have me overcome with emotion and I lean into her hug, squeezing my eyes shut against the sudden prick of tears.

"Speaking of wonderful people, where's *your* date, darlin'?" Fran asks.

I shake my head. "I don't have a date. Way too busy."

Fran smiles her knowing smile. "I would've thought you'd come with James."

"James?"

"Yes, aren't you two finally together?"

I blink in surprise. "What?"

Then, Grams adds, "oh, Franny, if only!"

The two women laugh loudly. And Pops joins in.

"The entire town has waiting for this for *years*," Grams goes on, animated.

Wow. I raise an eyebrow, voice flat. "So glad to hear that James and I have kept the Mirror Valley rumor mill busy."

"Honey, you still do." Fran places a hand on my arm. "We've had a wager going. Why do you think I made you and James pose together that day at the photo studio?"

"And the day the car ran out of coolant," Grams adds.

My mouth is wide open. "You did—"

"That was nothing," Pops chimes in. "After we sold it to you, we meant to zip by and fill it up. But then, James arrived. With the way that boy looks out for you, we figured that if you needed a hand, he'd be there."

Grams nods. "It seemed like things started going in the right direction after that, so we had to meddle less."

"There's no reason to be embarrassed, darlin'," Fran says, clearly seeing the blush rising to my cheeks. "That boy brings out your child at heart, and that's so important. Especially given how quickly you had to grow up."

I give my head shake. This is... a lot to take in.

I suddenly have the almost overpowering urge to spill my guts. To confirm their beliefs about James and me. To say that their meddling worked, because I am totally and completely into him, and it's scaring the pants off me.

I open my mouth, but Pops's ancient brick-sized cellphone dings. He takes it out of his pocket, put on his glasses, and checks the screen. He shoots Grams a look.

"It's about the *meeting*," he says quietly, though not so quietly that I can't hear.

Next to me, Fran straightens. "I'm going to snap some photos of the guests arriving."

She scuttles off and I should go with her, but I have a bad feeling rolling in my stomach.

Pops is still reading, and his mustache quite literally

droops with every second that goes by. "Ah. Mags, can you see this? Does it say Tuesday or Thursday?"

"Tuesday," she whispers. "Tell them the earliest we can meet is Tuesday."

"Meet who on Tuesday?" I ask at full volume.

Grams shifts on her feet while Pops turns his full concentration to powering down his phone and placing it back in his pocket. Grams clears her throat. "Tuesday is our meeting with the potential buyer."

My jaw hits in the floor. "THIS Tuesday?"

"It was supposed to be next Friday—plenty of time to talk through this decision all together. But the buyers were eager to move it up. They're actually already in town, so we compromised on Tuesday. Your Pops and I were going to speak to you about it tomorrow before Luke and Lenore leave for their honeymoon."

This is too fast. It's all happening *way* too fast.

"So this is it," I say, my voice much calmer than I feel. Blood is pumping in my ears so loud, I can barely hear. "We're selling the Brookrose."

"We need to talk about it properly," Pops says firmly. "As a family."

"This was never supposed to happen so quickly," Grams adds. "We didn't expect any of this. The buyer came out of nowhere and is pushing hard to do this soon. I'm not saying we'll do it, but we want to be prepared. But Ivy... just think. If we sell, you can finally get your dream job."

"My dream job is running the Brookrose."

"Thank you for saying that, honey, but your grandpa and I don't want you to be stuck or tied down here. You're our granddaughter, we love you so much, and with Luke leaving, we realized how unfair we've been. You gave up an amazing job with that hotel chain just to keep working at the Inn. When we retired, it wasn't fair of us to expect you to take over."

"You can do whatever you want, you'll be free," Pops says before I can get a word in. "And Luke and Lenore will have a nest egg to buy a house and start a family. Your grandma and I could retire comfortably..."

He goes on, but I don't hear any of it. Because he's right.

I could never be selfish enough to stand in the way of what they want. I keep acting like the Brookrose is *my* thing, *my* home, but this was never just about me. It's about my grandparents, who deserve to be well taken care of. And about Luke and his future family. They all deserve to get the happy endings this sale would give them.

Who am I to stand in the way of that? Who am I to ask them to take such a big risk?

So as much as my heart is aching, I put on a brave face. "It's fine," I manage, my voice cutting through my grandma's. I place a hand on her arm and force a smile. "It's all fine. I understand."

"We just want what's best for you."

"Thank you, Grams." I feel the edges of my facade falling away, fast. I gesture towards the bridal suite. "I better go. Need to check on Elly's suite before she arrives."

Before either of my grandparents can say anything, I bolt to the suite. The door slams shut behind me and I press my back against the cool wood, looking around for something to ground me.

My gaze lands on the table next to the couch, where I'd placed the items from the night at the market. The blue tea cozy, the penny, the headband, and Gemma's folded origami flower stare back at me.

I shut my eyes. My heart is racing again and I feel dizzy. Things are changing—too much and too fast. Luke is leaving, James is leaving, soon my home will be gone too. And it feels I can't do anything about any of it.

I sink to the floor and put my head between my knees.

Yoga breaths, Ivy. Just take yoga breaths...

If only something as simple as yoga breaths could save me.

34

IVY

I shouldn't be surprised when the door to the bridal suite opens.

I also shouldn't be surprised when the worried voice calling out to me belongs to James. "Ivy? Are you okay?!"

Yeah, I suppose I can see why he's asking. I've moved from the entrance of the suite into the bathroom, where I'm now spread-eagled on the cool marble floor with my eyes shut.

I wave a hand to signal that I'm okay as he runs towards me. He drags me into a sitting position so he can hold me against his chest. "What happened?!"

"I'm okay. Honest, I'm fine."

"Then why are you lying on the ground?!"

"It's cooler down here."

James is silent for a moment. Then, he presses the back of his hand to my forehead. "You sick or something?"

"Something." It occurs to me that this isn't a particularly flattering angle—my head is lowered into a quadruple-chin situation and my dress is scrunched around my midsection —but I can't be bothered to fix it. "You do know that this is the bridal suite. What're you doing here?"

"I was looking for you."

I sigh. "Do you have, like, a homing beacon strapped to you that tells you when I'm in distress?"

James snorts, relaxes slightly. "I'm your very own red alert."

"Well, that makes me feel eighty."

"You smell like it too."

I glare at him.

"What? I'm just saying that there's a *lot* of floral perfume in here. Maybe we should open the windows—"

"Don't!" I say sharply and James stops moving. When I speak again, my voice is quieter. "Just don't. Please. It's fine as it is."

James must hear something in my voice, because he doesn't argue. He sits back, holding me close.

I squeeze my eyes shut, trying to ignore the pressure building in my temples. "I'm sorry, I didn't mean to snap."

"It's okay, Brooks. I get it."

"It's just—"

There's a loud knock at the door, followed by a, "Lenore? Are you in there?"

James shifts slightly. "It's Fran."

"Here to take wedding photos. For the Wedding Review." Is there even a point? Why bother getting the perfect photos for a magazine if the Brookrose might not be ours as of this Tuesday?

I swallow thickly, suddenly nauseous.

No. Luke and Elly's wedding needs to be perfect. With or without the magazine, it needs to be perfect.

And here I am, lying on the floor. Slacking.

I jerk upright and scramble to a stand, pushing through the ache behind my eyes and ignoring my hyperactive heartbeat. I smooth down my skirt to regain my balance along with some sense of composure.

"What're you doing?" James stands beside me.

"I need to get back to work."

"Don't you want to talk about...?" He trails off, gesturing towards the floor where I was lying moments ago.

There's another knock at the door.

"Just a sec, Fran!" I call, then glance at James. "Talk about what?"

"I don't know. Maybe why you were on the floor? How you're feeling?"

"No time. I have to make sure everything's perfect for the wedding."

"Why?"

"Because it has to be," I answer. I've turned away and I'm arranging and rearranging the tiger lilies triple-time. But all I can see are the flaws—the flowers aren't big enough, they might be drying out. I need to get them water.

I grab an empty glass and stride over to the sink.

"Why does it have to be perfect, Brooks?"

"I don't want to get into this right now." My voice doesn't sound like my own, feels like it's coming from someone else.

I fill the glass with water and step towards the vase of tiger lilies, but James stands in my path. He takes hold of my wrist. "Why is it so important that Luke and Eleanor's wedding be perfect?"

"Because, it has to be, James. Why won't you believe me?" I look away, my chest hurting. I don't know where to look, what to focus on. The world is pressing down on me.

James takes the glass from me and puts it on the counter. Then, he grasps my other wrist and forces me to face him. The blue-green of his eyes captures me, and I focus on that. "Ivy. Talk to me."

"It can't go wrong," I manage in a gasp. My throat feels tight, but I don't want to blink. At least here, in James's eyes, there's some relief. "If it's not perfect, everything might fall apart."

"What do you mean?"

"If it's not perfect," my voice is a whisper now. "The worst could happen."

I don't know what happens next—if I fall or James does this of his own accord—but suddenly, he's sitting on the edge of one of the plush chairs with me in his lap. He wraps his arms around my waist and stays quiet, but I know he's listening. And I find myself speaking.

"Things have to be perfect. The day they went out, everything looked perfect, but it wasn't. There was a risk, and they went anyway." I take a shaky breath. "And that's when... that's why..."

I can't hold it in anymore, the tears leak down my face.

"They went. And they kissed Luke goodbye, and when they came to my room, I turned away from them. I was angry over something stupid, and I refused to acknowledge them. They told me they loved me, and I told them they were horrible parents. Those were the last words they ever heard me say."

My shame fills the air like poison. I never told anyone this—the last conversation, the last argument, I ever had with my parents. Luke's last memory is of telling them how much he loved them, and my grandparents have a similar memory.

Me? I carry the regret and guilt around my last words alone. And now, the pain and the sadness are rising up, threatening to bury me alive. I clench my eyes shut, waiting for it to take me.

James wraps his arms around me tighter, holds me closer. "They knew you didn't mean it. They knew you loved them."

"Did they?" I sob. "I said pretty much the worst thing

you could say to a parent. When they died, was that what they were thinking?"

James is silent for a long, long time. Then, he clasps both of my hands in his. "Listen to me. Your parents loved you and Luke, and you loved them too. I saw it every time I came to the Inn. You were a family. Families have disagreements and dysfunctions, but at the end of the day, you had each others' backs and that's what counts. Love isn't always perfect and beautiful, Brooks. Love is messy and vulnerable. And scary."

I hiccup a breath in. "How can you know that?"

He presses his fingers lightly to my chin and turns my head towards him. My eyes are all squinty and small from crying so hard, but there's so much comfort in meeting his gaze again.

"Trust me," he says quietly. "I know."

There's a weight behind his words that makes my breath catch.

"Your parents never expected you to be perfect. You *are* perfect, just as you are. They would've only ever wanted you to be happy."

His words fill my heart and I wish I could feel grateful. Instead, I just feel fear. I can barely speak around the lump in my throat. "But if I'm not trying to be perfect," I whisper. "What am I doing?"

To my surprise, James laughs. His chest vibrates with the sound. "You're being you. The real, honest, ridiculous, bad-comeback-giver, tone deaf Ivy Brooks."

And just like that, my last barrier breaks down, my last wall. I crumble against him. "You make it sound so simple."

"It is... And it isn't. But I need you to believe me. I need you to believe that your happiness is worth it. Because if you're not happy, there's no way I can be happy."

I look at James, look at this wonderful, amazing man

who's come through for me at my very best, and my very worst. All of a sudden, I feel something click, deep in my heart. All of a sudden, I'm not afraid anymore.

"I love you," I breathe.

James's face softens, his eyes sparking. But then, he pauses. "Ivy, there's something else I need to tell you..."

But before he can say another word, the door to the bridal suite slams opens.

Luke strides into the room, his brow furrowed and his mouth twisted into a grim line. "Lenore was supposed to be here a half hour ago. Have you seen her?"

35

JAMES

"Eleanor isn't here?" Ivy asks as we rush towards Luke. My news about moving to Mirror Valley will have to wait.

For once, Luke doesn't correct the name. He tugs his fingers through his hair, and only then do I notice the deep purple circles beneath his eyes. "I assumed she arrived and came straight here to get ready, but Fran said she still hasn't seen her."

"I'm sure there's nothing to worry about," I say. "Have you tried calling her?"

"No answer."

"She's got to be around somewhere, or on her way, at least." Ivy nods reassuringly. "Let's go look for her, and James, maybe you could try calling her again?"

"I left my phone in my room. I didn't want any work calls getting in the way today."

There's a flash of something in Ivy's expression, but the next moment, it's gone. Ivy shakes her head. "I don't have my phone either. James, why don't you get your phone and try calling her, and Luke and I will start walking through the Inn. She's probably caught up with some of the guests or something."

Luke continues picking at his watch, preoccupied. What a way to start off your wedding day.

"Listen, Lukey, we're going to find her and get this show on the road," Ivy says calmly. "It's going to be great. Even if things feel a bit shaky right now, your wedding is going to be perfect. Just as it is."

She glances at me and my heart skips. I'm happy that my words got through to her.

Ivy and Luke head out towards the parking lot, while I go back to my room. I should be thinking about Luke and Elly, but all I can feel is a warm glow radiating through my limbs. Ivy finally opened up to me, she was real with me. I can't imagine how hard it must've been to share her thoughts and deepest fears, and I don't take it for granted. I love that she trusts me, and with every piece that she shows me, I fall for her even more.

As I walk back to my room, I keep an eye out for Elly. Instead, I meet the gazes of Mirror Valley locals, all staring at me with weirdly knowing expressions. I give them an awkward wave and disappear down the hall towards my room.

I'm unlocking my door when my eyes fall on the window at the far end of the hallway. It looks out over the garden and the gazebo, both of which are all kitted out for the wedding. As expected, Ivy did an amazing job with the decorator.

What I'm looking at, though, isn't the gazebo, but the two familiar men talking to an equally familiar older couple.

I freeze for a moment, then pause my mission to head outside.

Guests are milling about, catching up and laughing in

anticipation of the wedding, but I barely notice any of it. As I approach the gazebo, Martin spots me and waves.

"Howdy, James!" he calls. "Your ears must've been burning."

I sidle up to the group and stand—somewhat protectively—next to Richard and Maggie Brooks. "So good to see you again... so soon."

"We were just talking about you," Maggie says in her usual bright tone, but the corners of her eyes are strained. "Well, we were talking about Penumbra Hospitality's generous offer, and your name came up."

Hold up.

Offer? From Penumbra?

I gawk at Maggie and Richard. "I'm sorry?"

"Surprise!" Martin bursts out. "We want the Brookrose Inn to be the pilot hotel for your campaign!"

There's a heavy, gut-churning silence before I shake my head, hoping—no, convinced—that this is some sort of joke. "I don't get it."

"What's not to get?" Xavier says. "Your 'start small, go big' campaign was focused around small towns, right? Mirror Valley is the *perfect* place. You should see the stats, the buzz around this town. Incredible!"

Xavier goes on animatedly, waving his hands towards Richard and Maggie, both of whom are staring at him with tight smiles.

"And, the coincidence of all coincidences," Xavier finishes. "You happen to know the current owners of the Brookrose. Could this be any more ideal? This inn is our golden nugget."

"Well, the deal's not done yet, but it will be come Tuesday," Martin agrees. "Mr. and Mrs. Brooks were hard, determined negotiators, but I think we've settled on an amount that we can all agree is reasonable. Wouldn't you say?"

Richard's arm squeezes protectively around Maggie's shoulders. "Sure."

I feel like I'm in some bizarre, backwards alternate universe. These two worlds of mine should have never collided—they're like oil and water, and I don't like it one bit. I don't like what this *means* one bit.

Because if I'm understanding correctly, Maggie and Richard aren't selling the Brookrose to just any big conglomerate. They're selling to *my* conglomerate, *my* company. Based on an idea that *I* presented to Xavier and Martin weeks ago.

The thought makes me feel physically ill. I have to stop this.

"Xavier, Martin." My voice barely conceals my alarm. "Can I talk to you?"

I walk a few paces away to a spot where Maggie and Richard can't overhear our conversation. I'm sure this impromptu meeting with my bosses is the last thing they want to be dealing with on their grandson's wedding day.

I know Xavier and Martin, though. Know they wouldn't want to wait until Tuesday if they didn't have to. They probably cornered the Brooks to rush them into a decision.

"What you do you think, James?" Xavier asks grandly. "Isn't this great? You'll be taking on the acquisition of the Brookrose."

"No." I try to keep my voice level and calm. "That was never the intent of my pitch. I never expected—"

"That we'd look at acquiring small, family-run inns and hotels in small towns, as you suggested?" Xavier's brow furrows. "What *was* the intent of your pitch then?"

"That we frame ourselves in the image of locally-owned, mom-and-pop hotels," I say tightly. "That we present ourselves as welcoming and hospitable, create a community. Not that we *acquire* them."

"We loved your pitch, James, loved everything about it," Martin says, palms open. "We just figured we could cut out the middle man."

"You should be thrilled about this." Xavier pops an eyebrow. "Our first acquisition is in the small town *you* grew up in. An inn that so happens to belong to people you know."

"But that's the problem. I know the Brooks family, I know how much this inn means to them and their family. You can't do this to them."

Xavier's smile loses its sincerity. "We can, and we will. Frankly, I'm shocked that you're not on board. This is your project, you'll be overseeing the Brookrose and revamping it. Once we tear it down and rebuild in the style of our other hotels, of course."

"And once that's done," Martin continues. "You can get to work doing what you do best. You'll get that huge bump in salary we talked about, full benefits, extra weeks of vacation... you can use the company's jet whenever you need. This is your ticket to the upper echelons of Penumbra Hospitality."

"Not to mention a guaranteed fast track to a C-suite position." Xavier's gray eyes are piercing right through me. He hasn't blinked. "Isn't that what you've always wanted? You're just like us, James: hungry, driven, success-oriented. This is your chance to shine. And if you do, I can't see why you wouldn't be a Senior Director within the next five years."

His words—words that would've made me so happy just a couple of weeks ago, words that would've kicked my butt into gear—fall on deaf ears. Yes, I wanted to rise in the company. Yes, I wanted to succeed. The pay raise and all of the perks sound amazing.

But they sound amazing for the person I once was.

Things are different now, I've changed. Or maybe, I've come to terms with who I really am. No salary bump or prestigious position at Penumbra Hospitality is going to be make me happy.

I've already found happiness here in Mirror Valley, and I'd be an idiot to give it up.

This time, when I speak, my voice is calm but firm. "I don't think you should move forward with this sale."

"Well, I'm afraid we can't do that. The wheels are already in motion. This is your job, James."

"Then I can't take it." I exhale a deep breath. "I quit."

Xavier's eyes widen a fraction. "You *quit?*"

"Yes. I'm grateful for the opportunities and everything I've learned at Penumbra, but I don't think we're a good fit anymore." I have no idea where these words are coming from, but I know they're the truth. "I'll come into the office to do my final handover, but please, I'm asking you not to go through with this. Find another hotel with more willing owners."

Xavier snorts. "The Brooks were willing to sell, let me tell you."

"And how many times did you have to up your offer?" I ask, knowing full well how Martin and Xavier work. They likely didn't leave Maggie and Richard alone, called repeatedly to raise the offer by increments. I'm sure it took time and a lot of money for the Brooks to agree to meet with them. "For the record, I don't think it's right that you're going after a kind, elderly couple and their family inn."

"Well, that's none of your concern now, is it?" Xavier says coldly. "The sale *will* go through and we'll move forward with this campaign, with or without you. Now, if you'll excuse us, I believe there's a wedding happening today and we don't want to spoil the fun."

With that, Martin and Xavier walk away, leaving me

standing alone with a cold, unsettled feeling raking through my body. The Brooks have disappeared, and given that neither Ivy nor Luke are in the garden, I think it's safe to assume that Elly is still missing.

This wedding day *really* isn't turning out as planned.

36

IVY

"Okay, let's go to the garden," I say, willing my voice to stay calm. "She has to be here somewhere. Or someone must've seen her."

Luke stays silent, his hands dug deep into his pockets. I'm trying to stay positive, but with every minute that we don't find, or hear from, Elly, I'm becoming more nervous.

Like clockwork, Daisy appears on the porch outside the Inn. I wave her over somewhat frantically—we are in desperate need of a dose of positive energy. She walks over, her adorable baby blue dress hugging her slim body, but as she approaches, I notice that she seems preoccupied.

"Happy wedding day, Luke!" she says, fiddling with the hem of her dress. "Are you excited?"

Before Luke can answer, I lean towards Daisy and drop my voice. "Have you seen Lenore this morning?"

Daisy frowns. "She's not here?"

"We haven't seen her. But I'm sure everything's fine." I force a reassuring smile in Luke's direction.

When Luke initially said that he couldn't find Elly, I wasn't all that concerned. Elly's often late, and she usually

295

has a reasonable explanation for being so. But this is cutting it close.

Even her parents seem concerned about her tardiness.

Daisy takes one look at Luke's pale face and concern flashes in her eyes. "What can I do?"

"Would you check inside for us? Ask around without raising suspicion?"

"On it. I'll get Dee and Noah to help too, they're around here somewhere." Daisy then places a hand lightly on Luke's forearm. He blearily looks at her. "It's okay, everything's still going according to plan. We'll find Lenore."

Luke manages to nod before Daisy takes off. She waves at a group of her coworkers from the gym as she bolts inside the Inn.

"Let's take a sweep through the garden, then we can circle back towards the parking lot," I suggest. "She'll be here soon if she isn't already."

Luke and I move quickly around the perimeter of the garden. I wave at wedding guests but keep moving quickly so no one can waylay us for a chat. There's no sign of Elly anywhere in the growing crowd of people.

As we approach the gazebo, I do a double take.

Is that James?

I tilt my head. He isn't in his room calling Elly, but talking to the two men in suits who've been lingering around the Brookrose all day. He's waving his hands around, his expression dead serious.

I stare at them in confusion. It looks like James knows the men, but how?

"You're doing that thing again."

Luke's voice is so quiet and somber, I barely hear it. I turn to him. "Doing what?"

"That thing. You know, when you look at James." He sounds weary, bored. "You turn your whole body towards him whenever you see him, like he's giving off a bat signal or something."

A rush of heat climbs up my cheeks. "I don't do that."

"Sure you do." A humorless smile flashes on his lips. "And he does the same whenever you're around. It's kind of annoying. Was *really* annoying in high school when we were playing soccer. Made him miss a few goals."

I clear my throat, feeling awkward. "Sure you weren't imagining that?"

"I wasn't. And I'm not now, either." Luke shrugs. "I know you like him, Iv."

The blood drains from my face and alarm bells start going off in my head. "What?"

"Don't worry, he likes you too. I'm happy for you, I think you'd be a good match. You've been at each other's throats for years, but you weren't fooling anyone except yourselves."

I swallow. Is he serious? I debate whether to play my "I don't know what you're talking about" card, but Luke's expression is clear as day: the jig is up. "You're not upset?"

"I used to be. Back when we were in school, it was irritating the way you guys would flirt and give each other a hard time. James was always distracted whenever you were around. But I've learned that love does things to people, changes them. I can't hold it against either of you."

"Luke..."

"That's what happens when you love someone," he continues quietly, looking towards the creek. "You commit to them. You make that choice to love them every single day. Even if they change so much that you no longer recognize who they are."

I have the sense that we're no longer talking about James and me. I hold my tongue, waiting for Luke to continue.

"When I first met Eleanor, I would've never expected that we'd be here." His voice sounds faraway, and I can't ignore that he used "Eleanor" instead of "Lenore" this time. "She was my lifeline for so long. I relied on her, and I loved her for listening to me and being there for me. I did my best to be what she needed. But sometimes, people change and it can be hard to continue being what they need."

"What do you mean?"

He cracks his knuckles. "I mean that... Life is hard, Iv. And love is a lot of work. Eleanor isn't the person she once was, but that's okay. I love her and I'd do anything for her. I want to keep working to be with her, and I think she feels the same way about me."

I place a hand on my brother's arm. It breaks my heart to hear him say these things, to see him looking so dejected. I wish there was something more I could do.

"Come on," I say gently. "Let's go inside. Maybe Daisy, Dee and Noah have found her."

We're walking into the Inn when we run right into Daisy. Her normally smiling mouth is twisted into a deep frown and her eyes are wide.

"Come to the front desk," she whispers so no guests can hear. "Val just found a note taped under the reservation book." She swallows loudly. "Eleanor isn't coming."

37

IVY

Daisy's words echo in my mind.

"What?" I breathe. I feel like I've been punched in the gut.

"There was a note." Daisy's voice is tearful. "She left a note. Could've been last night or this morning, Val doesn't know. She's gone."

Luke suddenly takes off in long strides towards the front desk, and Daisy and I follow close behind. Val wordlessly hands him a single sheet of paper and he scans it, his eyes practically piercing holes through the page.

After a heart-stopping second, he lifts his gaze, his mouth in a line. "That's it then."

"Hang on," I say, opening my palms. "There must be something we can do. She might've *just* been here. Maybe I should go back to the parking lot..."

Luke shakes his head. "She's gone, Iv."

"But she can't be." My heart is breaking, tearing into tiny, irreparable pieces for my brother. "It's not over yet. I'll find her."

Before Luke or Daisy can say anything, I bolt for the door. More guests are arriving and waving at me as they walk in, but I can't even force a smile. This can't be happening—not to Luke. Elly wouldn't do this, she wouldn't pull a Runaway Bride without telling a soul.

I dash outside and the parking lot is full, but I can't see any cars that might belong to Elly.

"Brooks!" A firm hand lands on my upper arm. "Brooks, I need to talk to you."

I glance at James, wishing that tearing my eyes from the parking lot could change the fact that Elly isn't here. "Now's not a good time."

"I have to tell you something."

"No, James. You don't understand." I drop my voice and lean in close. "Elly's gone."

His face pales. "What?"

"She's not coming." I shake my head, finally coming to terms with it myself. My mind is in overdrive, working five steps ahead. How on earth are we meant to resolve this? What is Luke going to do now? Are we supposed to send everyone home now?

Why would Eleanor do this?

"Luke's inside with Daisy," I manage. "Can you keep an eye on him, bring him to your room? I'm going to find my grandparents and we'll figure out how to deal with this."

James inhales sharply and he looks so conflicted for a moment that I almost ask him what's going on. But the next second, he releases his breath. "Okay. But I *need* to talk to you as soon as possible."

"We'll chat later. Let's get this under control first."

James takes off inside the Inn while I continue searching for my grandparents in the sea of wedding guests.

I'm circling back towards the garden when Fran appears out of nowhere. She pulls me aside, all red rhinestones and shining eyes. "Hey, darlin', is everything okay? I noticed that Lenore and her party haven't arrived yet."

300

I press my lips together. "Everything's fine. Nothing to worry about. The wedding is going exactly as we planned it."

"Are you sure? Because if there was a problem, you could tell me. Did I ever tell you about the time I was engaged to John D'Amelio? Rather short, stubbly fellow, but my goodness, I loved him. Anyway, we were meant to get married, but the day of the wedding—"

"I'm sorry, Fran," I cut her off, knowing full well that this is the start of a story I simply don't have time for right now. "I'm on an urgent wedding errand involving the... boutonnieres."

With that, I high-tail it away into the garden.

Unfortunately, it isn't long before I'm stopped again. This time, by the two mysterious men in suits that James was speaking to earlier.

They stand directly in front of me, rather rudely blocking my path. I force a smile, even as I look over their shoulders for my grandparents. "Can I help you gentlemen?"

"Did we hear you say that you planned this wedding?" the taller man asks. He has a slight Southern twinge that indicates he's not from Mirror Valley. Which checks out. He's quite an imposing figure, I'd remember him.

"Uh... yes. I was involved with the wedding planning. I'm actually the granddaughter of the owners of this inn."

"So you must be Ivy," the other man says, his gray eyes cool as steel. "You did a wonderful job, the venue is beautiful. Especially for a wedding."

How does he know my name? Unless...

Everything falls into place.

Two men in suits. Here to check out the Inn. Saying it's a beautiful wedding venue. And they know James.

Could these men be from the Colorado Rockies Wedding Review?

If so, this could *not* be a worse time. One, because there might not even be a wedding here today. And two, because this inn might no longer be ours this coming Tuesday.

I smile cordially, not wanting to burn any bridges while also desperately needing to get out of this conversation. "Thank you, that means so much to hear. I'm so thrilled you like it. But—"

"We're thrilled we like it too," the man with steel eyes interrupts. "Especially as we have plans to buy it."

The world stops turning.

Tilts on its axis.

And promptly drops me into thin air.

"What did you say?" I croak.

"We put an offer on your inn," the taller man answers. "We're from Penumbra Hospitality. We've been in touch with your grandparents and are excited to take this place under our wing and see it reach its full potential."

My entire body jolts with the shock. I couldn't speak if I wanted to.

"This is such a lovely inn you have," the man continues. "And there is so, *so* much we can do to make it shine. We can't wait to get started. You might even know the person who's involved with this project—James Weston?"

My knees almost give out. "What?"

"So you do know him!" The man with eyes of steel smiles wide. "He's been with us for years. Hard worker, totally dedicated and professional. All about corporate gains and rising in the company ranks. Or he was... He was meant to be leading this project seeing as it was his idea."

I have lost the ability to breathe. Truly. There is no oxygen in my lungs at the moment.

"I have to go," I squeak, before I shove past the two men.

302

I stumble forward blindly, my stomach twisted into a burning knot.

James? My James was the one who started this whole nightmare? My James is the reason we might be losing the Brookrose?

Is that what he was trying to tell me earlier in the bridal suite? Right after I said I *loved* him?

I feel it rising within me—the urge to shut down and shut him out forever. This time, with impenetrable cement and diamond-grade steel. I try to fight it, fight against the tide of betrayal, and tell myself that there must be an explanation... as implausible as that may seem.

But I can't do this right now. I need to find my grandparents and help Luke.

I'll deal with this mess later. Deal with James later.

38

JAMES

The rest of the day passes in a blur.

And not the good kind of blur. The kind that makes you wonder if this fever dream is going to end anytime soon.

I manage to get Luke into my room and I sit him down with a tall glass of water. He calls Elly every five minutes like clockwork, sometimes leaving voicemails, sometimes not. Eventually, he tires himself out—or her mailbox is full —and he just sits, staring blankly at the wall without moving.

On the surface, he appears calm and composed, but my best friend is the kind of person who feels everything way, way below the surface. Things look easy and calm, but deep below, there's a fierce undertow.

I also know that prying and asking questions will get me nowhere with Luke in this state. I need to smoke him out, wait for him to talk first.

Ivy takes on the task of canceling the wedding. I leave the room every once in awhile to grab Luke another glass of water or some food, and I find Ivy in full damage control mode. Her glasses are on, her hair is back up in a ponytail, and her dress has been replaced by gray slacks and a white shirt.

The guests file out of the Inn slowly, and noises of shock and sympathy seem to fill the entire space. No one can believe that Eleanor did this.

The rumor mill will be spinning stories about this day for years to come.

Every time I see Ivy, I try to meet her gaze, wave her down. I've even gone so far as to place myself directly in her field of vision while she was looking towards the dining room, almost knocking over a cart of food from the caterer in the process.

Nothing. If I didn't know better, I'd say that she was avoiding me.

I'm bursting at the seams with what I have to tell her—that I know who's buying the Inn, that I've quit my job, and that I will do everything in my power to save the Brookrose.

If only she would meet my eyes, just once.

Finally, it's mid-afternoon. The guests have left with no small amount of clamoring to see Luke and pass on their sympathies—good on Ivy to suggest that he come to my room—and the catering staff have driven off with the last of the food. The decorations in the garden have been taken down, and the gazebo is back to its regular, unadorned self.

All evidence of the wedding has disappeared, save for mine and Luke's tuxes, currently laid across my bed. I'm wearing a white shirt and blue jeans, and Luke's changed into the clothes he was wearing when he arrived this morning.

Feels like ages ago.

"How's it looking out there?" Luke asks when I walk back into the room with some snacks.

It's the first thing he's said in a couple hours, but I try not to make a big deal of it. "Pretty normal."

I hold out the carrot sticks I got him, but Luke opts for the greasy cheese bun I scrounged for myself. He takes a massive bite. "'Normal' as in...?"

"As in, it's only Ivy, Val, and hotel guests out there. Your grandparents have gone home to get changed and deal with a few things before they come back."

"Right," Luke says heavily. His head droops and I shift on my feet. I wish there was some way I could help my best friend, one thing I could say to make everything better. But no magic words will ease his pain. If only a simple phrase could heal heartbreak. Luke lets out an exhale and slaps his palms to his knees. "I should get going."

"You sure?"

"It's time. I need to get home and sort myself out. There's a lot to do in the next few days. I'm sure Eleanor's already packed the stuff she had at my place, so no chance I'll be seeing her there."

"I'll come with you. I still have Betsy."

A smile crosses Luke's lips, but it doesn't reach his eyes. "Thanks, man."

And so, for the first time since the news broke, Luke stands. We step out into the hall and I can feel his agitation, the tension as he looks around for any nosy neighbors. But Ivy did a good job clearing everyone out.

Together, we make our way to the lobby, then outside to Betsy. No one looks at us twice, and I'm doubly grateful that Xavier and Martin are nowhere to be seen. The last thing Luke needs right now is to meet my bosses.

On that...

I give Luke the car keys, then tell him I'll be right back. I jog inside to the front desk, where Ivy's bent over her clipboard, twirling a pencil in the tendrils of dark brown hair framing her face.

"I'm going to take Luke home, Brooks. But I'll be back later and I'll give you a hand if you need it."

Ivy barely reacts, barely looks up at me. "Nope. I'm fine."

My brows draw together. "Is everything okay? You've been avoiding me all day."

"I haven't been avoiding you." Ivy picks up the clipboard and tears out a page. She still won't meet my eyes. "I just don't have time for you right now."

I nod slowly. "It's been a disaster of a day."

She mutters something I barely hear.

"What?"

"I said that there've been a few disasters today," she says, tight-lipped. She turns away from me. "One of which being that I found out that the person I've fallen in love with is the very same person who's responsible for the sale of the Brookrose."

Crap.

Cold fingers of dread crawl through my stomach. "Brooks... How did you—"

"Find out? Well, these two *lovely* men cornered me earlier. Told me that they work for your company and they want to buy the Brookrose. Is it it true that *your* pitch brought this on?"

My stomach is in a tight knot. "Yes, but—"

"Is that what you do with your stupid, fancy job title? You search for places that were built on the blood, sweat and tears of hardworking people, and you poach them? You should be ashamed."

"No, you don't understand—"

"I'm an idiot. Is that why you're really here in Mirror Valley? Was this all just business?"

This, I can't let her get away with.

I take her wrist and force her to look at me. "No. Absolutely not. These couple weeks have been the best of my life, Ivy. There's nothing remotely 'business' about how I feel for you or this town. I'm crazy about you."

Ivy's eyes finally meet mine, but the normally sparkling emerald depths are flat and empty. When she speaks, her voice is bored, emotionless, and totally unsurprised.

"Then how could you do this?"

Before I can respond, she wrenches her wrist from my grasp and marches to the back office, leaving me standing alone.

I feel sick.

For years, Ivy would only ever look at me with the heat of hatred in her eyes. Then, for a brief moment, those eyes filled with something else—something tender and sweet and unbearably beautiful.

But to see her stare at me so indifferently, so unsurprised by my perceived betrayal? That will haunt me until the end of my days. I'd rather Ivy hate me with a passion than look at me like she wanted to believe the best, but expected the worst.

It's like we're back to where we started. After everything we've been through together, how can she think that I'd set out to hurt her? How can she believe I'm still the man she once thought I was?

39

JAMES

"Are we out of Gatorade?" Luke hollers as I collapse on the sofa in the living room.

"I don't know, man. I haven't had any, so it's all on you."

Luke sighs loudly, and I hear him close the fridge door. He walks into the living room, his running shoes squeaking on the hardwood floors. His eyebrows knit together as he grimaces at a bottle of red Gatorade. "I could've sworn we had a few more of the blue."

"Don't look at me. I've been running on coffee, water, and potato chips."

"Healthy."

I snort and raise the bottom of my shirt to wipe my face. Luke and I just got back from a ten-mile run. My cardio is not what it used to be when I was in college, and I spent a lot of the time keeping my own pace while Luke more or less ran circles around me.

Freaking Energizer bunny over here.

Though, to be fair, the guy's probably running on a lot of emotions right now.

It's been three days since Elly no-showed at their wedding. I've been spending a lot of time at Luke's house, sitting on the porch with him on warm evenings, playing video games, watching movies with huge pizzas we ordered in.

Luke hasn't cried once, hasn't broken down. He managed to kick himself into gear fairly quickly—the day after the wedding, he canceled their honeymoon, told work that he'd be back a few days early, and started reaching out to thank guests for coming and apologize for any inconvenience. All with that same neutral, flat expression.

I'm kind of waiting for Vesuvius to happen. For *something* to happen.

Luke tosses me a bottle of cold water and I take a swig. Then, he grabs his phone and sits on the other end of the couch. His dark blond hair is damp with sweat and his cheeks have a red, shiny glow.

"Anything?" I ask.

Luke shakes his head. "I shouldn't be surprised. Why would she reach out now?"

"To apologize for running off? To give you a proper explanation? To be less of a terrible human?"

"Hey now, that was my fiancée."

"Was. She made her decision."

"Maybe if I'd just..." Luke trails off, runs his fingers through his hair. He clenches his eyes shut, then exhales deeply. "Forget it. I'm gonna shower."

He launches to a stand and chugs the rest of his Gatorade. Normally, Gatorade isn't in the approved list of drinks in Luke's diet regimen, but if you're ever going to fall off the wagon, your fiancée leaving you seems as good a reason as any.

I lay across the sofa. The sun is shining through the high windows in the living room, heating it up. Luke bought this place a few years ago with the intention of having Elly move in after they got married. When she decided that she wanted to move to San Fran after the wedding, Luke was bummed that he'd have to sell this place. Thankfully, he hadn't found a buyer yet.

I always liked it here—it's the kind of house that would be perfect for a family. I can picture the kids running through the yard out back, curling up on the sofa in front of the fireplace, spending Sunday mornings cooking breakfast in the huge kitchen.

I wonder if Luke wants to keep it, or if it's too full of hopeful memories for a faded future.

Luke's phone vibrates on the coffee table.

I jolt upright and he freezes. We both stare at the phone like it's an alien life form.

"You gonna get that?" I ask unevenly.

Luke takes a deep breath, then answers the call.

"Hello?" His voice is rough as sandpaper. A moment passes, then he deflates. "Oh. Hey, Iv. What's up?"

At Ivy's name, my heart pounds even as my stomach twists into a knot. Ivy and I haven't spoken since our fight at the Inn. She hasn't reached out, and as much as my fingers itch to text her, I'm holding off.

The flat, empty look in her eyes has stayed with me. That, and the fact that she never gave me a chance to explain.

I've done everything I can the last couple weeks to show her that I'm here for her, to show her how much she means to me. It breaks my heart to think that she might never get there. For every step I take towards her, it's like she takes a half-step back.

Relationships don't work like that, they *can't* work like that. I want to put in the hard work, invest in and commit to her, but it's like Ivy has one foot out the door.

We can't move forward if she can't let go of the past.

"That's today?" Luke's voice brings me back to the moment. "Can't they put it off a little longer?"

I strain my ears, hoping to hear Ivy's voice.

Finally, Luke sighs. Pinches the bridge of his nose. "I hope so too. I'll talk to you later. Love you."

Luke hangs up and places his phone back on the coffee table. After a moment, he gives his head a shake. Straightens and starts collecting his stuff.

Curiosity gets the best of me. "That was Ivy?"

"Yeah, the meeting with the buyer is happening today. Our grandparents are going to ask the company to postpone the sale due to a family matter, but apparently, these people are quite pushy."

"Right, the sale..." I trail off. With all of the drama around the wedding, I never told Luke about the mess with Penumbra. Now seems as good a time as any. "Luke, there's something you should know. On Saturday, before every-thing happened with Lenore, I found out that it was my company that put the offer on the Brookrose."

Luke pauses, frowns at me. "You want to buy the Brookrose?"

"My *company* wants to, I didn't want anything to do with it. I told them not to go through with it, but obviously, they didn't like that. So I quit."

"I was wondering why you've been hanging around. You're not exactly a 'call in sick' kinda guy." Luke smiles humorlessly.

"Yeah, well there you go. And I'm happy I quit, it was the right thing to do."

In another universe, I'd be back in the office in Denver, drowning in paperwork and new ideas for my promotion. Or maybe I'd be in the meeting with the Brooks right now, trying to convince them to give up the Brookrose. I don't know who that guy is anymore.

Luke bites the inside of his cheek. "I can't imagine saying bye to the Brookrose."

"I wish I could help. There must be some way we can stop this."

Luke is silent for a long moment. So long that I have to look at him. He's staring at me curiously.

"What?" I ask.

"You really care about the Brookrose, don't you?"

"Of course I do. We practically grew up there."

"We 'practically grew up' in a lot of places." Luke waves a hand. "I didn't see you getting this upset when the school gutted the locker rooms."

"*That* was a tactical move. Those locker rooms stunk like fifty years' worth of feet and athletic disappointments."

"Even so. You spent more time in those locker rooms than at the Brookrose."

"What can I say?" I shift on the couch. "The Inn is important to me."

"Or maybe it's important to someone who's important to you."

I screw up my mouth, unsure where this is going. "I guess..."

"Come on, man." Luke laughs. "You're really not going to admit that maybe you love the Brookrose so much because you love my sister?"

My mouth drops open. "You know?"

Luke sighs, rolls his eyes. "I know. And it's about time you two got together."

I raise a hand. "To be clear, we're *not* together. We expressly agreed we wouldn't be together until after the wedding."

"Seriously?" Luke suddenly stands to his full height—intimidating, given my seated position—and glowers at me. I see that protective older brother, the one who'd do anything for his family.

I instinctively shrink back a bit, tense my forearms.

"You better not be leading my sister on," he growls. "Or I'll—"

He breaks into laughter. Shakes his head.

"Sorry, can't keep a straight face."

I relax. Yeah, Luke in scary-big-brother mode is kinda terrifying. And he has every right to be upset. "We didn't want to start anything until we could talk to you about it."

His expression softens. "I appreciate the thought, but you didn't have to walk on eggshells around me. I knew you two would end up together sometime."

"Yeah, but right before your wedding? Not a great time to create a stir."

"Look how that turned out." He chuckles dryly. "I love you both, I think you're good for each other. You push and challenge each other, and you guys could actually *be* something now that you've put down your weapons. I know you have her back and she has yours, and you would never do anything to hurt her."

I bite the inside of my cheek, looking down. "If only she believed the same."

Luke pauses, then nods. "Don't give up on her. She's stubborn but she's not dumb. She knows you guys belong together."

With that, he jogs up the stairs to take a shower.

That was not how I expected that conversation to go. For one thing, I thought I'd be armed with a few bags of his favorite chips, along with plenty of prepared variations of "I want to spend my life with your sister and would never do her wrong." I also figured that he'd be happily married, but life changes quickly sometimes.

I just hope it isn't too late to keep *some* things from

314

changing. To stop the woman I love from walking out the door altogether.

Suddenly, I sit up straight on the couch.

I'm an idiot. Things have been so crazy, I didn't even think to check. And if all has gone according to my plan, there's something I need to make sure Ivy sees.

I grab my car keys and head out the door.

40

IVY

Another day, another hour spent staring at the landscape painting across from the front desk.

No. I need to do better.

I shake myself off. Push my glasses up my nose and take a swig of my now-cold black coffee. That's right—no cream, no sugar, certainly not an iced chai. Today is not an iced chai kind of day.

I press my cheeks into my hands, forcing myself to read the wordy fine-print on Cam's latest contract. Yes, Cam Harris came by this morning to talk about Clear Reflections' contract with the Brookrose. No, I did not want to face him. It's hard enough to stomach the thought of what the future brings for the Brookrose, let alone speak to the man I once crushed on, who now makes me wonder what I was thinking.

Fun fact I learned during our awkward (on my part) encounter: Cam and Gemma are now dating. It's the one piece of page-six-equivalent news that squeaked through all of the glaring headlines surrounding the end of Luke and Elly's engagement.

Poor Luke.

My heart aches for my brother, for everything he's lost, and for the ways this might change him. None of us have heard from Elly, and her parents seem as perplexed by her behavior as we are.

She's gone on the lam. Literally—it's rumored that she ran off to a sheep farm. More likely, she packed up and moved to San Fran alone. But I'm not going to oppose the rumor mill without evidence.

After another few minutes spent staring blankly at the page, the words are still not sinking in. Probably because this contract may not be mine to sign in a few hours.

My grandparents are meeting with the Penumbra guys at Morning Bell right now, and it's all I can think about. With the wedding cancelation, my grandparents want to ask the buyers if they can postpone making a decision, but honestly, I can't imagine a world where they won't sell. I won't ask my grandparents to take a chance on me and risk their retirement.

Although, now, I'm totally preoccupied with that last conversation we had. They kept alluding that they didn't want me to feel "stuck" or "tied down" working at the Brookrose.

If only I'd been able to prove to them how much I wanted this before any of this "selling the Inn" business came up.

I've tried to do my stupid yoga breaths, to re-center myself, but James keeps popping into my head. Always with the great timing, that one.

James and I are on shaky ground. I haven't seen him around the Inn, haven't heard from him. Anytime I think about him, I remember that last fight we had.

It took me some time to calm down, but once I did, I started to see things more clearly. See that maybe I jumped to conclusions. Again. There's a chance that I don't know the full story, but I didn't exactly give him an opportunity to tell me his side. As hard as I tried to fight it, my walls went back up again.

For so long, I put James in my "wrong" category, and it blinded me. I interpreted everything for the worse, but then, I was boxing myself in to one explanation. Did I just do that again?

I've never been good at trusting people. I believed that I had to be independent and do things alone. Admitting I needed help meant admitting that I couldn't do something to perfection all by myself, and I've never been ready to do that.

But then James appeared back in my life, and he crashed on into my heart. He saw my shortcomings and weaknesses, my deepest flaws and imperfections, and he reminded me to laugh. To recognize that I don't *have* to be any certain way, and that I can ask for help and care without it meaning that I'm not enough.

I love him for that. Love him for showing me what love feels like.

And I've been awful.

I went ahead and shut him out when it was my turn to fight for him. Refused to give him a chance when *he* appeared to be less than perfect.

Needless to say, I'm a mess today. And the person I want to talk to more than anyone else is the one person I can't reach out to. Isn't it, like, a conflict of interest or something to fall for someone when they're trying to buy your business?

This has a mild *You've Got Mail* vibe to it. And just like Meg Ryan, I can't expect to come out of this with both the man and my sweet little bookstore.

But the more I think about it—whatever James's explanation is for his behavior—if someone is going to buy the

Brookrose and manage it, it *should* be him. I trust him with our inn, know that he would go above and beyond for it. So if I need to give up this place, it couldn't fall into better hands.

I can't take it anymore. Forget conflict of interest, I need to talk to him.

I reach for my phone and open a message thread with James.

My fingers hover over the screen.

How does one say "I am the worst, please forgive me for pushing you away, and if you could find a way to somehow, maybe, possibly love me despite my behavior, I will grovel at your feet forever" in a chill, casual, easy-breezy sort of way?

Suddenly, Val bumps my shoulder with hers. "Mail's arrived. Check out what's on top."

I put down my phone—my super eloquent, poetic text will have to wait.

On top of the stack of periodicals, bills, and flyers, there's the latest issue of the Colorado Rockies Wedding Review. I feel a pang for all of the hopes and dreams I had for the Brookrose.

"Ah, I wonder who they featured this month," I say as I open the magazine and start leafing through. This month's feature is a gorgeous ranch house south of Denver that's dripping with rustic elegance. Massive wine cellar and Swarovski chandeliers included.

I continue looking through the magazine, feeling the weight of my dashed expectations. But it'll be okay. I'll be okay.

I flip to a new page and stop. My fingers clasp the paper so tight, it crinkles.

"Wha...?" I breathe, my eyes scanning the page once, twice, three times. Am I dreaming?

Because right there, on page 10, is a bonus feature titled "Up and Coming."

And the hotel is none other than the Brookrose.

I swallow thickly, my eyes jumping across the page. I recognize the photos—taken by Fran right before the wedding—and the text—started by me, then finished by someone else.

I can't believe it. The Brookrose Inn is featured in the Colorado Rockies Wedding Review.

But I didn't do this, I can't take the credit. There's only one person who could've done this.

I pick up my phone.

Ivy: I saw what you did. Thank you, and I'm so sorry for everything I said. You've been nothing but amazing to me, and I never should have doubted you. I meant what I said the other day—I love you. And if you could find it in your heart to forgive me, I need your help.

Not the most skillfully phrased text message, but I hope he gets it.

I bite my nail as the seconds tick by. Logically, rationally, I know that he probably won't get back to me right away. He's probably in the meeting with my grandparents right now.

But I no longer care about that. Because the thought of James no longer being in my life? The thought that I lost him because of my own stupid behavior? It's too painful to bear.

Please don't let it be too late... Please don't hate me...

My phone dings and I jump on it hungrily.

James: I'm already here.

There are truly no better words in the English language.

My heart skips and I'm flooded with emotion. Because, once again, James has come through for me—he's taken a chance on me, even when I pushed him away. I don't deserve this man.

I drop my phone and dash out to the parking lot. Straight to where he's waiting, leaning against Betsy and holding the latest edition of the Colorado Rockies Wedding Review. I fly towards him, landing in his arms and almost knocking him over.

"Woah, Brooks!"

"I'm sorry!" I say at the same time.

James laughs that rich chocolate laugh of his and wraps me in his arms. He kisses the top of my head, and tears sting my eyes.

"I'm so sorry, James," I say again quietly. "I should never have assumed—"

"Don't apologize. The situation didn't look good. I don't blame you."

I glance at the magazine in his hand. "I can't believe you did this."

"I believed in you. Believed in your vision for the Brookrose. The future you saw for it."

"Hang on." I pull back. "Why aren't you in the meeting with my grandparents right now?"

A smile tugs at his lips. "I quit."

My eyes go wide. "You quit your job?"

"That's what I was trying to tell you—I'm moving back to Mirror Valley. I quit Penumbra because I realized that there was something I wanted here more." Then he adds, "and because they were being jerks about buying the Brookrose."

I shake my head. "I can't believe it. I thought you loved your job."

"I did. But I love you a million times more."

My breath catches and I press my forehead to his. "I want you to know that, no matter what happens with the

Brookrose—whether my grandparents sell or keep it—I'm all in with you. As long as I'm with you, that's all I need to be happy."

James smiles that gorgeous smile of his, tucks a strand of hair tenderly behind my ear. "As long as you're happy, I'm happy, Brooks."

I bite my lip, completely overcome by my love for this man.

I stand on my tiptoes and bring his mouth to mine, tangling my fingers into his hair. His arms lock tight around me, and he swivels me to press my back gently against the car door. Once again, I get lost in another of his amazing kisses.

Right now, it doesn't matter what happens next. Because as long as I'm with James, everything will fall into place. He's the best enemy I ever had, the best competitor, the best friend, the best partner. I sigh against his mouth, so happy I could explode.

I pull back to catch my breath. "I love you, James Weston."

He beams, kisses the inside of my wrist. "And here I was thinking I was the worst thing to happen to you," he teases.

I meet his eyes, get locked into those turquoise depths. "Maybe the next worst thing."

"I'll take it," he says in a playful growl. "But don't tell me that's the end of the story."

"What do you mean?"

"I know you, Brooks. We've got an inn to save. What's the gameplan?"

My lips tug into smile—this man really does know me. "Here's what I'm thinking…"

41

IVY

One Year Later...

Okay, Ivy. You can do this.
Yoga breath in... yoga breath out...

I suck in another inhale, my eyes closed against the sunlight. I clear my mind and allow the mantra to fill my body with warmth. The anxiety ebbs, bit by bit, and by the time I open my eyes, I'm smiling.

"Miss Brooks, are you ready?" Tina bustles over. She tugs at the ends of her hair while balancing her overflowing clipboard in her other hand. Maybe I can give her pointers on clipboard organization later, but for now, Tina's in charge.

"Ready as I'll ever be," I say and she leads me into the garden.

The interviewer—none other than the amazing Ramona Proctor—waves from the gazebo, where she's set up with the photographer. My stomach twists with anticipation, until I see that tall, familiar, smirking presence off to the side.

My eyes lock with James's and a stupidly huge smile

takes over my face. He matches it, and even from here, the connection between us feels like fire. Is it crazy that, even after all these months together, I still get butterflies when the man so much as glances my way?

He cocks an eyebrow in that teasing, flirty way of his and mouths "good luck" with those perfect lips. Lips I already can't wait to kiss again.

Tina ushers me into the gazebo, and I see Luke, standing in the garden with his arms crossed. Daisy isn't far away, and she's literally glowing with excitement as she waves at me. My grandparents are on the other side; Pops has his arms wrapped sweetly around Grams's waist. If James and I could look even half as happy as my grandparents do at their age, that would be more than enough for me.

"Hello, Ivy," Ramona booms, flicking her iconic pink quill-pen in the air. I have a feeling she and Fran would get along. "Take a seat and we'll get started."

I nod, slightly breathless, and sit in the brand-new porch swing. I adjust my coral blazer over my cream dress, fiddle with my hair, which I'd put into a half ponytail—partly because I love how it frames my face, and partly because I know how appreciative James is of ponytails.

The cameraman snaps photos as Ramona takes a seat in her designated CRWR chair. She shuffles her papers and we get into the interview.

"Thanks for sitting down with us today," Ramona starts, quill-pen held aloft. "The Colorado Rockies Wedding Review has been wanting to get you for an interview for awhile, but it sounds like the Brookrose is keeping you busy! You took on the management of the Inn a year ago, is that correct?"

I go over my mental notes. Can you blame me? I *had* to prepare for this. "That's right. The Brookrose Inn has been with my family for generations, but last year, my grandparents received an offer that was almost too good to refuse. Luckily, my partner, James, and I managed to sweep in at the nick of time and save our beloved inn from being bought out by a huge conglomerate."

"Sounds like it was high stakes." Ramona laughs.

"It was! And the CRWR played a part in it..." My eyes land on my grandparents. Grams's eyes are shining with pride, and even Pops looks teary. I have to swallow a sudden wave of emotion. "My grandparents—Maggie and Richard —are some of the best people in the world, and they didn't want me or my brother Luke to have to give up our dreams in order to run our inn. What they didn't know was that managing the Brookrose *is* my dream."

"We heard about that." Ramona shuffles through her papers. How surreal that she has notes about *me*. "You did your degree in Hospitality Management, correct? And you were offered a job with one of the country's top hotel chains."

"Yes, but the job wasn't for me. Mirror Valley is my home, the Brookrose is my life. I'd do anything for my town and my family, but my grandparents didn't fully believe it until they saw the Brookrose featured in the CRWR. That was enough for them to see how serious I was about wanting to run our inn, and they insisted on taking a chance on me."

"It's a lot of responsibility for one person though, isn't it? All the late nights, the stress, the unhappy guests... doesn't it get exhausting?"

"Not at all. Because I'm not doing this alone. My family and friends are huge supports, of course, but I couldn't do this without James."

"James also has a background in hospitality, doesn't he?"

I smile as I look at him. We lock eyes and my entire

body lights up. "That's right. He was actually more involved with the sale last year than either of us knew at the time. But now, he's running the place with me, and I couldn't be happier to have him as my partner."

"Why don't we get James up here?" Ramona asks. "You two clearly can't keep your eyes off each other."

I wave for James to join me. He seems unsure for a moment, then runs up the steps and sits on the swing next to me. The photographer snaps a couple more photos as James wraps an arm comfortably around my shoulders.

"Hey, Ramona," he says, the English lilt in his voice sending shivers down my spine. "I'm just here to support Ivy. She's worked hard to get the Brookrose on the map."

"And she's done a wonderful job. It's rare to see a family-run inn take off on the wedding circuit like the Brookrose has in the past year. It's a staple on our 'Top 10 Wedding Venues' list, and we get calls and requests for more information all the time. The first feature we ever did on the Brookrose is still a top performer."

"You know what's funny?" James smiles. "I sent that information to a contact of mine at the CRWR. I sent him everything I had, which was a stack of unedited photos, and a half-finished description. He went nuts for it. It's not like I talked it up or anything—the Brooks have just created such a wonderful inn on their own."

I'm glowing with happiness at James's words, bathing in his support. "I wouldn't be here without him."

James stays next to me as Ramona runs through the rest of her questions for me. His arm feels safe and secure around my shoulders, and for the millionth time, I know that I've found perfection. *My* perfection. With the man I'm still deeply in love with, and who loves me so well.

Finally, the interview comes to an end. As Ramona and

the rest of the CRWR crew drive away, Daisy and I break into a happy dance.

"Iv, that was amazing!" she squeals, throwing her arms around me and lifting me off the ground. "They *loved* you!"

"Great job, sis." Luke wraps an arm around my shoulders and squeezes tight.

"Come on, Luke!" Daisy teases him. "Surely you can muster more enthusiasm."

She jokingly pokes him in the side and Luke chuckles as he takes her hand. "Better watch your fingers, Dais."

"Or what?" She brings her hands to her hips.

Luke squares up to her, but Daisy doesn't back down. His lips twitch a little—he's amused by this. "You don't want to know."

James and I exchange a glance. Luke has had a tough year and some days are harder than others, but Daisy always seems to find a way to make him smile. Maybe someday soon, he'll be ready to date again...

But I mustn't pull a classic "Mirror Valley" and start meddling.

I leave Luke and Daisy to their conversation, and wrap my grandparents in a big hug.

"Ivy, we're so proud of you," Grams says, her voice thick with emotion as she pats my back. "Just look what you've accomplished in the past year."

The three of us turn to look at the Inn. We finally decided to invest in a paint job for the Brookrose, and it's looking a lot more like the English country manor I always dreamed of. Though with the same blue "Welcome" sign—*that* will never change.

"And we're so happy about you and James," Grams says. "He's done *such* a great job with the garden... Turning into his father, that one."

"Thankfully, without the visor."

We both laugh. It's true—James's favorite place in all of Mirror Valley is very clearly the Brookrose garden. I can picture him running through the plants someday with a child or two, playing tag, being a great father.

Maybe I'm getting ahead of myself.

Happy tears sting my eyes as I wrap my arms around my grandparents. "This all happened because of you two. I so appreciate you thinking of my future when you wanted to sell, but I'm even more appreciative that you didn't." I chuckle, remembering when James and I crashed into Morning Bell to stop the meeting with Penumbra. "All I ever wanted was to be like you."

Pops beams with pride as he nods towards James. "I think you've found an excellent partner."

"I think so too."

I leave my grandparents and walk over to James, tucking myself back under his arm. He kisses the top of my head. "Hey, Brooks," he says and my heart skips a beat.

"Hey, Weston."

"Have I told you today how much I love you?"

"I can't remember. You can say it again."

He smiles. "I love you."

"Guess you're okay."

James snorts and pulls me around to face him, holding my chin tenderly as he brings his mouth to mine for another heart-stopping kiss. I swear, I could spend forever kissing James Weston.

He takes my hand. "Come with me, I want to show you something."

I bite my lip. Honestly, I'm so in love with this man, I'll follow him wherever he wants to lead me.

He takes me back to the gazebo, to the stairs where, a few months back, I first pressed my hand against his chest. It feels like so long ago, and yet, it might've just been yesterday. Time is kind of elastic when it comes to James and me.

He faces me again, his expression so sweet, it takes my breath away. He stands on a step below mine so we're closer to eye level.

He doesn't say anything, just looks at me.

"What?" I finally ask, weirdly self-conscious.

"Ivy..." he breathes my name and heat rushes through my body. "When I was seven and you were six, I had no idea that I'd met the love of my life."

My breath catches. What's going on?

"For years, you were all I could think about," he continues. "Usually, because you hated me and I thought I hated you. You embarrassed me in front of my dates, and I gave you a hard time in front of yours. I didn't realize at the time that I was doing it because I was jealous. Because *I* wanted you."

His eyes are boring into mine and it's all I can do not to fall headfirst into the tropical ocean blue.

"And the truth is, I still want you. I'll always want you, now and forever. I never understood where my future was leading me, never knew what home was, until you came back into my life. *You* are my future, and *you* are my home. And if you'll let me, I will spend the rest of my life trying to give you what you give me every day..."

James is reaching for something behind his back. He pulls out...

A boutonniere.

I exhale in a breathy laugh, barely aware of the tears streaking down my cheeks. Because within the flower arrangement is a stunning diamond ring.

"Ivy Brooks, will you marry me?"

A rush fills my body and I can barely breathe. I have never been happier than this very moment.

"Yes! James Weston, I will absolutely marry you."
Nothing has ever felt more right.

Thank you so much for reading!

If you enjoyed this book, please leave me a review. As a new author, reviews mean everything to me. I appreciate each and every one of them.

THANK YOU FROM SJ

You know that feeling when you're so eternally grateful that someone made it through to the end of your book?

<3

If you've made it this far, THANK YOU! Thank you for *taking a chance* on James and Ivy's story, and thank you for reading! This is my first sweet romcom, and it was an adventure. High highs, low lows, lots of chocolate and snacks. It took me longer to write this than I could've anticipated, but being funny takes time, y'all!

Okay, maybe it's the hours I spent *getting inspired* by Schitt's Creek and Friends (anyone else a fan? <3) This is also the longest book I've written, so I appreciate you taking the time!

So, to my fantastic beta reader and editor, to my phenomenal ARC team that I couldn't do this without, and to you, dear reader, thank you! I could not be more grateful, and I hope you enjoyed reading Ivy and James's story as much as I loved writing it.

Now, back to my next story (after a quick happy dance, of course).

Happy reading,

XX SJ

Made in the USA
Las Vegas, NV
03 July 2022